MARY CRAWFORD

Hearts Set Free

A HIDDEN HEARTS NOVEL 8

COPYRIGHT

HIDDEN BEAUTY SERIES

Until the Stars Fall from the Sky
So the Heart Can Dance
Joy and Tiers
Love Naturally
Love Seasoned
Love Claimed
If You Knew Me (and other silent musings) (novella)
Jude's Song
The Price of Freedom (novella)
Paths Not Taken
Dreams Change (novella)
Heart Wish (100% charity release)
Tempting Fate
The Letter
The Power of Will

HIDDEN HEARTS SERIES

Identity of the Heart

Sheltered Hearts

Hearts of Jade

Port in the Storm (novella)

Love is More Than Skin Deep

Tough

Rectify

Pieces (a crossover novel)

Hearts Set Free

Freedom (a crossover novel)

The Long Road to Love (novella)

Love and Injustice (Protection Unit)

Out of Thin Air (Protection Unit)

Soul Scars (Protection Unit)

OTHER WORKS:

The Power of Dictation

Vision of the Heart

#AmWriting: A Collection of Letters to Benefit The Wayne Foundation

DEDICATION

This book is for the
people who have loved
and lost, yet dare to
love again.

CHAPTER ONE

STUART

I SLIDE INTO THE booth, throw down my messenger bag and look at my best friend, Mitch. "What's so urgent it couldn't wait? I don't have long. I need to clean up an arthritic knee in an elderly Schnauzer later this afternoon."

Jessica grabs her husband's hand. "This will be quick. We want you to be the first to know. Well, the first behind my grandpa — but we didn't mean to tell him, he guessed."

My stomach clenches as I set the menu down and study Jessica. She is beaming at me, bursting to tell me her news. I recognize that look. Nora had the same one when she informed me she was having our child.

I glance over at my best friend who is closer than a brother. He is the picture of quiet contentment as he gently massages Jessica's back. Mitch's happiness radiates from him like sunshine. Watching them bubble with excitement sends me back to another time and place where things might've gone very differently in my life. I was once in this situation, but I didn't handle it nearly as well. Not for the first time, I wish I could travel back in time and make different choices.

Looking back, I realize I should've reacted to the news more diplomatically — but I was petrified. Nora and I weren't even married yet. We'd talked about marriage many times, but decided to wait until things were calmer. Being parents was not something we had considered yet, but once Nora was pregnant, I was thrilled to be a dad. We figured we had time to sort it out and pull it all together. I was proud of my growing family.

Despite my protests, Nora had been involved in the search and rescue field long enough there was no way she was going to let a simple pregnancy stop her. She cleared it with her doctor and went on a rescue mission. I could not go because I had to take my final exams. The plan was for me to meet up with her after the school year. I never got the chance.

Even though it's been years, I still remember being called into the Dean's office. In her shock, my mom called the school instead of me and there in front of a bunch of strangers, I learned the love of my life and the mother of my child had been killed trying to rescue other people. My heart permanently broke.

Jessica clears her throat. "Most people don't find me boring — but it seems like I've lost your attention."

I rub the back of my neck. "I'm sorry, it's been a long day. I started before the chickens got up this morning."

Jessica looks glum. "Oh, bummer! I was hoping you were pining for someone you recently met."

"You're downright hysterical. Unless you count four-legged creatures or my buddies with fins or feathers, I haven't met anyone lately. My practice is crazy these days."

"Not an awful problem to have." Mitch takes a sip of his milkshake.

"Nope, it's not. Sometimes, I wish I could be cloned. Even if the perfect woman walked into my life right now, I don't think I could do anything about it."

"I'm sorry to hear that. But you won't be less busy soon," Jessica reveals with a huge smile.

"Are you going to tell me you're having a baby, or did you want me to guess?" I respond.

"How does everyone know?" Jessica turns to Mitch. "I swear I said nothing."

"I think you forgot I am a veterinarian. I deal with pregnant animals all the time. Pregnant is pregnant. I can tell by your expression and the way your hand is placed protectively over your abdomen you're expecting," I explain with a soft smile.

"Well, that takes the fun right out of it," Jessica pouts good-naturedly.

"I'm sorry." I gulp my coffee and wince when it scalds my tongue. "I should've let you tell me. Congratulations, guys. It couldn't have happened to a better couple."

"Thanks, man. I appreciate it. We are nervous, but we've been waiting for this for a while," Mitch explains.

"I can imagine. I bet everyone in your family is ecstatic. Walter will be the ultimate doting great-grandfather."

"Yeah, he will — but his health isn't as good as it was. I worry about him."

"I'm sorry to hear that. Walter is one of my favorite people," I respond.

Before I can say more, my cell phone beeps. I glance down and see a familiar name. It's odd for Darya to call me in the middle of her workday. I turn toward Mitch as I get up from the booth. "I better take this."

"Jessica and I need to get to her appointment anyway," Mitch says. "We'll touch base with you later, but Jessica couldn't resist the opportunity to tell you."

"It's great news. Congrats!" I collect my belongings from the booth. I throw a few dollars on the table. "This should cover everything."

"You didn't need to," Mitch protests. "After all, we were the ones who invited you here."

"Don't worry about it." I shrug. "You need to save all your pennies for diapers and baby clothes."

Jessica laughs. "Mitch has taken the preemptive step of taking away my credit cards. He knows me well enough to know I'd buy a complete wardrobe for a boy and a girl." Jessica sighs. "I wish I could argue with him, but the man has a point."

"There's a good reason I'm single. I don't want to mess with that kind of conflict." I chuckle as I head out the door. When I reach my car, I return Darya's phone call. She picks up on the first ring.

"Thank God! You *are* there. Are you in your office?" Panic edges into Darya's voice.

"No, I was having lunch with Mitch and Jessica, but I can be back to my office in a couple of minutes. What's up?"

"There aren't words. You need to see this in person. I'll meet you at your clinic."

"Okay, I'm headed there now. I'll talk to you in a bit."

The sheer terror in Darya's voice disconcerts me. As a police detective, not much puts her on edge. Something has her spooked. This can't be good.

Darya arrives at the clinic at the same time I pull into the driveway. She runs to meet me with what looks like a football formed from a beach towel. When I shoot her a quizzical glance she explains, "I'm sorry, I didn't have anything else in my car. I'm borrowing someone else's cruiser today because my favorite rig is in the shop." Gingerly, she holds out the bundle she's been guarding. "Technically, I'm not supposed to be the one in charge of this. Still, I couldn't leave him there. Fortunately for this little guy, medical had to attend to my witness so I could get away and bring him to you."

I still can't spot what she's talking about. My first thought is she found a litter of kittens and this one was left behind. Finally, I see movement in the bundle. When I gently pull back the towel, I see it is not a kitten after all. Rather, it's a tiny, malnourished Chihuahua. As he shies away from me, I see the whole left side of his body is bright red.

Alarmed, I ask, "Do you have any idea what happened?"

Shaking her head, Darya whispers, "No. I don't. The suspected perp was a witness in one of the cases I'm investigating. Maybe he got burned or something was spilled on him. I was hoping you could tell me."

"I don't know. It could be a lot of things, but I'm afraid this looks disturbingly familiar. I recently took care of several kittens with burns like this. I pray I'm wrong." I sigh as I try to move the towel so I can get a better view. I cringe as I see his raw skin. "Unfortunately, I don't think I am."

"How could someone be so deranged? This tiny little dog isn't strong enough to harm a flea. Why would anyone deliberately try to hurt him?"

I glance down at the tiny, bedraggled puppy and shrug. "No matter how long I do this, I've never been able to come up with an answer to that question."

"I know what you mean. When I first started out with the police department, I was hopelessly idealistic. Time has taught me very hard lessons. I'll never understand the harm humans do to each other."

"I need to examine these injuries more closely. I'm taking him back to the surgery room where my lighting is better and I can give him pain medication."

"Do you think he'll be okay?"

I gently open the pup's mouth and examine his gums. "It's still too early to tell much. I'll know more if he makes it through the night."

"Umm … I brought him here on the spur of the moment because I couldn't leave him to suffer. It might take me a while to pay off his bill — you know, public servant and all."

I stop my examination and meet Darya's gaze, "Seriously, don't worry about it. Consider it my contribution to making my neighborhood a better place to live."

Darya looks pensive. "Are you sure? I don't want to make you pay for my twisted sense of moral responsibility."

"If what you did is considered twisted, count me in. You saved this puppy's life. You are not the twisted one in the situation. The person who did this to him is the one who needs help. I take a few charity cases from the local animal shelters. I'll consider this one of those. Sometimes, you do things because it's the right thing to do."

Just then, my stomach growls. Darya looks startled and then covers her reaction with a laugh. "I thought you said you went to lunch with Mitch and Jessica. What did you eat?" As soon as she asks, her eyes grow wide and her mouth opens in surprise as she gasps. "Oh, shoot! I need to go pick up Maya from daycare."

"Who is Maya?" I'm losing track of the conversation as I try to multi-task and work on the puppy as we chat.

Darya stops petting the top of the puppy's head. After a moment, a pained expression crosses her face. "Maya is my daughter. She's eight and a half. Don't forget the half — it's very important to her."

"Seriously? We've been friends for a while, and I didn't know you had a kid."

Darya seems embarrassed. "Yeah … Sorry. I guess it's an occupational hazard. I don't talk about my family very much because of my profession. I don't want her to become a target of some deranged person I'm investigating."

"I suppose I can understand. You know I wouldn't do anything to hurt you or your daughter, right?"

"Oh, I know. I got into the habit of never mentioning Maya. It's safer for her. I hope you understand… it's not personal."

"Don't worry about it. Do what you have to do to keep your family safe. You don't need to justify anything to me."

"Thanks. It's hard to know how much to share. Anyway, I need to go. My daycare might give Maya's slot away to another child if I'm late. I've had to work overtime a couple of days this week. My childcare provider is less than happy with me right now — I don't want to give her another reason to be mad."

"Go on. Take care of your kiddo. I've got everything handled with our little survivor here."

"I appreciate it. Thank you for all you're doing. I feel better knowing he is in great hands. I'll call you later to see how he's doing — not because I don't trust you — there's something about this little guy. I don't think I'll rest well until he turns the corner."

"I completely understand what it's like to be a pet parent when your little one is hurt. Feel free to call anytime."

"You know the dog isn't mine, right?"

"I know. The question is … does this little guy?"

While I stroke the little pup's ear, I ask him, "What do you think I should call you? You seem a little sad. It's like you have the weight of the world on your shoulders. Maybe I should name you Atlas. Hopefully, that will encourage you to grow big and strong. If things don't go well, Darya will be devastated. So, you need to concentrate on getting better."

Atlas nuzzles my hand and licks my finger. "Good enough for me," I respond as if it's perfectly reasonable to conduct late-night chats with a puppy I can fit in the palm of my hand. "Atlas it is."

Gently setting him down on his blanket, I make Atlas dinner. I mix canned wet food with puppy formula. After I dip a tongue depressor in the mixture, I hold it out for

Atlas to eat. At first, he is hesitant, but soon he begins eating it as if there's no tomorrow. "Been without food for a while, I see." I laugh at his newfound enthusiasm over food.

Atlas looks up at me as if I've completely ruined his dining experience. "Okay, I'll shut up so you can eat. You're a bossy little thing."

Atlas is happily ignoring me as he eats every scrap of food I offer him. After he finishes, I take him to the side yard and let him take care of business. My grass is almost taller than he is. Even so, he is a good, sweet pup. It makes me wonder what happened to him. As a veterinarian, I try not to think about the horrors my rescue dogs go through, but in this case, it's hard not to because the evidence of abuse is written all over his tiny body.

Darya surprised me in so many ways today. Whenever we are together, she always strikes me as having a great sense of humor and an ability to laugh at herself. This emotional, empathetic side is interesting because she is known for being so tough. When I interact with her on the job, she is the consummate professional. I didn't expect her to break down in tears over the plight of Atlas.

I'm not sure I've ever thought about Darya's home life, but it's difficult to envision her as a mom. Although, the revelation makes some things make much more sense. Darya is known in the community for her wild, over-the-top ties. When she became a detective, she decided men and women shouldn't have to dress differently to do the same job. So, she began wearing suits tailored to go together with goofy ties and brightly colored suspenders. I suppose it's her tongue-in-cheek salute to archaic dress standards. Her daughter may explain the fun themes.

The announcement she has a daughter is mind-boggling. Most parents I know brag incessantly about their children. Even though I understand the reason she needs privacy, I'm still having a hard time wrapping my brain around the fact we've been friends for years and she never said a word.

Then again, I can't say much. I've never shared my whole story with anyone. If I'm not willing to disclose everything about my personal life, I'm not sure why I expect her to be an open book — especially considering her occupation.

"Sleep well, Atlas," I instruct as I place him down in a nest of bedding in the corner of his kennel. "Be sure not to let anything bite. You need to save your strength for a bigger fight."

Atlas turns his head as if he's confused by my ramblings. I laugh at his baffled expression. "Oh, don't mind me. It's been a long day. I'm calling it a night. I'll check on you in a few hours."

Atlas's response to my announcement is to curl up in a ball with his back facing me as he tucks his nose under his tail.

"Well, I guess I've been dismissed. I'll check on you in a few hours."

What is it about 3 AM and puppies? They all seem to run on the same internal clock, I think to myself as I roll out of bed and throw on some sweats.

I carefully feed Atlas more food and give him another dose of pain medication. Even though the area is still raw and painful, the antibiotics and pain medication seem to be helping the puppy. After he goes outside, I pick him up and carry him in the crook of my arm. When he feels my warm sweatshirt, he breathes a sigh of relief and closes his eyes.

I look down at him as he gives a soft snort. "I know you would like me to hold you all night, but I need to get to bed because I am performing surgery in the morning." Atlas opens one eye and shakes his head as if to say, "You're not doing any of that crazy stuff to me."

My phone rings at six forty-five in the morning. "Hello. The Critter Clinic, this is Dr. Eastwood," I greet as I put water in Atlas' bowl.

"Oh … hi," Darya replies tentatively. "I'm sorry, I thought my call might go to your answering machine. I didn't mean to disturb you so early, but I'm going on shift and won't be reachable by phone today. I'm checking in to see how the puppy is doing. I barely slept last night because I was so worried."

"I just got done taking him outside. He seems much stronger and in a lot less pain this morning."

"He must be quite the little fighter to be able to survive what he did."

"Very true." The puppy pulls on the sleeve of my lab coat. "I hope you don't mind, I named the puppy. I figured since you didn't know the details of the puppy's living situation, you probably don't know his name."

"I don't. Trust me, if I knew anything more about this situation, heads would roll."

"I hear you. Hopefully, there's video that can help catch the punks who did this. Anyway, I named the little puppy Atlas."

"Mighty big concept for a teeny-tiny dog." Darya

laughs.

"Exactly why I named him something so lofty. Perhaps, he'll be inspired to live up to his mighty name."

"Oh, you mean like parents who name their kids after famous athletes in hopes they'll acquire athletic talent?"

"Exactly! Maybe he'll grow up to exceed everyone's expectations. After all, Atlas is a legend."

"Did you know all the artwork with Atlas holding up the world is historically inaccurate?"

"I'm such a fan of Greek mythology I happen to know that. Atlas was the God of the heavens and the skies. I don't know why no one notices the discrepancy."

"You know, I've never run into another soul besides me who knows that bit of trivia. How did you know?"

"I had to study something to give me a break from all my science classes in college. Classic literature let me escape."

"I didn't know we shared a passion for geeky things. Someday, we should explore that more. Unfortunately, I need to get Maya ready for school and get to work myself. Thank you so much for being such a hero. I'm sure Atlas appreciates it too."

I chuckle as Atlas tries to crawl his way into the pocket of my lab coat. "It would probably depend on whether I'm performing a procedure on him. He wasn't such a big fan when I was cleaning up his skin."

"I can't even imagine. A bad sunburn is awful enough. I plan to spend as much time as I can today trying to figure out who did this to him."

"I hope you kick bad guy butt. I'll be working on helping this guy feel a little better."

Chapter Two

Darya

"Mom, how come I don't have a dad like all my friends?" Maya asks as I tie her tennis shoes.

Her simple question is like a bayonet to my soul. I always knew this day would come. I didn't realize it would hurt so much.

"What's with all the questions this morning?" I hedge as I tickle Maya's knee.

"Mom, stop!" she protests. "I want to know the answer."

"Why do you suddenly want to talk about your dad?" I scoop her up and hold her in my arms. She is getting so tall it's a little hard to do this.

"Everyone is making presents at school for Father's Day, and I don't have a dad. I don't know who to give my present to. It seems like everyone has a daddy except me. You never tell me the whole story."

While I grab my purse and walk toward the front door, I struggle to come up with an appropriate answer for my child. Even though I've rehearsed this little speech almost since the day Maya was born, I didn't expect to give it while I was rushing out the door to work. I envisioned we would be having a wonderful mother-daughter interaction and have the luxury of time. I take a deep breath and let it out.

"Are you mad at me? I haven't been bad — I swear!" Maya panics when I let the silence linger a bit too long.

"No, sweetie, I'm not mad at you. I'm trying to figure out the words to help you understand."

"Understand what? Did you and my daddy get a diborce? My friend, Lizette says that's what happened to her."

"No, your dad and I did not get a divorce." I put a little extra emphasis on the word divorce to gently correct Maya's speech.

"Why is he gone?" she presses.

"Great question, Maya. I don't think anybody knows the answer."

"Then what do you know?" she asks with a puzzled expression on her face.

Instead of walking to the car, I sit down on the front porch swing and reposition her on my lap as I prepare to have one of the most difficult conversations of her life.

"Maya, this story might make you sad. Are you sure you want me to tell you?"

"Yeah, one of the kids in my class said I don't have a dad because he's probably in jail. That's not right, is it?"

The thought of Sergio Javier López ever being in jail strikes me as funny and I smile. "It's a good guess, but no. You don't have a daddy anymore because he was killed while he was fighting to put bad guys in jail," I reveal as I try to keep my voice from breaking. Whoever said time heals all wounds has never been in my shoes.

"Did Dad get scared and run away from the bad guys?"

I shake my head. "No, your dad was one of the most courageous, kindest and smartest people I've ever known. When I was in school to be a police officer, your daddy came to show my class how the professionals make it so bombs don't blow up. I thought he was the bravest, most handsome man I had ever seen."

Maya's eyes grow wide. "My dad got blown up?"

I nod tightly. "Yes, he was killed in an explosion. But, it wasn't one he was working on, somebody set a bomb off in your daddy's car when he was driving to the gym."

"Dad couldn't fix the bomb so it didn't work? No fair!" Maya squirms around on my lap.

"He didn't know the bomb was even there until it was too late, sweetie."

"When he's done being dead, can he come visit me?" she asks, as she accidentally digs her heels into my shins.

The innocence of her question reminds me again how young and vulnerable my daughter is. Most of the time, she's so mature it's easy to mistake her for a much older child.

"No, Maya. That's not the way it works. Once a person is dead, they can't come back like they're on a play date."

"So, my daddy can never come back and be with us?" Maya asks, her eyes shining with tears.

I hug her. "I'm sorry. I wish Sergio could still be in your life, but that's not the way things worked out."

"How come I don't remember a man named Sergio?"

I have to swallow hard before I can utter the next

words. "You don't remember your dad because you never met him. Sergio died about three weeks before you were born."

"Do you think Daddy misses me as much as I miss him?"

"I'm sure of it. Sergio was looking forward to the day you were due. If he were alive, he would have done everything in his power to be there. It would have upset him to miss something like that."

Maya's shoulders hunch, and she blows out a breath. "I don't want my daddy to be sad. I want to give him the presents I made at school."

"I know, sweetie." I choke back tears.

"Mom?" Maya asks tentatively. "You're a policeman now. Are you going to catch the bad guys who hurt Daddy?"

I kiss the top of Maya's head. "I work on it all the time."

"Is it okay if I stop by to see Atlas?" I ask when Stuart answers the phone. "It's late, but my neighbor was kind enough to pick up Maya and take her to a movie, so I have a couple of hours."

"One of the reasons I practice from my home is so I can accommodate other people's schedules. Feel free to stop by whenever you can."

"I hope you mean that because I'm about five minutes away."

"I mean it. Skye and I will be waiting for you."

"Who is Skye?" I'm strangely let down there'll be

another person there. After the day I've had, I don't feel like being sociable with Stuart's girlfriend.

"Oh, don't worry about Skye. She is my geriatric Siberian Husky. These days, she's half deaf."

"Oh, I see. I'll be there in a few."

"See you soon."

When Stuart opens the door, I'm surprised to see him in a muscle shirt. He is surprisingly built. Usually, he hides all that underneath professional clothes. His usually artfully styled hair is askew. It doesn't look much like an impressive pompadour at the moment. It makes him seem more approachable. Although Stuart is a very handsome man, there is a boyish charm hidden right under the surface.

He catches my open perusal and blushes. "Sorry about this, I was brushing down Skye. She gets hair everywhere — I was trying to limit the damage."

Despite the stress of the day, I quirk the corner of my mouth up as I confess, "Please don't apologize. The sight of you dressed like that might be the highlight of my day."

"Then I don't even have to ask how your day was. It must've been terrible. I'm not exactly a poster child for hot guys."

"My day was awful. But I disagree with your assessment that you're not sexy. I've never noticed all the hotness you hide under your work uniform. Scrubs and long lab coats don't do you justice."

Stuart looks befuddled by my compliment. He steps out of the doorway and takes my duffel bag from me. "Who knew lifting people's overweight pets all day would have such positive benefits?" He walks down the hall, talking over his shoulder. "How about I make your day a little better? I'm happy to report Atlas is doing much better today. He's no longer running a fever, and he seems to be moving around a little easier."

"Great news! I worried all day about whether this little guy would make it."

"Any word on who caused this?"

I practically snarl. "No, can you believe everyone in the neighborhood is claiming not to own this animal — including the person we arrested on site?"

"I can. People do horrific things to their pets. Very few of them want to take the blame for their actions."

I follow Stuart into the room with the kennels; he opens a tiny one and removes Atlas. I gasp when I see him. "He looks worse than yesterday. Oh, poor baby!" I reach out to hold him.

"It takes a special kind of faith to believe me when I tell you he is doing much better, but trust me — he is. He looks worse because I shaved around his burns to make sure I could debride them properly. From a vet's point of view, they look much better."

Stuart picks up the tiny Chihuahua and pulls up his lip. "I don't know if you can see this, but look — his gums have much better color today. He's not running a fever at the moment, and he is eating and drinking well. Those are all very positive signs."

"I don't know what we will do with him. I don't want to place him back in the neighborhood he came from. After all, no one there is claiming him."

"It'll be a while before he is ready to go home with anyone. He's burned extensively for such a little thing."

I lean down and study Atlas' tiny face as I move my thumb to scratch between his eyes. "I wish I could take you home. I think you are adorable — owies and all."

"Why can't you?" Stuart asks bluntly.

"I don't know how Maya would do with a dog. She was bitten when she was younger. She is afraid of most dogs."

"It's hard to say. Eight-year-olds are not always consistent. Some kids don't understand how easily an animal can get hurt. Others seem to have an empathic ability to feel the animal's pain. So, I would have to see Maya with Atlas to evaluate how they get along."

I fiddle with my tie tack. When I put on my tie with big bright smiley faces this morning, little did I know my day would not be so bright. "I don't know. We'll see. Maya already has a cat named Mrs. Sprinkles. I'm not sure how she'd treat such a little dog. She might think he's a cat toy, for all I know."

"Like I said, let's cross that bridge when we come to it. Atlas needs to regain his strength before he meets any new friends."

"I'm pretty sure Maya would fall in love with Atlas. She'd probably try to dress him up in her doll clothes. The more I think about it, adopting Atlas would be a spectacular idea. Maya could use a little happiness in her world right now."

Stuart shoots me a questioning glance. "Is there something wrong? Is Maya sick?"

I shake my head. "No, Maya isn't physically ill. She just discovered a lot of kids have another parent and she doesn't. She wants to celebrate Father's Day. But, unfortunately, her father is dead. He was blown up by a nameless, faceless creep who took my daughter's chance at happiness without even so much as a backward glance."

"I'm so sorry. Was he a cop too?"

"Not in the way you think. Sergio was a member of the bomb disposal team."

"Was he killed in action? I don't remember anything like that happening around here."

"No, he was driving his personal car. He never saw it coming. If it had been a bomb he was working with in the line of duty; it would've been safer. At least he would've known what he was up against and could've had a chance to disarm it. Disarming devices was his specialty. He could unarm nearly every mechanism put in front of him by the bad guys. He had an intuitive sense about that kind of thing. He had nerves of steel. It sucks beyond all belief he was taken out by the very thing he could've dismantled if he'd known it was there."

"Have they solved his murder yet?"

"Negative. The gas tank in the car caught on fire after the initial explosion, and there was nothing left for them to put back together — even the metal parts melted. Unfortunately, even the experts could not figure out the bomber's signature from the mess left behind."

"Well, it seems to me the fact he left a bomb is probably signature enough."

"You would think so, but usually each bomb has a signature which ties it to all the rest of the bombs a perpetrator has put together."

"So, does that mean the guy was a rank beginner who hasn't set off any other bombs?"

"The team won't tell me much — even though I'm a police officer. The task force investigating Sergio's death is looking into it, but they don't like to talk to me. Apparently, I've been a little too pushy in trying to find answers."

"Oh, I know exactly how you feel. I was calling the investigators every single day — sometimes multiple times a day when I was trying to figure out exactly what happened to Nora."

"Who is Nora?"

"Nora was my first love. We were engaged to be married, and she was expecting a baby when she went on a search and rescue mission in the aftermath of a severe earthquake. Unfortunately, she and the baby were killed in a freak accident."

I feel that familiar stab of pain as I process his words. "Oh my gosh! I lost Sergio, but at least I was blessed with Maya. I can't imagine losing both."

"It's not something I talk about much," Stuart admits. "Most people don't expect men to take it quite so hard. Our baby was smaller than a peanut when Nora died. She used to have this book that showed every week of development. Nora photocopied the picture for each week to show me. She would tuck it in my backpack. I never knew which textbook it would be in. It became a game between us. I was remarkably attached to the little white spot on her ultrasound."

I flash Stuart a sad smile. "Oh, I believe it. Sergio used to sing to my belly before Maya even had ears. Every time I used to complain about not fitting into my clothes or my feet swelling, he would kiss my baby bump and tell me what a wonderful job I was doing. He always said growing a baby was the hardest job in the world and he was so proud of me for doing it."

"Exactly how I felt about Nora. She was superstitious and didn't want to tell anybody until the very last minute because she was afraid if people knew, something would go terribly wrong. So, we kept our news to ourselves. It about drove me crazy. I wanted to announce it to the universe. I had been in love with Nora since we were kids. Even though her pregnancy wasn't exactly planned, I wanted to be a dad. I didn't know how I would juggle it with my class load, but I was ready to be the kind of parent I didn't have."

"I'm so sorry for your loss." I reach out and take Atlas from Stuart and go sit in one of the chairs he has in his makeshift waiting room. I bunch the towel up on my lap and Atlas makes teeny tiny circles as he tries to find a comfortable place to sleep. "I have a strange question, do you mind?" I blurt impulsively.

Stuart looks over at me with a wary look. "Sure, why not? It's not like we haven't been sharing personal stuff."

"Are you tired of people asking you about whether you want to start over again with another family? People ask me that all the time about Maya and it drives me crazy. I can't instantly fall in love with someone because my daughter wants a father. It would be nice if she could take part in all the holidays without feeling like she's being left out, but I loved Sergio so much I can't even seriously consider falling in love again."

Stuart works on changing the bedding in Atlas' kennel and replaces the water. He glances up at me. "I always thought it was me. Since college, people have been trying to match me up with their friends. They didn't understand what Nora and I had together. No one besides us knew about the baby. Most people thought I would get over her death in no time at all."

"I know it's hard. There is a big part of me that will never get over the loss of Sergio."

"Growing up, Nora, Mitch and I were inseparable. People figured we were dating out of convenience and eventually I would move on to a 'real' girlfriend. But, Nora was as real as it gets for me."

I smile. "Maybe we should date each other to take the pressure off. It would make my family happy to see me do something social for a change."

"That would probably be an awful deal for you. Ask Mitch; I'm terrible to hang around. I play practical jokes on people and I hate to do the dishes. I've been known to drink milk straight out of the carton and put a near-empty container back into the refrigerator. I eat my breakfast cereal dry and like my toast on the burned side. According to Mitch, this makes me virtually un-datable."

"I have a confession. As long as Maya isn't watching me, I drink straight out of the carton too. However, I like almond milk and Maya won't touch it. So, there's no cross-contamination or anything."

"My grandmother would be scandalized if she could hear us. She was so fastidious and formal she would pre-chill glasses before pouring a beverage in them. She wouldn't know what to do with the likes of us."

"I do have company manners. I simply don't display them very often. After all, I work with a bunch of guys. Sometimes being gross is a way to fit in," I admit as I loosen my tie.

"Darya, I've known you for a long time. I can tell you honestly you will never, ever fit in anywhere. You are one of a kind."

I bristle at his words because I work hard to be one of the gang. "What do you mean?"

"Have a look at yourself, darlin'. Sure, you are wearing a traditional suit befitting your position as a detective. Still, you take it up a notch with all of your funky ties. I look forward to seeing you just to see what you're wearing on any given day."

I shrug. "What can I tell you? I like to follow the rules, but I also love to stretch them as far as humanly possible."

Stuart gently picks Atlas up and hooks a small leash to his little red collar. "Are you ready to take your fur-baby for a walk?"

"I suppose so. Is he up to going outside?"

"He is. We have to be gentle and patient with him."

"Of course, I'll be careful."

As I leave the room in front of Stuart, he places a hand on my shoulder. "Thanks for understanding what I'm going through. I know you meant it as a joke, but maybe we could be each other's plus-one for a while. I'm sick of going to events solo."

I smile shyly. "Okay, it's a deal. Next time you need a stand-in girlfriend, I'm your girl."

My heart skips a little beat as I watch Stuart gently cradle Atlas as he dries off his paws and offers him water. When his refrigerator's ice machine makes a noise and startles the puppy, his soothing voice calms us both. It's weird after all these years how I'm suddenly seeing my friend in a brand-new light. When did Stuart get so sexy?

CHAPTER THREE

STUART

I WALK INTO HOPE'S Haven, with Atlas tucked in the crook of my arm. The trip in the car unnerved him a little. He's shaking, but after he settles into his favorite resting place, he calms down.

"That small fry looks a little too young and size-challenged to be a search and rescue dog," Mitch jokes as he walks toward me with a smile on his face.

"I wasn't planning to turn him into a working dog quite yet. I need to see how he does with kids. Do you have any around so we could do a behavior evaluation?"

"How young are we talking?" Mitch takes Atlas from my arms. "Our new receptionist meets her grandkids at the school bus and if I ask her, she might bring them by."

"How old are they?"

"I believe one is in the first grade and the other is in the third."

"That'd show me what I need to see. Could she do it today?" I look at the time on my cell phone. "I had a dog owner change their mind about surgery this afternoon, so I'm open. I'm dismayed at their decision, but it opened up my afternoon."

Mitch shrugs. "I can try. Let me send her a text message."

Mitch puts the puppy in a playpen while he sends a text message. A curious puppy greets Atlas with a chorus of happy yips.

At first, Atlas cowers in the corner when the bigger puppy barks at him, but then he gets the message the other dog would like to play. I observe the interaction carefully. I'm curious to see how Atlas does with other animals. So far, he's been alone at my clinic except for his brief interactions with Skye. However, Skye has never met another canine she doesn't like. By the time Mitch comes back, the dogs are playing in the middle of the pen. The big dog has rolled over on his back and Atlas is valiantly trying to climb onto his belly, but he keeps slipping on the long hair. He's like a little kid playing in the ball pit at the fair as he sinks into the other dog's long coat.

Mitch smirks as he watches them romp around the pen. "Your little puppy has nerve. Starsky here is about ten times his size, but your little guy is holding his own."

"He is full of character, that's for sure. Were you able to get a hold of your receptionist?"

"Yeah, she'll be here with her grandkids in about fifteen minutes. Mind if I ask you what's up?"

Mitch's question catches me off guard. I almost tell him Darya's secret, but I catch myself.

I shrug in what I hope is a nonchalant manner. "I have a potential adoptive family for this little pup and I want to make sure an eight-and-a-half-year-old kid can handle his attitude."

"Do you expect him to have a problem?" Mitch asks

with open curiosity.

"No, actually I don't. For such a little guy, he's got the soul of a St. Bernard. He isn't aware he's a microscopic dog."

"I've seen dogs like him before. Hopefully, he won't take the typical small dog attitude toward the kiddos."

"That's what I'm hoping; it's only one part of the battle. The owner also has a cat."

Mitch laughs out loud. "Okay, buddy. I know you are a complete miracle worker when it comes to training animals. What will you do when the cat decides your little guy is about the size of a large rat and would make a nice appetizer?"

I make a comic showing of covering Atlas's ears. "Hey! You and I know that, but he doesn't need to. He has the heart of a lion. Let's see how it goes."

Mitch squats down and pets Atlas on the head. "Okay, whatever you say. He seems like a real sweetheart though, given what he's gone through." Mitch looks up at me as he adds, "Don't forget; we've got the awards banquet with the Chamber of Commerce this weekend."

I rub my short beard. "I hate to get cleaned up for this kind of thing. I'll probably have to wear a tie, won't I?"

"I hear you. It sucks, but Jess wants to go all out for this event. It's the first one that recognizes Hope's Haven's involvement with the young offender program. She thinks it will generate positive PR. I'd rather not wear a monkey suit either, but sometimes you gotta take one for the team."

"Easy for you to say, you have a team to play on. I hate going to these things alone. People are wondering if

I'm completely inept."

"Don't you have a single friend you could drag along? Some people like this kind of thing."

"I do. In fact, we were just joking about this a couple of weeks ago."

"Who are you talking about?" Mitch asks, looking doubtful.

"I ran across Darya the other day, and we were comparing notes about our relationship status. She made a joke about being my plus one."

"Dude! I'd take her up on it if I were you. We can count on Darya to make things fun and interesting — not like that bimbo your vet tech set you up with. I swear, she never had an original thought not lifted from a soap opera."

I cringe. "Yeah, that was the most excruciating ninety-five minutes I've had in a while. I didn't need to know the genealogy of the characters on all her favorite soaps."

"Very few people need to know that knowledge off of the top of their head."

"Seriously … What do you think of the idea of me going out with Darya?"

Mitch chuckles. "Well, it would keep Jess and me on our toes for sure. Darya has a wicked sense of humor, sort of like yours. The two of you together might be dangerous."

"I don't know if it's her dark, exotic looks or if it's her quick wit, but I find Darya very intriguing."

"I assume your next step would be to actually ask the woman out. She can't read your mind."

"I forgot how much I hate this part of the process. I never know how to approach it."

"If I had to take a guess, I would say Darya didn't give you that opening for nothing. She probably wants you to ask her out — even if it is as friends. She already did all the work for you. Tell her you would like to take her up on her offer."

I frown. "Are you sure? Sounds clinical to me."

"Stuart, you are asking the woman out to a banquet, you're not asking her to marry you. I think there's a little leeway there."

"I told you I'm rusty as heck. I'm not kidding. If it weren't for random people in my life setting me up on blind dates, I wouldn't go out at all."

"You are way too close to becoming a *Doctor Phil* episode. You've turned into the male version of the cat lady. Go be social for once."

"I thought you liked my quasi-cat-lady status. After all, who else would treat all the dilapidated, broken down dogs who come through your doors?"

"Speaking of … did you find homes for those little puppies who were dumped at our gate the other day?"

"I did. Surprisingly, they looked like they were almost purebred cocker spaniels. I don't know who would dump a bunch of defenseless puppies."

"The puppy at your feet tells you how low people will stoop. I'd think after as many years as you been in practice, nothing much would surprise you anymore."

"I guess I'm not exactly surprised. Disappointed is more accurate. Sometimes working in this field is exhausting."

"Okay, take a break Friday night and ask Darya to come with us to the banquet."

"I might. I've got nothing to lose."

Mitch laughs out loud before he advises, "You might want to work on your approach. I don't think even Darya will be impressed if you pitch it to her like that."

"Says the happily married man. You've forgotten how rough the game is."

Mitch hands me his phone. "Stop being such a wuss and call the lady already. The suspense is killing me."

I was saved from further embarrassment by the arrival of Lillian's grandchildren. Surprisingly, Atlas did well with them. He was shy at first, but once they gave him treats, he turned into a complete ball of cute.

I give Atlas his last dose of antibiotics for the day and place him in his kennel. When he gets adopted, I'll miss him something fierce. For such a little thing, he's quickly wormed his way into my heart. Mitch could have a point about me turning into a stereotype.

I take a deep breath and blow it out before I dial Darya's number. She sounds sleepy when she answers the phone, and I immediately apologize, "I'm sorry I didn't mean to wake you up."

Darya answers in a husky voice. "It's all right; you couldn't have known I would be asleep at this time of day. We had a stakeout go late last night — or should I say — this morning. I was just trying to catch a nap before Maya gets home from her friend's house."

"Still, I'm sorry. I know I have had overnight patient

watches. It sucks to be woken up when you're trying to catch up on your sleep."

"Is there something wrong with Atlas?" she asks with concern in her voice.

"No, can you believe I'm not calling about him? Atlas is terrific. He only has a few more days of treatment left. Otherwise, he is ready to be placed in a permanent home."

"Do you still believe he would be a good fit for our household?"

"I hope so. I haven't met your cat, but Atlas seems to do fine with Mitch's cat. He passed with flying colors at Ketki's house as well."

"So … if you didn't call me to talk about Atlas, why did you call?"

"I'm calling about our conversation the other day regarding being each other's plus one. Were you serious?"

"I might've been. What do you have in mind?"

"You may not be aware, but I serve on the Board of Directors at Hope's Haven. The Chamber of Commerce is giving us an award for our work with the youth offender program on Friday night. As much as I enjoy Jessica and Mitch's company, I get tired of feeling like a third wheel. I thought it would be fun if you came along."

Darya snorts with laughter. "That's your big sell? Banquet food where people give long, boring speeches? Way to sweep a lady off her feet."

I cringe. "You're right. I suck at this dating thing. Maybe I should call you back when I have something more exciting to offer."

"Relax, Dr. Eastwood. I was yanking your chain. I'll

have to find a sitter for Maya, but I think I can go."

I sag with relief. "Perfect. Can I pick you up around five? The banquet starts at six."

"Sounds good. It'll be nice to dress up for a change."

I try to focus on our conversation as I envision Darya dressed up. If she is wicked sexy in an oversized suit and novelty tie, I can't imagine how she'll affect me when she dresses up fancy.

"Great! I'll pick you up then."

After I hang up the phone, I kick myself for my inane conversational skills. It's amazing Darya wants to even talk to me, let alone go out with me after our stupid interaction. You'd never guess I have multiple diplomas on my wall. I sounded like a blubbering idiot.

I sigh as I plug my phone into the charger and sit down to do chart notes. I can't help but think how boring and sedate my life has become. Nora would be disappointed in my unwillingness to take chances. Maybe this friendship with Darya is a good place for me to rediscover the person I once was. Before Nora's death, I actually enjoyed life — now I feel as if I'm just existing from one day to the next. Something needs to change. These days, I even bore myself. It's time to take some chances again.

Chapter Four

Darya

I MAKE A SLOW twirl in front of Tinley. "Do I look okay? I haven't been this nervous about a date in a while. Thank you so much for volunteering to babysit."

"No problem, Ms. Vick. I was studying for my English Literature final anyway. This is a break for me too."

"All the emergency numbers are on the refrigerator, and there are fish sticks and tater tots in the freezer. I don't know if Maya will be hungry because I think she made pizzas today at the sitter's house. At least, that's what I hope was on her shirt. If it wasn't, I'll have to have a talk with Shirley."

Tinley giggles. "As a police detective, does your brain automatically go to the worst-case scenario? I already talked to Maya about it. She was telling me she put seven slices of pepperoni and eleven olives on her pizza."

"Funny, when I asked Maya how her day went, she told me, 'It was okay.' Maybe you should be an interrogator. You seem to be able to get details I can't."

Tinley glances up from her smart phone. "I know you meant that as a joke, but I seriously am considering majoring in criminal justice."

"Good for you! We need more smart people like you in our profession."

The alarm on my phone beeps and I draw in a deep breath. "Well, I guess this is it. Stuart should be here any time."

"No worries, Ms. Vick. You look killer. Dr. Stuart won't know what hit him. Don't worry about Maya, she and I will have a great time. If you want, I can spend the night if things go well on your date."

"Tinley! Stuart and I are friends. It's not that kind of date," I assure her as I try to hide my blush.

"I'm just sayin' if you guys have a special spark, I've got you covered," Tinley winks.

I shake my head in utter disbelief as I realize I'm taking dating advice from a sixteen-year-old.

"How about I play it by ear? I'll text you and let you know what my plans are."

"Well, the minute he sees you in that dress, all bets are off. I think I'll be staying the night."

"Don't get your hopes up. This is the first time I've gone out in a while."

"I'm not worried. My mom met my new step-dad and decided she would marry him two minutes into their first date. My mom said dating was just like riding a bicycle. Once you know how to do it, you know how to do it forever."

Before I can formulate a response, my doorbell rings. Stuart and I have hung out with Jessica and Mitch many times. I'm not sure why this feels so different to me, but somehow it does. I take a deep calming breath before I answer the door, yet I'm still a little shaky. My knees are knocking together. I open the door and smile as I resolve to make the best of my night out.

If I thought Stuart looked handsome in his scrubs and lab coat, this look is enough to knock me off my feet. He has his beard trimmed, his hair artfully coiffed, and he's wearing a conservative suit with a beautiful patterned tie. Instinctively, I do what my grandpa taught me to do. He always told me a man who shines his shoes would take care of you and everyone around you. Sure enough, Stuart is wearing black wingtip shoes, and they are shiny and clean.

Stuart catches me studying his shoes. He lifts his foot up and examines the bottom. "I don't think I tracked anything in the house." He shrugs as he flashes me an embarrassed smile. "I have lots of animals boarding this week, so you never know."

I blush. "Oh, it's a habit my grandfather taught me."

He grins. "Let me guess? You're checking to see if my socks match?"

I laugh softly. "Close enough. My grandfather had a thing about people shining their shoes. Whenever I see someone who's dressed up, I always have to see if they paid enough attention to detail to wear nice clean, shiny shoes."

"How funny. my grandfather was the one who taught me to shine shoes. He used to be in the military, and he was fastidious about that kind of thing. He would be thrilled to know you noticed my shoes. Speaking of shoes, those are some kind of shoes. You look marvelous. I don't think I've ever seen you in a dress, but it's a great look for you."

I flex my ankle and show off my sky-high heels. His open perusal makes my heart beat faster. "Thank you. I spend so much time struggling to be one of the guys; it's nice to dress like a woman for a change."

"I'm glad I could provide a change of pace for you — even if it does mean going to an awards banquet."

"I went to a wedding there a couple of months ago. The food is decent, so we'll be okay."

Stuart's stomach lets out a growl. "Good, I'm so relieved to hear that. I could do with some quality food. I've been living on protein bars and trail mix the last few days."

"Why?" I ask. The man clearly doesn't need to diet.

"A backyard breeder dumped a bunch of puppies on Craig's List who were positive for Parvo. I finally sent the last one home today. I saved four out of the seven who were brought in. I wish I could've saved them all. Unfortunately, that's not the way it works in my job."

"That must be the hardest part. How do you find time to mourn the animals who pass when you have to keep treating new sick ones?"

"It is hard, especially the ones who didn't get a fair shot at life or whose owners are really attached to them. Sometimes I wonder if I am more like a pastor than a veterinarian."

"I know the feeling. The hardest thing to do is console the family after a tragedy."

"Death notifications for human beings must be so much more challenging than for pets. I wouldn't want to be in your shoes."

"Fortunately, I don't have to do them much anymore.

Very rarely, they happen when I am investigating a missing person case, but for the most part by the time I'm called in, people already know their friend or relative has passed."

"I thought you were handling robberies and theft cases?" Stuart asks.

"At one point I was, but we are short staffed in the detective bureau, so I end up traveling around to different specialties."

"Well, I suppose your job isn't boring."

"No, I'll give you that. My job is rarely dull. I'm not a huge fan of stakeouts — but depending on who your partner is, they can be fun too. Whenever Dylan Palmer and I are together, we challenge each other to trivia contests. The man is wicked good. His skill level makes the time go by quickly."

"I know you probably get sick of shop talk, but what you do fascinates me. Do you have any stories you can share with a civilian?" We walk out the door and get in his truck. Before he shuts the truck door, he pulls the seatbelt over me so I can comfortably reach it.

I have to think a moment before I answer his question, "Yes, I guess I can tell you this one because it has already hit the news. This gentleman came to me because some of his most valuable antiques were gone. He was certain someone was coming in during the middle of the night and stealing his belongings. He was very disturbed by this. The man wanted us to put his house under round-the-clock surveillance. However, there was no sign of forced entry or anything else. His own security cameras never picked up a thing."

"Weird. Those cameras generally pick up almost

everything," Stuart remarks as he pulls out of my driveway.

"I know! It's so unusual for something that's being filmed to go missing. The story behind this is so sweet it'll give you a toothache."

"I love stories with happy endings."

"It turns out the victim in this case wasn't actually a victim after all. It was his wife trying to give him an epic anniversary present for their fiftieth wedding anniversary. She was cashing in antiques she figured he'd never miss so she could pull the money together to buy a vintage roadster for him. She was sneaking all the loot out of the house under her mu-mu or coat."

"So, was the husband more excited about his car or more upset about his missing valuables?"

"Let's put it this way ... a shiny, candy apple red vehicle in mint condition tends to put you in a better mood."

"That was a lucky break for the wife. I know my parents would not be pleased if things were missing from their various collections. My dad is a hoarder and keeps everything from labels off of pop bottles to historic newspapers. If you try to throw anything out, he has an anxiety attack. It makes it impossible to deal with either one of them. I worry about their health every day," Stuart replies as he scrubs his hand down his face.

"I saw a couple of episodes of those hoarding shows on TV. It must be emotionally draining to deal with that kind of situation."

"You're right — but the one thing those shows don't ever convey accurately enough is the terrible stench that goes along with hoarding. My parents would like me to visit more often, but I can't bring myself to deal with all the chaos. Maybe that's why I like things more orderly. I can be a little obsessive about neatness. When I was growing up, I was afraid I might end up like them — which is why I spent so much time with Mitch and Nora. I couldn't stand to be in my own home."

"Did Nora and Mitch understand what was going on?"

"It was hard to miss. They were the only people who I ever invited over to my house. Eventually, I moved out into a heated garage so I could be separate from the rest of the house. It was only then I felt comfortable inviting Mitch and Nora over. I was separated enough from the colossal mess that was the rest of my life, I felt safe to invite them into my world."

"Mental illness in any form is difficult. When it hits home, it's even worse."

"I spent years plotting to escape. I saw academics as my way out. I worked exceptionally hard in junior high and high school to get the highest grades so I would be eligible for scholarships. I played high school basketball thinking I might get a scholarship. Unfortunately, I just missed the cut. My academics were strong enough I still got almost a full ride to undergraduate school."

"Sounds like me. My father was very old school. He didn't believe women needed an education. He paid for my brother's college, but he didn't cover mine because he considered it to be completely unnecessary. If I wanted to go to college, I had to apply for every scholarship I could find. Eventually, I pulled just enough together to go to college and get my degree. I joined the Police Academy right after college. That's also where I met Sergio. In many ways, my husband was the perfect anecdote to my parents' attitude toward me. He believed I could do everything."

"I miss having a cheering section too. Nora thought I would be a world-famous veterinarian who discovered every cure to every problem in the animal kingdom. She never had a second of doubt about who I would be, or what I would accomplish."

"*Argh!* Listen to me go on and on. I promised myself I wouldn't talk about Sergio while I was on this date."

"Why would you do that?" he asks quizzically. "I'm a great listener."

"For one, I think it's rude. Two, I want to be able to put the past behind me. It seems like Sergio comes up in every single conversation I have. He is still a part of me even after all this time. I don't know if that will ever change. It sounds like you feel the same way about Nora."

"I do. Partially because Nora, Mitch and I were friends for as long as I can remember. Before she passed away, there weren't many memories in my mind that didn't involve her or Mitch — or both. Even all these years later, I feel a huge void."

"I've never spoken to anyone who feels the same way about all this as I do. I could force myself never to say Sergio's name again, but that feels unnatural to me. He was the center of my existence. He is the reason I made the detective ranks. He pushed me to be a better cop."

"I don't want you to feel any pressure because of the deal between us. This is supposed to be a fun solution to our dating woes. So, if you want to talk about your husband, please feel free. He was a big part of who you are. I want a chance to get to know you and Sergio was part of who shaped you. After all, he is the person who made you a mother."

I sag against the door handle. "Oh my Gosh! Thank you so much. I was worried that I would have to bite my tongue all night. I don't try to talk about Sergio, but it's hard to be who I really am when I avoid talking about him."

"I totally understand what you mean. On some of the blind dates I've been on, I've pretended Nora didn't exist. I found cutting her out of my vocabulary leaves a huge gaping hole in my past that's difficult to explain."

"That makes more sense than you could possibly know," I remark as a cloud of sadness settles over me.

I tuck my feet further under my chair to give Matilda a little more room under the table. She sighs and stretches out a little further. It's all I can do not to snicker at her antics. She is a very expressive service dog. I try my best to studiously ignore her. The couple next to us signals the waitress and asks to move. Curious, I turn to Mitch. "Are people always like this when you take your dogs into a restaurant?"

"Surprisingly, no. Most people are more in awe my dogs are so well behaved around all the food. It's hard to say what their issue was. It might've even been something as simple as allergies."

Stuart laughs under his breath. "To be fair, Mitch, you have to acknowledge Matilda isn't your usual service dog. Most people expect to see Labradors or Golden Retrievers — they don't expect to see a dog as big as a horse."

"True enough. Matilda will be a balance aid for a person who is losing their balance because of multiple sclerosis. Her size as a Great Dane makes her a perfect companion. This guy is about six feet four, so he needs a very tall dog to help him."

"I think it's great you were able to find him the perfect match. Matilda is very sweet — but even though I am a dog person, her size is intimidating."

"It is my hope when people see her working and supporting the client, all those stigmas will go away. She is the best-behaved dog in the class. I use her to show the younger dogs what to do."

"You should see his class. He's training everything from miniature border collies to Matilda. It's like a magical menagerie," Jessica comments.

When the wait staff drops off our meals, Stuart looks ready to dig in. As soon as the domes are removed Jessica slaps a hand over her mouth and runs toward the restroom.

I look around the table blankly as I ask, "Will she be okay?"

Mitch looks uncomfortable for a moment before he answers me. "It was our intention to keep all of this a secret, but it seems like Jess's body keeps betraying her."

My eyes light up as I decipher his clue. "How many weeks is she?"

"Almost to our second trimester. She's been sick every day since she found out — or maybe even before. Pregnancy is rough on her. It's so hard for me to watch her be sick and not be able to make her feel better."

I gaze over at him sympathetically. Mitch reminds me so much of my husband. Sergio worried about every item that went into my mouth and every symptom I ever had. He either worried my symptoms were too severe or not severe enough to be healthy. The man drove me crazy.

"Been there, done that," I blurt without thinking.

Mitch looks at me with a surprised expression. He raises an eyebrow in question.

I take a deep breath and confide, "For reasons I can't fully explain, I don't usually tell people this, but you and Stuart are such good friends it would be difficult for me not to tell you. Yes, I had morning sickness every day until I delivered my daughter, Maya. She's eight and a half now, and I still remember how awful I felt when I was pregnant."

Jessica arrives back at the table in time to hear my odd announcement. "Shut up! You have a kid?" she exclaims as she sits down next to Mitch.

"Yeah, I do. She starts third grade soon. I have a hard time even saying that out loud. It's shocking to me she has grown up so much."

Jessica looks stunned as I watch her process the information.

"Wait! I've known you longer than that. How were you pregnant without any of us knowing?"

"Remember when my dad had a stroke and then fell and broke his hip? I had her when I was there," I explain.

"I can't believe you never breathed a word. I can't imagine keeping this private," she adds, gesturing toward her invisible baby bump.

"You'll think I'm a terrible friend, but I didn't mean to keep all of it from you. It happened so suddenly; I didn't know how to break the news to people. My husband, Sergio and I met while I was in the police academy. Sergio worked as part of the bomb unit. Ironically, he was killed by a car bomb, but it wasn't one he was working on. So far, we haven't been able to solve his murder. I don't tell very many people about Maya's existence — for her safety."

Jessica's eyes tear up. "I'm sorry you had to go through this alone. If we had known, we would've been here for you. That's the kind of friends we are. I thought you knew."

"I do know. During that time, I wasn't thinking clearly, and I got in the habit of keeping Maya a secret from the world. I guess it never occurred to me you would want to know about my personal life. I know we've done some social stuff together. Still, I was never sure if I was included in the group because I helped figure out who stole Hope or if you considered me to be your friend."

Mitch shakes his head. "Darya, with all due respect — Hope is old enough to be retired now. From the moment we met you, I thought you were my friend. We invited you to our wedding!"

I blush. "I'm sorry. I didn't mean to hurt anyone's feelings, I just didn't know what end was up and I didn't want to assume things."

Stuart places his arm around my shoulder. "Don't worry about it, Darya. This group is big and forgiving. We are also very careful about what we share with other people. If you need Maya's existence to be kept a secret, she will go no farther than this table."

I fiddle with the cloth napkin. "I don't even know if Maya is truly in danger. It just feels necessary for me to not talk about her. No one ever figured out why Sergio was killed — so who knows, this person could have a vendetta against my whole family."

Jessica blanches. "Oh, I hope not. That would be awful."

"Have you considered getting a protection dog for Maya?" Mitch asks with a thoughtful expression.

"Now that the cat is out of the bag, I can tell you Darya and her daughter are the clients who are interested in adopting Atlas," Stuart reveals.

Mitch crosses his arms. "Not that there's anything wrong with Atlas, he's a sweet little pup. But, he won't afford you much protection against bad guys."

I sigh. "I know. I looked into becoming part of the canine squad, so I would have a trained dog around, but their waiting list is a mile and a half long. Evidently, they prefer people with dog training experience. I would've automatically been at the bottom of the list."

"I run a different list. I evaluate clients based on the urgency of their need. You would automatically go to the top of the list."

"If you're worried about Maya all the time, it likely affects your whole life," Stuart points out.

"True. I don't get much sleep."

"Come out to Hope's Haven. I'll see which dog works well with you, if you'd like."

"I'm overwhelmed by your generosity, but I don't know. Maya is so little I'm afraid she wouldn't know what to do with a dog that size. I told Stuart the other day she got caught in the middle of a dog attack as a toddler. She's uncomfortable around dogs in general."

Jessica pats me on the knee. "Hang around these guys for a while, you will become a fan of all breeds."

"I'm not concerned about me. It's Maya I'm worried about. She's petrified when she sees a big dog. I don't want to stress her out any more than she already is."

"I understand. Hope's Haven can help with that too. If you decide to adopt Atlas, let me know. I can set up some special dog training classes and involve Maya to help her get used to the presence of other dogs."

I pull my hair off my neck and nervously rub my dress. "Thank you so much for your kind offer. I don't know what decision I'll make about the dogs. I don't even know if Maya can tolerate a dog as small as Atlas. Right now, we're in a wait-and-see pattern. We'll have to see how well she does with him."

"Would you like me to bring Atlas over tomorrow? We can have a meet-and-greet."

I shake my head. "I don't know how, Maya has baseball practice."

"Lucky her," Stuart replies."

"Well … maybe she has baseball practice. The coach is in the process of quitting. Every other week, he sends an email out saying the next practice will be his last one. We've been going like this for about two months. I hope he doesn't quit because Maya loves to play."

Mitch pins Stuart with an intense gaze. "Someone I know knows how to play baseball extremely well. He needs to get more involved in the community. He lives where he works and that's not healthy for anyone."

"So do you," Stuart protests.

"Yeah, but my business operations don't take place

in my personal residence. You don't have enough of a separation between your work life and private life."

"Stuart, I thought you played basketball in high school?" I ask, as I try to follow the interplay between the two friends.

Mitch smirks. "Oh, he did. He considers himself a better basketball player than a baseball player, but the truth is he played both equally well."

Stuart shrugs. "I participated in every sport I could fit into the school year, but, the recruiters didn't come after me for baseball. It was all about the basketball."

Mitch shakes his head as he argues, "That was a pure fluke. You were gifted at both sports."

Stuart blushes. "Enough about me. Did you play sports when you were in school?"

I nod as I take a bite of my food.

"Well, don't keep us in suspense, what did you play?" Stuart presses.

"I did two things well — and one thing very poorly."

"That's not much of a hint," Jessica observes.

"I won't make you guess; you probably wouldn't in a million years, I was one of those square, nerdy kids. I didn't play the popular sports."

Jessica leans forward in her seat. "Okay, now you have me intrigued. I'd love to see if your hobbies beat mine for obscurity."

I laugh out loud. "Chances are they do. I was on the archery team and the shooting team. The sport I was awful at was tennis. You'd think if I had the upper body coordination needed to shoot at clay pigeons, I would be able to hit a tennis ball. Apparently, it involves a different process in my brain. I never got any good at tennis, despite trying for two years."

Stuart whistles through his teeth. "That explains so much. Tristan and Isaac were wondering why you shred their averages at the shooting range."

I blush as I take another bite. "I've always enjoyed shooting, but I don't do it much now. In my opinion, it's the number one downside to being a detective. I don't have an excuse to train in the shooting range very often — only when I re-qualify. I miss keeping my skills sharp."

Jessica puts her hands on her hips. "I wish you would've said something. There are a bunch of us who go out and shoot for fun. Savannah could use some competition. Rogue is good with firearms, but she's no match for Savannah. I guess Savannah took a boatload of personal safety classes and is an expert now."

"I'd love to, but any time I'm not working, I have Maya. I have a few friends who help out, but I try not to rely on them any more than I need to."

"All you need to do is ask. Rogue's twin sister, Ivy, loves kids. Ivy and Marcus don't have any yet, so I'm sure she would enjoy a little girl time with your daughter."

"I'll think about it. Maya can be shy around strangers."

"But, we're not strangers," Jessica argues. "You know all of us."

"I know all of you, but my daughter doesn't. I might have to bring her to some get-togethers and stick around so she can become accustomed to all of you."

"Oh, I have the perfect plan!" Jessica announces.

Mitch rolls his eyes. "I foresee a very spendy trip to

the mall in my future."

Jessica turns toward Mitch. "How'd you know what I was going to say?"

"It's easy to guess your plans. Every time you want to bond with your girlfriends, you all go on some industrial-strength shopping marathon. Now that you're pregnant, I can't even imagine what your shopping excursions will bring."

I look over at Jessica as I whisper, "You're so busted."

Jessica pulls her hair out of her eyes and takes a sip of her lemon water before. "I probably am, but he would've figured it out sooner or later. He knows I'm dying to shop for the baby — but we need to figure out what gender it is first. So, are we on for next weekend?"

"I don't know. I haven't looked at my schedule since it was posted this morning. I'll let you know."

The MC for the event taps on a glass as he tries to get our attention.

Stuart leans over and murmurs in my ear, "How is this for a full-service date? I found you a shooting club, a shopping club, and a dog trainer."

I smile at him and wink. "Well, you are doing better than one guy I went out with — he took pictures of women's cleavage and then rated them on a scale of one to ten," I tease.

Stuart grimaces. "I should hope so. If I can't do any better, I'm in serious trouble."

"Just so you know, the dating pool is very shallow."

"I am aware. That's why I am thrilled to be here with you. You are renewing my faith in the process."

I reach out and squeeze his hand. "The same holds for me. This is the most fun I've had in a while."

"Hold that thought — the speeches are about to start," Stuart warns.

"It's the company that matters, not the content," I comment as I turn my chair toward the stage.

"I'm not sure why you're my best friend," Mitch observes as he walks by Stuart and taps him on the shoulder. "You know good and well I'm the first one up."

Stuart grins up at his friend. "I didn't want to spoil the surprise. I figured Darya might actually be interested in your speech."

I look up at Mitch as I warn, "You better get up there. If that guy hits the glass any harder to get our attention, it's going to break."

Mitch calls Matilda, and she immediately falls into a heel position as they walk toward the stage. Mitch looks over his shoulder at Stuart. "Come on. Your name is on that award too."

Stuart looks at me helplessly. "I'm sorry. I usually stay behind the scenes."

"Go! You earned this award," I urge as I take the napkin from his lap.

Reluctantly, Stuart gets up and follows Mitch to the stage.

Jessica is tearful as she watches them walk toward the stage. "Aren't our guys something?"

"They do phenomenal work — you should be commended."

Jessica smiles at me. "Half of the team is attached to you. You get to be proud too."

I swallow hard and nod slightly, shattering a little inside as I acknowledge what Stuart and I are doing is just pretend. For a fleeting moment, I wonder what it would be like if we truly were a couple.

Chapter Five

Stuart

In the couple of days since our date, I don't think my feet have touched the ground. I'm grinning like a fool. It's been forever since I've felt this happy. I can't remember a time I've felt so connected to a person. Mitch was right; Darya and I have extremely similar senses of humor. It was almost as if we could finish each other's sentences. It says something about the quality of our friendship that we could have so much fun in the middle of an otherwise very boring event.

I take a large box out of the back of my truck and place Atlas' kennel on top. Admittedly, I'm giving Darya and Maya a lot more than I typically donate to a new adoptive family. I can't even pretend this adoption isn't special.

Darya opens her front door. I take a moment to drink in the sight of her. Today, she is decidedly dressed down. Her Levis have holes near the pockets and the knees. She is wearing a T-shirt and flip-flops.

Attached to her leg is a little girl with dark hair and dark brown eyes strikingly similar to Darya's. She is giving me a skeptical look as if she's trying to decide whether I am, in fact, an ax murderer.

I squat and set the box down as I take Atlas' kennel out of the box. Holding her gaze, I ask, "I brought a friend along with me, do you want to see him?"

Maya shakes her head no as she crouches further behind Darya.

Darya tries to disengage her daughter from her leg. "It's okay. I've met this puppy before. Remember the day I told you I rescued a puppy from the bad guys? This is the same puppy. His name is Atlas."

Maya pulls on Darya's sleeve. Darya leans closer to hear Maya whisper in her ear.

"You're right. Usually, we don't talk to strangers about animals. Dr. Stuart is the veterinarian who took care of Atlas. He's also a friend of mine. I've known him since before you were born. It's all right if you look at the puppy and talk to Dr. Stuart."

Maya examines me carefully as she tentatively takes a step forward to look.

She peeks through the metal gate and smiles. "He's little," she whispers to Darya.

I nod. "He is tiny. Would you like me to take him out of his crate so you can see him a little better?"

Maya looks up at her mother for guidance.

"It's all right, Maya. I've held Atlas several times; he is a very nice dog."

"He looks kind of like a weird kitty," comments Maya, as she steps closer to the kennel.

"He's a Chihuahua puppy. He's not very old. He is probably about three months old."

"He's like a baby," Maya realizes as she sticks her fingers through the openings in the mesh gate. She glances up at me and her brow furrows. "Why is your hair so weird?"

I reach up and touch my faux-hawk, as some would call it. I shrug. "I use a bunch of hairspray and stuff. I like to wear it this way. It keeps it out of my eyes. It helps people remember who I am, I suppose it's like my signature thing now."

"I never seen a grown up with hair like that before. I want to dye my hair purple, but my mom says I'm too little. I keep telling her I'm almost a teenager, but she says I shouldn't rush growing up too fast."

"Your mom is right. You're perfect the way you are. Being a kid is fun. You should enjoy it while you still can."

Atlas frantically tries to lick her fingers though the kennel bars. He is trembling with excitement as he tries to connect with her.

"Would you like me to open the kennel for you?"

"Will Mrs. Sprinkles eat the puppy?" Maya asks in a worried tone. "She likes to catch mice from the yard."

"I don't think so. Most cats try to steer clear of dogs they don't know."

"Mom, will you hold me? I want to see the dog, but I don't want him to bite me."

Darya smiles gently as she hitches her daughter up on her hip. "I'll keep you safe. Dr. Stuart will watch Atlas and make sure he doesn't do anything dangerous."

"Atlas has played with several other kids before, but he is a little shy at first. If you give him a treat, he'll come right around," I instruct as I open the kennel and gently lift Atlas out.

Maya's eyes widen as she looks at the tiny puppy, who is smaller than my hand. "Oh, poor puppy!" she exclaims. "He's cold. Mom let me down. I want to get the puppy a blanket."

Darya sets Maya on her feet, and she runs down the hall. Darya grins at me. "So far, so good. Maya is nervous, but not more than she usually is."

"Is she always this reserved, or is this something special for me?"

"Wait until she is more comfortable. Then you'll wonder where the shy child went. She tends to be timid at first, especially with men. I don't bring many of them around. To her, you might seem like an interesting specimen to be studied."

"I'm used to people reacting oddly to my presence. Sometimes, people forget I only treat animals. The other day, a mother brought her pug in for routine vaccinations, but her seven-year-old twins thought for sure I was going to give them shots too. They were inconsolable. My receptionist had to take them outside with sidewalk chalk before they calmed down."

Darya reaches out and takes Atlas from me. She holds him up in the air and examines him closely. "I can't believe he is already growing hair over his bald spots. I was afraid he would be half bald."

"The antibiotics helped clear up his skin quickly. I have a hunch when he is a little older, he will have long hair on his back and sides."

"Most Chihuahuas I've seen look like drowned rats."

"I think he may have a bit of Yorkie in him."

"I wonder what's taking Maya so long?" Darya says as she glances down the hall.

Apparently, Maya heard her mom because she yells, "I'm coming. Don't take the puppy away."

"Maya, don't worry. Dr. Stuart brought the puppy for you to see."

Maya runs into the living room carrying a small doll blanket. "I think this is the perfect size for the puppy."

Darya sits cross-legged it in the middle of her living room floor as she holds Atlas. "I think you're right. Why don't you see how Atlas likes your blanket?"

Gingerly, Maya walks up to the puppy in her mom's lap and covers him with the small fleece blanket. Atlas pulls the blanket off with his teeth and bunches it up before plopping down in the middle of it.

"How come he did that? If he's cold, he should leave the blanket on."

"I don't think Atlas is cold. I suspect he's shaking because he's nervous to meet you."

"Sometimes I get nervous too. I shook when I had to ride the school bus for the first time," Maya admits. "Atlas must like my mom. See, look, he is trying to take a nap."

"Atlas likes your mom a lot."

"Will he like me too?" Maya asks as she peers into her mother's lap.

"As long as you're gentle, I am sure he will love you."

I show Maya a pouch attached to my belt loops. "Do you want to give Atlas a treat?"

Maya nods slowly.

I pull the soft treats out of my goodie pouch and hold them out with my palm flat. "This is how you give the puppy treats. Can you do that with your hand?"

Maya nods again as she turns her palm skyward.

"Very good. Squeeze your fingers together so the treats don't fall through."

Maya immediately places her fingers closer together. I deposit a treat in the middle of her palm. "Now, put your hand where Atlas can reach it."

Atlas immediately takes the soft kibble from Maya's hand and devours it quickly.

"Mom, nobody taught the puppy to chew with his mouth closed," Maya says sternly.

"That's all right, Maya. Dogs can't chew that way; it's sort of a human thing."

Atlas pokes his nose up to sniff her palm again to see if she has another treat. He licks the side of her finger.

"That tickles!" Maya exclaims. "Do you think he wants to eat me?" she asks dubiously.

I shake my head. "Atlas is searching for more treats. He likes treats a lot."

Maya looks at Darya and grins. "Kinda like me and caramels, huh?"

"Exactly. To Atlas, dog treats seem like a special goodie."

Maya makes a face. "Does that mean the puppy has to drink milk and eat his vegetables to get strong like me?"

I grin. "Atlas has puppy food he eats that has special

vitamins to help him grow up big and strong. It is better for him to eat the puppy food than to eat people food."

Maya sits down beside her mom and copies her body language. "Do you think Atlas will sit in my lap?"

Darya shrugs. "I don't know. Let's give it a shot." She gently lifts up the puppy, blanket and all and places him in Maya's lap.

Atlas' back end wiggles a mile a minute as his tail wags. He puts his paws on Maya's torso and tries to chew on the ends of her hair.

Maya's eyes light up. "Look! The puppy is trying to give me a hug. He likes me."

Darya's eyes grow misty. "I see that. Do you think you are big enough to help me with the puppy?"

Maya nods enthusiastically. "I promise! I'll take good care of him."

Darya looks directly in Maya's eyes. "Sometimes, it probably won't be so fun. Atlas might need you to take care of him while you are watching cartoons. Or, you might have to take him outside in the rain to go potty."

"I don't think I like cartoons as much as I want Atlas."

"One of the most important things I tell new puppy owners is they have to be careful to keep things up off the floor so their puppies don't chew on them and get hurt," I caution.

"Yeah, Legos would be bad for a dog," Maya agrees.

"Mom's other friends, Mitch and Jessica teach classes to help the puppy learn manners. You'll have to help me teach the dog to behave. Are you up to that?"

"Are you joking me?" Maya asks. "A puppy this little

has to go to school?"

I nod. "Absolutely. You want your puppy to behave and not have bad manners."

"Boy, having a dog is hard work," Maya proclaims.

"It is. Do you think you're ready for that?"

Maya nods solemnly. "You said I was a big girl. Big girls can handle having dogs. 'Sides, this one is so little, he could fit in my doll's bed."

"That's probably true," Darya answers. "But, he is not your doll. You have to treat him gently."

Darya looks up at me as she announces, "I guess Atlas has found a new home."

"I think it is a great match," I declare as I spot the cat sitting on the back of the couch. "Let's see if Mrs. Sprinkles agrees. Can you hand me Atlas? I need to make a formal introduction."

"Atlas is going to curtsy like a princess?" Maya asks with astonishment.

Darya chuckles softly. "Not that kind of formal introduction, honey. He is going to show Mrs. Sprinkles the puppy isn't here to hurt her."

"Okay, that makes way more sense. I was confused!" Maya draws her knees up to her chest.

I walk over to the couch and let the cat smell Atlas. The puppy barks in a series of yips, but the cat does not seem to be bothered. After about half a second, Mrs. Sprinkles turns around and stretches out on the couch.

"Atlas barks funny," Maya announces. "He sounds like he's broken."

"Atlas is such a little dog, it's hard for him to make a

deep sound like a bigger dog."

"Will he always sound like that?" Maya asks.

"His bark will change as he gets older, but it won't ever be like a large dog."

"Weird."

"Every dog makes a different sound when they bark." I turn to Darya. "Apparently, your cat isn't too bothered by Atlas."

"That's good, right?" Maya confirms.

"It's a very good sign."

"Mom, does that mean Atlas is my dog now?" Maya asks as she looks over at her mom.

"I guess so. Everyone seems to be getting along well."

Maya stands up and jumps up and down. "I can't believe it! I have a dog. Wait until my friends see."

"Whoa," Darya says as she places her hand on her daughter's back. "Calm down before you scare him. We have to wait until Atlas is used to us before we introduce him to a bunch of people."

"How long will that take?" Maya asks in a dejected voice.

Darya smiles as she ruffles her daughter's hair. "Patience, little one. It will take how ever long it takes."

"There's another reason to take Atlas to puppy class. He can get used to being around other people and other animals."

Darya looks up at me. "Okay, I'll call Mitch and schedule a few classes."

"Maya, I'll see you in class. I have a new puppy I'm

helping to train too."

Darya looks at me with a puzzled expression. "You do?"

I shrug as I respond, "My older dog, Skye needs a friend and Sol is one of the cutest Bull Terriers I have ever seen."

Out of the corner of my eye, I see Atlas start to sniff around.

"Maya, when you see him do that, it means he needs to go potty."

"Where does a dog go potty?"

I ask Darya, "Where would you like me to take him?"

Darya looks a little startled before she answers, "I guess the side yard would be the best. It's fenced in."

"Maya, can you show me where the side yard is?"

"You have to go through the laundry room. Sometimes, our washer leaks, so you have to be careful. Don't slip."

I scoop Atlas off the floor and follow Maya. When we reach the side yard, I set Atlas down. After a few seconds of sniffing, he squats and defecates.

Maya watches with utter fascination. Finally, she comments, "His poop is as little as he is."

I chuckle at her observation. "True, but it can still make a mess. You'll need to take him outside often to make sure he learns to go to the bathroom outside instead of in your house."

Maya wrinkles her nose. "Gross."

"Puppy accidents are no fun, but all puppies have them. After all, he's just learning."

"There is this one kid in my class who has accidents too. The teacher says the same thing about him."

I wasn't expecting her to share that story, so I choke back a laugh as I struggle to find something to say. Before I can comment, Darya gives her daughter a hard look. "Amaya Vick, do we tell other people's private business?"

Maya looks subdued. "No, ma'am."

I can tell Darya is struggling to keep a straight face too as she agrees, "I didn't think so."

Maya goes back to watching Atlas explore the yard. A few seconds later, she pulls on my shirttail as she asks, "Where will the puppy sleep?"

"That's up to your mom. But, I brought a kennel for Atlas and a small dog bed. You and your mom can choose where he sleeps."

"Did you bring food too?" Maya adds.

"I did. It's all in the big box I brought in. I also brought Atlas' favorite toys."

"Does he know how to play fetch?" Maya asks hopefully.

"Not yet, but that's something you can teach him."

"I'm a pretty good teacher. My teacher says so because I taught some of my friends to play hopscotch."

I smile. Darya was right. Maya seems to be warming up a little. "Well, after hopscotch, fetch should be easy. Our friends, Mitch and his wife, Jessica, will help you learn how to teach Atlas new tricks."

"I can't wait! Maybe Atlas can be like one of those circus dogs I saw on TV."

"Maybe… You never know what the future might

hold," I respond as I catch Darya's eyes over Maya's head.

CHAPTER SIX

DARYA

My hands are sweating as I stand outside my supervisor's office. I have no idea why he asked for a meeting with me. As far as I know, I have done nothing controversial or even made a close call recently.

He opens his door abruptly. "Don't just stand there; Come on in."

"Captain," I greet with a nod.

"I bet you're wondering why I called you in here." He shuffles through a file.

"The thought did occur to me," I admit.

"At least this time, it's not a complaint about your choice in neckwear."

I roll my eyes. "Yeah, who knew a Bugs Bunny tie would be so controversial?"

He chuckles. "I never understood that one. It was a tie, for Pete's sake — not a protest sign."

"Well, the upside to the whole ordeal is I got permission from HR to wear novelty ties as long as they have no offensive speech on them."

Captain Allegheny clears his throat. "I didn't bring

you in here to talk about your fashion choices."

My heart sinks to my toes as I scramble to figure out what I've done.

"There is no easy way to introduce this topic, so I'll just tell you."

"Please do," I croak as I try to catch my breath.

"I'm sure you'll remember they found a degraded DNA sample in your husband's car which they could not match to known exemplars."

I nod slowly. Of all the things I expected him to say, this was not it. "Has there been a new development? Last I heard, they thought they wouldn't be able to retrieve anything definitive that would hold up in court."

"DNA technology has advanced to the point where they can make matches even from a partially degraded sample."

"Have they?" I press as I focus on keeping my breathing even and containing my excitement.

"The good news is, they were able to make a match, the bad news is the suspect was killed in a gang fight in prison."

All my hope drains away. I can't tell you how many false leads we've had in Sergio's case. "Then why did you even bother to bring me in here? It breaks my heart every time we can't follow-up on one of these so-called leads. I don't know how much longer I can put up with this. I'm losing hope. I don't think we'll ever find my husband's killer," I vent.

Captain Allegheny nods sympathetically. "I can understand why you're so frustrated. The reason this lead is so critically important is because Mr. Johnson has ties to an active neo-Nazi group."

My eyebrows shoot up. "Sergio was killed because he was Hispanic?"

"It may be too early to determine that, but crimes involving this group tend to be violent and racially motivated. So, it's good to be aware."

"Are they rounding up Mr. Johnson's associates to question them?"

"Yes, because we suspect this might be a hate crime, there is a special task force within the FBI leading the investigation. That might move things along a little faster. They have more resources than we do."

"Captain, I'll be honest with you. Not a day goes by that I'm not mistaken for a radical Muslim. Most people associate people who look like me with terrorists. As Maya grows up, I fear the situation will be even worse for her. How am I supposed to cope with a threat I cannot see or identify? How do I keep my daughter safe? It's been years since Sergio was killed and now the threat seems more imminent than ever. I don't know how much longer I can cope with this. Some days, I feel like running away, but I don't know if there is a safe place on the planet to hide from hate."

Captain Allegheny takes off his glasses and rubs his eyes. "I wish I had better news for you. Unfortunately, there are segments of society which are dark and ugly. I'd like to shield you from all of that. Even when someone has expertise in the field, it's not always enough."

I slump down in my chair. "Don't remind me. I am haunted by that thought every single night. If Sergio were here, he would not want me to live like this."

"I know this sounds like an empty promise, but we

are still working on your case. It's slow and plodding, but bit by bit we're making progress."

I take a tissue off of Captain Allegheny's desk and wipe my eyes. "I understand, but it's still hard. Can't you do something to make it go faster?"

Captain Allegheny sighs. "Darya, you're a valuable asset to our police force. If I could've moved heaven and earth to solve this case years ago, I would've. We have to be careful to work within the system. We don't want to bust whoever did this without following proper procedure. If we don't, we run the risk of allowing them to go free. We have to go by the book."

I stand up and pace around his office. "I understand. You're right, Captain. Sometimes I want to take that book and feed it through a paper shredder."

Captain Allegheny nods. "There are days I want to say the hell with my job title and my responsibilities and figure out who did this any way I can. But, that helps no one in the long run."

When I return from investigating a bogus lead in a shoplifting ring, I wearily walk to my desk. I'm surprised to come face-to-face with Stuart. He is carrying two cups of coffee.

He grins when he sees my Star Wars tie. "I approve of your fashion choices today, Detective Vick. It makes me wish my usual attire required a suit and tie instead of scrubs. Your collection of neckties is beyond impressive."

When he reaches me, he thrusts a cup of hot coffee in my hand. "I hope this is the way you like it. In case it isn't, I brought sugar and cream on the side."

I smile at his thoughtfulness. "Thank you so much. I have to admit even though I am a seasoned cop, I've never developed a taste for black coffee. I will gladly take the cream and sugar."

When I look up from putting the cream and sugar in my coffee, I notice Stuart is studying me intently.

"What? Do I have dirt on my face?"

"No, I'm wondering what kind of case you're handling that's taken the sparkle out of your eyes," Stuart asks.

I look up at the clock and realize I haven't even taken lunch yet. "Do you have a moment to get something to eat? There is a good food truck up the street that serves barbecue. I'm starving and I need a break from this place."

"Yeah, actually I do have time. For some reason, my schedule today is exceptionally light."

I walk over to the bulletin board and mark myself out as I tell the receptionist, "I'm going to take a few minutes for lunch. If it's an emergency, I'll have my cell phone on me."

"Thanks for letting me know, Detective Vick," Kelsey says with a smile. "Do me a favor, don't hurry back. You've been running yourself ragged. You deserve to take a full lunch hour for a change."

I smile wanly. "I may take you up on that. It's been a long morning already. The day has barely started and I'm ready to go home and call it done."

Kelsey gives Stuart a hard look. "Make her take care of herself, will you?"

"I'll do my best," Stuart pledges as he places his arm around my waist and escorts me out the door.

As we stand in front of the bank of tables beside the barbecue truck, I'm quietly lost in my thoughts as Stuart methodically unpacks our lunch and organizes it in front of me. "I'm sensing whatever is wrong is bigger than being hungry or needing caffeine to get through your day. Can you tell me what's happening or is it related to a case?"

"It *is* related to a case. Unfortunately … it's *my* case. Every time it seems we're making progress on Sergio's murder, it's another dead end. I'm about to give up hope. Sometimes, it feels like a waste of our resources to continue to chase leads in a case that's colder than ice."

"This isn't my area of expertise, but I watch television and it's my understanding one tip can set the case in a whole new direction. You never know when that clue will show itself," Stuart says carefully.

I shrug. "You're right. Still, how many clues will surface on their own after this much time? It's hard to not feel like we lost the battle before we've even begun. It's been too long. Nobody cares anymore."

Stuart shoots me a sympathetic look. "I'm sorry today has been so tough. I hope things get easier soon."

"I don't know how they'll ever get better. Our strongest lead to date ended up dead. How do we recover from that blow?"

"I don't know. I wish I did. If nothing else, I'm here for moral support."

"It might be easier to deal with if that was my only problem, but it's not. I have to deal with Maya too. Right now, she's next to impossible to live with. She is so emotional about not being able to play baseball, I'm not even sure how to deal with it."

"Did your coach finally throw in the towel?"

"Threw in the towel and apparently absconded with a big portion of our budget too. They won't even let me investigate the case because I'm one of the victims. I am so frustrated I could spit. I want to find this jerk and nail him to the wall. Maya and I even made homemade cookies for the bake sale. She is devastated."

"What a scumbag! That does suck. I'm so sorry."

I drag my hand through my ponytail and flip it behind my back. "Losing the money is only part of the problem. The kids worked hard to make it to the playoffs, and now if they don't have a coach within the next three days, they have to forfeit their spot. It's so unfair — the guy should've stuck it out until the season was completely over. Talk about being a bad role model."

"I agree. It's wrong to take it out on the kids."

"Rather than blindside Maya with the truth, I tried to warn her what might happen if her coach stepped down. When she figured it out, Maya went ballistic. She was counting on being the star catcher. I feel like a failure as a mother because I can't fix this. I bet Sergio would know what to do."

"Oh, poor Maya. At her age, disappointments like that run deep."

"Tell me about it; she's been crying herself to sleep every night. The only bright spot in her world is Atlas. He is so sweet — he can tell whenever she is upset and he can't get close enough to her."

"I understand how he feels. I wish I could take away your pain and make it easier."

I take a sip of my coffee. "Thank you, the fact you want to make things better, is a step in the right direction. The rest of it, I have to figure out on my own. Thank you for lunch and the coffee."

Stuart gathers up our garbage and throws it away. When he comes back to the table he says, "Not so fast. I'm supposed to make sure you spend your whole lunch hour with me. So, instead of rushing back to your desk, we're going to take a nice walk around the park."

"But I have so much work to do," I protest halfheartedly.

Stuart flashes me a grin. "That's the thing about paperwork, it'll still be there when you get back to the office. You need to give yourself a mental health break — especially today."

Stuart pulls me up against his side and puts his arm around my waist. He has no idea how comforting I find this gesture. Although he feels different from Sergio, the sensation of warmth and protection is much the same. I lean my head against his chest. "Thank you so much for taking care of me when I'm too scatterbrained to do it on my own. Usually, I'm much more put together than this."

He pulls away from me and looks me in the eyes. "Darya, I've been your friend for a long time. I know you are. Every once in a while, you have to give yourself permission to relax and become unwound. Otherwise, you'll break."

I take a deep breath as I try to clear away my stress. "I know you're right, but I have so many things to do. It's hard to prioritize my life."

"Lucky for you, you have me around to help remind

you you're important — not only to Maya — but to me too."

"Thank you, I can't tell you how much that means. It's been a long time since someone watched out for me."

"If you need anything, let me know. I am happy to help."

A warm glow passes through my body as I consider what a difference Stuart has made. He may think he only treats animals, but he has helped me feel immeasurably better.

As we walk back to my office, I slide my hand into his. "If I haven't told you this already, I am beyond grateful you are in my life."

Stuart kisses my temple as he whispers, "Ditto."

Chapter Seven

Stuart

Hoisting a few folding chairs up on my shoulder, I place them in a large circle in the training room of Hope's Haven. The old German Shepherd, who is the namesake of Mitch's training center, lounges on a custom-made orthopedic mattress. I had to replace Hope's hip a few months ago and she seems to be getting along better these days.

"Are you ready for tonight?" Mitch asks me as he places little bags of treats on each chair.

"I think so. Solstice is making solid progress on his own, but I believe he needs more socialization. He's all goofy puppy, and he's a little rough with Skye."

"That's helpful information, but not what I was referring to. I'm more curious about whether you are ready to come face-to-face with Darya. It sure seemed like you guys were generating some heat at the awards dinner. Jessica and I could barely get a word in edgewise."

"What do you think about Alachua County Youth Baseball?" I ask abruptly.

Mitch snickers at me. "Give our little one a chance to be born before you enroll him or her in sports —"

"You're a regular comedian, aren't you? I was talking about Maya's team. Her coach quit in the middle of the season and if they don't have a coach by tomorrow afternoon, the kids won't get to compete in the playoffs. That's bogus. Who in their right mind would let a bunch of kids down?"

Mitch stops what he's doing and looks at me. "It's not as if you don't have the athletic prowess to do it. You competed in Little League all the way through school. But, are you sure you have the time?"

"It's a short-term commitment. I've got a recent grad from the University of Florida working for me. She could cover my practice in the afternoons. Dr. Austin is quite capable of handling almost everything that comes through my door. Sydney's surgical skills need practice — but overall, she's a talented vet with excellent people skills."

"It sounds like you've already made your decision. I mean, you've gone as far as to have contingency plans in the works. What's holding you back?" Mitch observes me.

"I guess it's because I'm new in Maya's life. I don't want Darya to think I am using the baseball team to get close to her."

"Well … aren't you?" Mitch asks pointedly.

I look away from Mitch's intense gaze and study the tops of my shoes. "I can't deny that it would be great to run into Darya. The kids really need a coach. Remember the time when I was ten, and I broke my arm? My team missed the playoffs because I wasn't pitching. Twenty years later, I still wonder what would've happened that year if I hadn't broken my arm. I don't want these kids to wonder what could have been if only the grown-ups in their life had gotten their crap together."

I hear Mitch sigh. "You have to be careful with how you present it to Darya. She has a powerful BS meter. If you try to go in there with a song and dance that isn't true, she'll be defensive. I'd tell her what you just told me."

"Even the part about hoping she comes around?"

Mitch shakes his head at my indecision. "I guess I'd play it by ear. It'll be interesting to see if you guys are throwing off sparks today or if it was a fluke because of the environment at the banquet."

"Remember, you're supposed to be teaching an obedience class, not diagnosing my love life," I tease.

Mitch grins at me. "Nothing says I can't multi-task. Good luck tonight. Darya is a phenomenal woman. I like her almost as much as I love my wife. I hope there's something between the two of you. It'd be a good thing."

"Wow! That's saying a lot … because you adore Jessica," I comment, surprised at by best friend's defense of Darya.

"I do. Don't screw this thing up. Playing referee between two friends is not a place I want to be."

"I'll try my best. For the first time in a long time I'm excited about my future."

Mitch looks at me solemnly. "I can't tell you how glad I am to hear that. Jessica has been crazy worried about you. She's convinced you are drowning in loneliness. You deserve a chance at the same kind of happiness Jess and I have."

I swallow hard and mess with my baseball cap as I try to put a lid on my emotions. "So, what do you say we put the ball in play? Do you want to be my assistant coach? Darya might be less suspicious if my game plan involves both of us."

Mitch rubs the back of his neck as he mulls over the idea. "Only because it involves you — I'm in on this insane plan to woo your woman. I might even recruit my grandfather-in-law to help. Walter loves baseball. As long as we've all moved back to Gainesville, we might as well start a family tradition. Our little one will appreciate it someday."

Even though I am practically a professional student in Mitch's dog training classes, I'm remarkably nervous. Every time someone comes through the door, my heart practically screeches to a stop.

Mitch walks behind me and whispers, "Breathe, my friend, I don't want to pick you up off the floor. Darya sent me a text message saying she's running a few minutes late because she has to pick up Maya from the sitter."

"Am I that obvious?" I ask Mitch as he walks away.

He pauses and turns around for a moment. "Probably only to me — I haven't seen you this excited since you asked Nora to the eighth-grade dance."

Solstice plays with my shoelace and I squat down to distract him. He seems to understand my emotional distress as he climbs onto my legs and kisses me in the face.

"Sol, sit," I command. His little butt hits the cement, but his tail never stops wagging.

From my left, I hear a voice, "Mom, look Dr. Stuart's

puppy is already doing it. Isn't that cool? That's what we're going to teach Atlas, right?"

I hear light laughter from Darya. "Maybe not today, I think they probably have a lot of information to share with us before we get started."

"I hope not. I want my dog to do what Dr. Stuart's puppy can do."

I stand up and face Maya. "I've taken Mitch's class before, so Solstice has a bit of a head start."

Maya looks up at Darya. "Is that the same is cheating?"

Darya glances over at me with an amused expression. Kneeling down next to her daughter, she says, "No, I don't think so. I bet Mitch counts on Dr. Stuart's help to run the class. So, Stuart needs to know his dog can demonstrate properly for Mitch."

I give Sol a treat and offer one to Atlas, who's comfortably perched in Maya's arms.

"It's a funny thing about dog training; some dogs like to practice obedience and learn quickly. Other dogs are more stubborn and take longer. Have you ever seen the dogs on television run all those fancy obstacle courses? Those dogs start out in a class very much like this one."

"I want Atlas to be a smart dog like those ones," Maya answers as she sets her dog down on the floor.

"From what I've seen, Atlas is very smart," I assure her as I sit in the chair next to her.

"My mom says I'm smart too. I can't decide whether I want to be a policeman like my mom or if I want to be a teacher like Mrs. Avery. I was thinking about being a baseball player, but Mom says it's not a very practical dream."

"I see," I answer. I'm not sure what else to say.

As I am trying to come up with an answer, Maya continues her story. "Anyway, my mom is probably right. I must not be very good at baseball because our coach quit."

"Amaya Vick! You know better. How good your team is has nothing to do with why your coach stepped away. The Pelican Sliders rock. You made it all the way to the playoffs," Darya corrects emphatically.

Maya foregoes the folding chair and sits on the floor as she cuddles Atlas in her lap. "I know — but we don't get to play no more because the coach left."

Maya's dejected posture spurs me to make an impulsive declaration. I catch Darya's eye and softly announce, "I don't know what the process is, but Mitch and I are willing to coach the team if the organization will let us."

Darya's mouth rounds in surprise before she stammers, "I don't suppose the two of you have criminal background checks handy, do you? Time is running short."

"We do. It's required by our liability insurance. All the people who work at Hope's Haven as staff or volunteers have to undergo routine background checks. Mitch and I recently completed ours. I can get you copies."

"Are you sure about this? Do you know anything about T-ball? Our kids run the gamut. Some of them, like Maya, are super talented, others just do it for the fun of it."

"It's been quite a few years since I competed in Little League, but I think I can get back into the swing of things. A community-based baseball league can't be much different from what I did as a kid."

Darya quirks her lip up. "You'd be surprised. The level of competition isn't quite as intense. We have an 'everybody plays' policy. We're not aiming for perfection — just good clean fun. Although, don't tell the parents, some of my fellow parents are a bit too enthusiastic about their children doing well."

"I remember that kind of thing when I was in Little League. One of the parents punched out another over a bad call. It was scary to watch."

Darya raises an eyebrow at me. "So, if you and Mitch take over the team, are you guys going to control stuff like that? I worry Maya might learn unsportsmanlike conduct from the parents, of all people."

"We'll make it a priority," I vow.

"You might be the person we need to whip our team into shape before the playoffs. I wish I could be more involved, but my schedule is unpredictable, and I can't be off in the afternoons. Talk to me after class, and I'll give you the contact information of the organizer."

"I look forward to it," I answer candidly. My mind whirls as I try to fit together the puzzle pieces I will need to make all of this happen.

The ambient sound in the family-friendly pizza parlor is almost drowning out Maya's enthusiastic conversation. I have to struggle to hear her over a crying toddler a few tables away.

"Atlas did the awesomest today in class, didn't he?"

Maya asks as she stuffs another bite of pizza in her mouth.

"He's a very talented dog."

"I know, right? I knew he was smart. He knows all the places to hide from Mrs. Sprinkles."

"I suppose they haven't made friends yet —"

"Sometimes, when Mrs. Sprinkles is sleepy, Atlas likes to sneak up and cuddle next to her to keep warm. But, when my kitty is awake, Atlas is scared of her."

"I don't blame him; the cat is bigger than he is," I reason.

"Will Atlas be a big dog when he's all growed up?"

"He'll be a little bigger, but he won't be a big dog like a Newfoundland or a Labrador."

Maya sticks out her bottom lip, "I was hoping he would get big like the dog in *Air Bud*. He seems nice."

"I'm sorry, Atlas is a small breed dog. He is designed to be small. He's not a Golden Retriever like the dog in the movie."

Maya turns to Darya. "Can I have a big dog too? Atlas is so smart; he could teach the big dog stuff."

Darya looks stunned by her daughter's request. "We can talk about that later. I thought you didn't like big dogs."

"I thought so too, but Matilda is the biggest dog I've ever seen in my whole life, and she is nice."

"I'll think about it," Darya hedges.

In a stage whisper, Maya responds, "Mom's gonna say no."

"Not necessarily," clarifies Darya, "it means I need

to think about it."

Maya crosses her arms and narrows her gaze at her mother as she challenges, "When was the last time you said that and you didn't say no?"

Darya slumps back against the booth. "Am I that predictable?"

Maya takes a long drink of her soda before she nods. "Uh-huh."

Darya looks at me helplessly. "I guess I better change up my game every once in a while. My daughter is too smart for me."

"I'm smart enough to have two dogs," Maya announces cheekily.

Darya reaches out to tuck Maya's hair behind her ear as she explains, "I know I usually mean no when I say I'll think about it. This time I really will think about it. There are a lot of things to consider. I work a lot. Who would watch two dogs?"

"I don't know. Atlas sleeps in my room, so you still need a big dog. How long will it take you to think about it?" Maya asks Darya in a frustrated tone.

Darya frowns. "Amaya Vick, it will take as long as it takes. It doesn't help if you get impatient."

Maya looks down at the table. "Sorry, Mom, I got excited."

"I know honey, but this decision will take a while. After all, we just got Atlas and he's barely settled into his new home. I don't want to disrupt him by adding another animal."

Maya sets her drink down as she looks longingly over at the play area. "I ate all my dinner. Can I go play with the other kids now?" she asks.

"Okay, let's go get you checked in." Darya looks at me apologetically. "I'll be right back."

As I watch Darya and Maya walk away, I'm amazed at Darya's ability to handle everything at once.

Darya comes back quickly and slides gracefully into the booth. "I need coffee, stat. I try not to drink too much of it in front of Maya because I don't want to be a bad example, but I am on call tonight. I'm already exhausted. I hope nothing gnarly comes in on my shift. Lately, I've been unlucky when it comes to that. I've been working an insane amount of doubles — often, that means there's a homicide involved. Those are so draining. I don't think I've stopped being tired since Maya was born."

"You weren't kidding. Maya does come out of her shell once she gets to know you. She asks a lot of insightful questions. She did amazingly well being the only child in Mitch's class. It's clear Atlas adores her."

"Sergio was brilliant, and Maya certainly takes after him. Sometimes, I struggle to keep up with her quick mind. It's hard to be both Mom and Dad."

"I never met Sergio, but I think Maya is a lot like you. She is compassionate, funny and smart. Those are characteristics she got from you."

"You think so? Some days I feel like all I do is tell my daughter she can't do things. It gets old."

"I wouldn't worry about it. Kids usually do better with structure. I think you are doing a remarkable job with her."

"Stuart, I have to ask you if you were serious about the coaching gig? The team is devastated they might not get a chance to compete in the playoffs. It would be great if you could step up and help out."

"Sure, give me the name of the organizer of your league and I'll set the ball in motion."

"For real? I don't want to get the team's hopes up if you plan to walk away like everyone else."

I reach out and touch Darya's arm. "Look, I know it seems like I take little in life very seriously, but one thing I do take seriously are my commitments to children and charities. If your daughter's team needs a coach, I'll happily volunteer."

"The guy I've been working with is Ramon Velasquez."

I groan as I hear the name. "The situation just got a little more complicated. Ramon and I go back a long way. The last time he saw me, a piece of my bat broke off and struck him in the cheekbone. He had to have surgery during our senior trip. I don't know if he's still angry with me, but I want you to be aware that we have a bit of a history."

"That is an unfortunate coincidence, but the fact remains you're the only person who's stepped up to help the Alachua County Youth League. I have to believe it's all going to work out in the end. My daughter deserves to play. She's worked all season for this victory."

I grimace as I tease, "Way to put on the pressure. Do you realize I've never actually coached a baseball team? Now, you're asking me to take a team who doesn't even know me all the way to the finals. I am a talented baseball player, but I don't know if I'm a miracle worker."

"The fact you're showing up in my daughter's life as someone she can count on means you are already a winner, no matter what happens in the playoffs."

"It's not a problem. I know from personal experience every once in a while, even the professional rescuers need help."

"I know you're being modest about this and about all of your accomplishments. It's no small deal. You'll be influencing not only her life, but the lives of the rest of the team. As my grandmother would say, 'You're putting lots of good karma in your bank.' I hope it pays off for you."

I look at her flushed face and warm brown eyes and see nothing but good things. "Some things are worth the challenge."

Chapter Eight

Darya

I HAND CAPTAIN ALLEGHENY a bagel and a cup of coffee. "I figure as long as we keep meeting like this, I might as well feed you." I sit down in the uncomfortable vinyl chair across from his desk as I wait for him to explain the reason for this visit.

"I have to tell you you're a godsend, Detective Vick. All heck is breaking loose in our department. This may be the only time I get to catch a bite to eat."

"I heard about the tasing. If it makes the officer feel better, I used to deal with that kid's family back when I was a beat cop. They don't have any respect for anyone's life — especially police officers."

"I'll be sure to tell the officer. He's freaked out because this was his first Tasing outside of the police academy. He didn't have a choice because the kid was coming at him with a knife, but he didn't know the boy had underlying heart problems, which made the Taser more lethal. He is feeling guilty the perp is in the hospital. However, it was a good call. I hope he can figure it out sooner rather than later."

"I've done that too. On one of my first arrests in

Gainesville, I broke a suspect's arm when he became combative as I was putting the cuffs on. He ended up having surgery to insert pins in his bones. The whole incident haunted me for a long time. Eventually, I concluded there was no way I could have known how fragile his bones were."

"I recall hearing something about it. The guy had that weird bone disease, right?"

"That's what the DA told me. Still, it took me a long time to forgive myself."

Captain Allegheny takes a long sip of his coffee before he runs his hand through his gray hair. "On days like today, I regret not following my mother's advice. I could have been a banker with a cushy corner office who puts in less than forty hours a week. I swear, I've put in forty hours today alone."

"I have been pulling long shifts myself. When do we get to add more staff?"

"I'm working on it. It doesn't help any when we get stuff like this thrown in our face. This crap doesn't do me any favors."

"I feel out of the loop. Do we have something else going on besides the Taser incident?"

Captain Allegheny slowly drags his hand down his face. "I'm so sorry, Vick … I thought someone told you. Let me queue it up for you so you are not blindsided on your own."

"Is this about the testimony I had to give to the grand jury?" I try in vain to read his expression.

Captain Allegheny shakes his head. "As far as I know, this has nothing to do with your testimony."

"I suspect this has a lot more to do with your husband's death than anything else. However, the powers-that-be are not being super helpful."

"I thought we were done fighting over jurisdictions. Didn't we sort them all out?"

"I thought we did too — but that was a different case in a different time. For now, I seem to be stuck between a rock and a hard place. Every place I go for answers, I hit a roadblock."

"You've already broken the bad news that it has something to do with Sergio's death. Lay the rest of it on me. I've learned to expect bad news."

Captain Allegheny twirls his pencil in his hand before he admits, "There is a whole task force of people who are trying to figure out what this means or even when it was posted. Apparently, they were monitoring an ex-felon, and he had this bookmarked on his Internet browser. It might've been floating around the Internet for several years, but this is the first time anyone has taken notice and attached it to our police force."

"I thought the IT guys could pretty much figure out the second something hit the Internet. So, what are we talking about?"

Captain Allegheny swings his monitor around so I can watch. I suck in a deep breath as ominous music plays. An altered voice comes on the video to narrate. "We have already taken one of your precious few. There is nothing to say we cannot come back for more. America is the land of the pure and untouched. The infidels shall not be allowed to propagate."

The video fades to black. I glance over at my Captain. "Why do they think it's related to us?"

"Just wait," he advises as he nods toward the screen.

As I study the monitor, the song *Eye of the Tiger* comes on as images from crime scenes appear.

"*Holy crap!*" I exclaim as I see a familiar picture. "That is a scene from a convenience store arson I investigated. Whoever did it burned out an entire family."

As I watch more, I recognize another horrific picture. "*Holy cow!* That is a picture from Dylan Palmer's case. Remember the woman who was killed in front of her three kids? Those pictures were so graphic; they were never released to the public. How did this creep get them?"

"We don't know. It would appear this video is not more than four years old based on the pictures included."

"I noticed no pictures from recent cases, so that might narrow it down."

"Yeah, our technicians are working on it. There are thousands of crime pictures in our archives, and not all of them were as high-profile as the ones you recognized. It is freaking scary that whoever is behind this had access to over two hundred crime pictures — some of which were not ever public, as far as we can tell."

"I hope I'm paranoid here, but as one of the few people on this force who is not Caucasian, I feel like the threat might be directed at me and my daughter."

"There's a reason you are sitting in my office, and it's not because you frequently bring me delicious things to eat," Captain Allegheny concedes. His lips are pressed into a thin line as he holds my gaze.

"What am I supposed to read into the fact all the crime victims featured in the video were minorities? Please level with me. I have Maya to protect."

"I'd wait before you jump to that conclusion until the task force is done with its work," he cautions.

"With all due respect, Captain, I don't have the luxury of waiting around for the task force. When I went to get that cup of coffee you're drinking, someone spat at me and told me to go home and read the Koran."

"Vick, please tell me you kept it together. I don't need another PR mess on top of all the stuff we're dealing with."

"It took industrial-strength tongue biting, but I said nothing. My badge was visible, and I was on the clock. I said nothing as I cleaned up and washed my hands. I even paid for the coffee because I didn't want to run afoul of ethics rules. The coffee shop owner saw what happened and offered to give me the food and drinks on the house."

"Will you press charges?" Allegheny asks with a look of resignation.

"No," I respond with an eye-roll. "If I pressed charges against everyone who was rude or discriminatory against me because of the way I look, I'd never get anything done. These days it's hard to tell whether people are angry because I have dark skin or because I am a police officer."

Captain Allegheny takes a drink of his coffee. "True enough. Still, I'm sorry; that kind of behavior is not acceptable — regardless of whether it's because of your race or your profession. People should treat each other a little better."

"I won't argue with you. People should, but they often don't. Unfortunately, my experience today was not unusual. I've learned to let it roll off my back. It doesn't seem that I am a third generation American. My grandfather was a respected physician in Pakistan, but he came to America to help prevent polio. It's all about hate. So, my question is how in the world do I keep my family safe from a threat I can't identify or stop?"

My captain sets his coffee down on his cluttered desk and leans forward in his chair. He takes a gulp of air before he addresses me. "Detective Vick, I won't kid you and tell you I know the answer. You've already lost your husband; I don't even want you to have to deal with all of this. Unfortunately, it is what it is. Be extremely cautious."

Grinding my teeth in frustration, I try not to let the seemingly simple admonition crack my broken heart wide open. Every morning I would tell Sergio to have steady hands, a bright mind and a cautious heart. Even that did not save him.

"I don't suppose I have to remind you Sergio López was one of the most cautious, aware people I've ever known, and he is dead. I've already basically hidden my daughter from the world. A lot of people don't know I have a child. In fact, I hurt a group of friends I respect a lot because I didn't share the information about Maya. I don't know what else I can do."

"I don't know either, Vick. All we can hope is this video helps lead to real suspects this time."

"Somehow, that doesn't feel like enough," I remark with a heavy sigh.

For the first time in several hours, my lips curve up into a natural grin. It is such a relief from the crushing anxiety

I've been feeling. It is impossible not to smile when I see Maya with Atlas. When I thought about getting a dog, I was worried Maya would quickly lose interest. Quite the opposite has happened; Maya is so attentive to the puppy's needs he has the basics of obedience training down pat.

I'm not the only person who has noticed her affinity with animals. Mitch has made her his unofficial teaching partner. She often is the first to demonstrate each new command. The other day, I caught her watching dog training videos on YouTube instead of her usual diet of *The Glitter Force*. I never considered Chihuahuas to be particularly bright, but Atlas is bucking the trend.

As I watch Maya walk Atlas around the training center, a shiver goes down my back as I get the feeling I'm being watched. My heart beats faster, and I have to consciously slow down my breathing. Carefully, I swivel on my stool to catch a glimpse in my peripheral vision. I hate what my life has become. I'm tired of being scared all the time. I'd give anything to go back to the days where I was oblivious to everything around me. I don't know if I'll ever be able to let my guard down. When I catch the perpetrator's eye, he blushes and looks away. His wife, who is a fellow student, cuffs him on the back of the head as if to say, "Put your eyeballs back where they belong".

Expelling the breath I've been holding, I try to steady my nerves. This time, it was an ordinary guy who finds me distracting. This time ... but what about the next?

Maya runs toward me with Atlas' leash in her hand. She has a wide grin on her face and is practically vibrating with excitement. As soon as she takes a moment to look at me, her demeanor sobers. "Mom, what's wrong? Are you cold? You're shaking."

I shrug, downplaying my fear for my daughter. "Yeah, I suppose I am. I just got a chill up my back."

"Weird; everyone else here is sweating — especially Doctor Stuart. He told Mitch if he didn't turn on the air conditioning, he could turn this place into a swimming pool because everyone is sweating so much. I told Doctor Stuart he was gross."

I choke back a snort of laughter. "You're right, that is disgusting."

"Guess what?" Maya hops from one foot to the other.

"What?" I play along. Maya adores guessing games.

"Atlas knows how to roll over. At first, Mitch thought Atlas did it on accident, but then I showed him again. Doctor Stuart says not even Solstice can do that," Maya brags.

"Wow! I'm impressed. Seriously, Maya, you've done a phenomenal job with your puppy."

"Does that mean we can get a big dog too?" Maya presses hopefully.

"I haven't made the final decision yet, but I'm thinking about it."

"Oh, I forgot to tell you. Mitch wants to talk to you after class."

Stuart comes up behind me and murmurs, "You look lovely today."

I look down at my tailored pinstripe suit and at my relatively tame tie. "Oh, this old thing? I just threw it on because I had a meeting with the prosecutor today. Honestly, Tori Clarkson is always perfectly dressed. She intimidates me."

"From where I stand, you don't have anything to be intimidated about. You look perfect."

"Thank you, I appreciate that. I'll take all the help I can get."

Stuart speaks quietly in my ear. "Speaking of that, Mitch needs to talk to you."

"Yeah, Maya told me."

"It's important, so don't leave without talking to him, okay?"

Stuart's tone sends my stomach lurching toward my throat.

"Is everything okay?" I ask anxiously.

"If everything goes well, I think things will be better soon."

"What do you mean?" I ask, searching Stuart's face.

"It's not my place to say. You really need to talk to Mitch about this. He's the director of the program."

I feel a lump in my throat. "Have we done something wrong? I thought Maya was doing well. We've been practicing all the commands we've been taught."

"Darya, take a deep breath. This has nothing to do with how well the class is going. It's an entirely separate matter. He just needs to speak to you privately after class."

Stuart places his warm hands on my shoulders and gives me a massage. Instinctively, I lean into his touch. I miss small moments like this more than I can say. I try to collect myself as I roll my neck and whisper, "Thank you. It's been an incredibly stressful day."

"I'm available for massages anytime you need them,"

Stuart offers. The smile in his voice is clear even though I'm not looking at him.

Resting my cheek against his knuckles. "Be careful, I might take you up on that. You may be sorry you offered."

Stuart grabs the chair beside me and straddles it backward as he looks at me intently. "If you need me, I'm here for you… all you have to do is ask."

Tears sting the corner of my eyes. "Today of all days, you might want to reconsider. My life is a complete mess at the moment, and there is no indication it's about to get better anytime soon."

Stuart runs his hand along my forearm. "I wish you'd let me help. That's what you do when you're dating someone — it doesn't matter that we're pretending."

Our conversation suddenly feels oddly intimate. I look up to see where Maya is. To my relief, Jessica is dancing with her in the middle of the training room — out of earshot.

I clear my throat. "I'll keep that in mind." Raising my voice a little, I add, "It looks like class is over, so I need to go speak to Mitch. It's been a long day, and I want to get Maya home and tucked in bed soon."

I straighten my spine as if I'm headed into battle. I walk over to Mitch who is putting his training gear away. "You needed to see me?" I stammer.

Mitch turns around and regards me carefully. "Are you okay?"

His question takes me off guard, and I sink into an oversized chair. "Yeah, I'm good," I instinctively answer. "Why do you ask?"

Mitch rolls his shoulder slightly. "Oh, it was just something Maya said."

"What did she say?" I ask with alarm.

"Nothing major, she mentioned she saw you crying in the bathroom before class. She's worried."

The idea that I am so stressed out I can't even hide it from my eight-year-old daughter is enough to crumble what's left of my reserve.

I use the back of my hand to wipe tears from my face." I lied — things are not okay. They are *so* not okay. I'm beginning to think being frightened twenty-four hours a day, seven days a week is my new normal. I'm so angry at myself. Sergio wouldn't have wanted me to live this way. He certainly wouldn't have wanted me to freak out our daughter because I'm afraid of my own shadow. I'm tired of living in fear."

Mitch puts down the dog leashes and walks over to give me a hug. "I can't fix everything and I can't make Sergio come back, but I might be able to lighten the burden of watching your back all the time."

"How? You and Jessica have jobs. You can't guard me all day. Besides, I'm not sure I would let you. I don't want to put anyone else at risk."

"One of my trained protection dogs came back to me. Dozer's new family can't keep him because one of their children wound up being severely allergic to dogs. I feel terrible because Dozer is an excellent working dog and you would be his third placement."

"Third placement?" I ask. "What kind of dog is he?"

"He is a Belgian Tervuren."

"A w-what?" I stutter.

"A Belgian Tervuren. It's a herding dog that looks a lot like a fluffy German Shepherd."

"He sounds beautiful. What's wrong with him?"

"Nothing. That's the sad part of this. He was trained by the TSA to be a bomb detection dog. Unfortunately, he turned out to be skittish around umbrellas so they washed him out of the program. Isaac is well connected within law enforcement and Hope's Haven is given a fast track for adoption."

"Wow, cool!"

"Yeah, it's great to give the dogs a second chance. I brought Dozer into our program and worked with him on his phobias. I trained him to do additional protection work and placed him with a musician's family here in Florida. Unfortunately, one of her children ended up being allergic to the dog. So, Dozer came back to Hope's Haven."

"Poor thing, he must be so confused."

"He does seem lonely for sure. Belgian Tervurens are social dogs. They don't cope well with being left alone."

"How does he do with kids, cats and minuscule dogs?" I ask in a resigned tone. Mitch knew exactly how to appeal to me. I'm a sucker for a sad story.

"Dozer plays with Jess' summer reading camp kids just fine. He likes our cats — even the ones who don't care for him. He's best buddies with the Yorkie we are boarding," Mitch explains as he addresses each of my concerns.

I look over at Maya. She is showing Jessica Atlas' new tricks. "You don't think Dozer would pose a risk to Maya?"

"I don't. He is very gentle around kids. I've put him through a battery of temperament tests and he passes with flying colors. I wish all my dogs performed as well as Dozer does."

"I'm off day after tomorrow. Can I bring Atlas over to see how they get along?"

"Sure. I'll throw stuff on the grill and we can make it a social thing."

Standing up, I give Mitch a half hug. "Sounds good. I need to go collect your junior trainer and put her to bed."

"Something tells me my 'junior trainer', as you call her, will be a very happy camper soon. Dozer is a real charmer."

I grimace. "I hope this all works out, because I would hate to get Maya's hopes up for nothing."

CHAPTER NINE

STUART

"I DON'T KNOW WHY I'm always surprised at the amount of hair this dog has. He looks like he should be radically overweight, but he's not. He's just fluffy."

"Yeah, fluffy and in need of a bath. Is your high school student still around?" Mitch asks as he takes off Dozer's collar for me.

"She sure is. Jenny has been champing at the bit for something to do. The animals I have in clinic right now are either too sick to be handled or self-sufficient. There are only so many things she can file."

"Do you think she would mind giving Dozer her most thorough spa treatment? I want him looking his best."

My eyebrow goes up. "Please tell me this is for who I think it is."

"It is. Darya is coming over tomorrow for a meet-and-greet."

"I hope Dozer here can give her peace of mind. Darya mentioned how little sleep she gets. Maya told me even more. Apparently, Darya has been reacting strangely to noises on the television."

Mitch looks surprised. "She hasn't always been afraid of stuff like that. I wonder what's going on?"

"It's hard to know because there's so much she can't tell us about her job. Still, I get the feeling it must be something big. Even Maya seems to be wound up and worried."

"I wish there was more we could do to help. Darya has always been there for us. It seems like she could use a hand now, but I'm not sure what she needs. I think she may find Dozer here to be an answer to her prayers. Do me a favor, take care of as much of his care as you can. I don't want Darya to have to worry. She has enough things on her plate."

"One super deluxe spa day at The Critter Clinic coming up. Consider it done." I look down at Dozer sprawled out on my exam table and address him, "You have no idea that all of your dreams are about to come true."

Mitch reaches out to scratch Dozer's ears affectionately. "I hope you're right. This dog could use a happy ending for a change."

Mitch is sitting in a lounge chair next to Dozer. He's busy taking pictures of Jessica while I man the grill. I don't mind because Mitch's grill is about twice the size of mine. I feel like a professional chef when I cook at his house. "Do we know if Maya likes hamburgers or hot dogs?"

Before Mitch or Jessica can answer, I hear a voice coming from the sliding glass door. "Maya doesn't care. Whatever you do, don't try to feed her onions," Darya replies with a chuckle.

Darya gasps. "Oh my Gosh! Who wouldn't want this dog? He's beautiful." She plops down on the deck beside Dozer. She looks up at Mitch as she asks, "Will he be okay with this?"

"I think you'll find precious little upsets Dozer. He's pretty mellow until he has a reason not to be."

"What if I'm the reason he's not mellow?" Darya jokes. "These days, I'm on edge most of the time."

"Well, we hope to change that with Dozer. He can handle whatever comes your way."

"May I pet him?" Darya asks.

Mitch nods. "Knock yourself out. Get comfortable with him. It's the only way you'll be able to tell if you guys are a good match."

"He's not working or anything, right?"

"Not at the moment," Jessica responds. "I was just playing fetch with him."

"Mom!" comes a voice from inside the house. "Can I bring Atlas out now? He wants to play fetch too."

"Wait a second, Maya," Darya answers as she looks to Mitch for guidance. "Do we have to do anything special here?"

"No, not in this case. Dozer has been trained to ignore other animals."

"Okay, Maya, you can come out now. Don't be bouncy. I don't want you to scare Dozer."

"Don't you remember? Mitch told us about that in class." Maya carries Atlas in her arms.

As soon as Atlas sees Dozer, his whole rear end starts

to wiggle. He struggles to get out of Maya's arms so he can get closer to Dozer. Although Dozer stays in his down position, his back-end is twitching just as much.

"Look how happy Atlas is. See Mom? I told you we should get a big dog."

Darya shoots a bemused smile at Maya. "You did say that."

Mitch makes a hand signal, and Dozer stands up and walks over to Maya. For several moments, he stands in front of Maya. It looks like he is making an assessment of her well-being. He lies down in front of her feet and puts his chin on the toe of her shoe.

"Dr. Stuart, I think the big dog likes me," Maya tells me with a wide, happy grin.

"It sure looks that way."

Dozer stands up and sniffs Atlas. Maya turns to me with wide eyes as she asks, "Is he going to eat my dog?"

"No, sweetie, he's just curious. They seem happy to see each other, so you can let Atlas run around on the deck."

"Geh spielen," Mitch commands softly.

Dozer's body language suddenly changes, and he relaxes.

"What did you say?" Darya asks with a startled expression.

"I gave Dozer permission to play with Atlas. When we train protection dogs, we teach the commands in German so it's unlikely someone could sabotage him when he is on duty."

"Smart. I never would've thought of that. I have one question though. How will I know what commands to give?"

"If you decide Dozer is a good match, you are welcome to bring him to the protection dog class, and I will teach you the specialized commands. I have a class meeting two weeks from Saturday for law enforcement and search and rescue teams. You are welcome to attend that one as well."

While Mitch and Darya talk about the class, I watch Dozer intently. He seems curious about Atlas, but not aggressive. Atlas walks up to Dozer's paw and grabs a tuft of fur with his teeth and pulls. I hold my breath as I wait to see how Dozer reacts. To my relief, Dozer collapses into a play bow and wags his tail with excitement. When Atlas barks at him, Dozer lies down and rolls over on his back. It is hysterical to see a dog as big as Dozer become submissive to such a tiny creature. Atlas walks around and tries to climb on Dozer's tail. When he can't get enough leverage on the rapidly swinging tail, he yaps at Dozer and runs across the deck. Dozer scrambles to his feet and chases after him. Of course, it takes the Tervuren only one step to catch up with the tiny Chihuahua. When he does, Dozer starts the play ritual all over again.

"I think it's safe to say these two will get along fine," I predict with a chuckle.

"Stuart, toss me a hot dog," Mitch instructs. "I have to run a couple of small tests."

"Oh, I saw you do this when Maya and Atlas were in class. This is a biggie," Darya remarks.

"Dozer, *hier*," Mitch commands softly.

Dozer immediately stops playing and runs over to Mitch, sits at his feet, and gazes at him expectantly.

"*Braver Hund!*" Mitch praises.

"What did you say, Mitch? It sounds like you're sneezing," Maya giggles.

"First, I told Dozer to come here and then I told him he was a good boy when he did," Mitch explains.

"Can I tell Atlas that stuff in regular talk?" Maya asks.

"Of course," Mitch says. "As long as your dog understands, any language will work."

Maya walks over to where Mitch is sitting and commands, "Atlas, come're."

Atlas' ears perk up, and he runs toward Maya as fast as his little legs can carry him. He screeches to a halt when he meets her and plops his butt on the deck. I laugh out loud when Maya gives Mitch a look that says, "Top that."

"Wow! You guys have been practicing," Jessica comments.

I walk over to Mitch and hand him a plate with a hot dog on it. Darya is gnawing on her knuckle as if she is waiting for the other shoe to drop. I walk behind her and place my hands on her shoulders. I lean down and whisper in her ear, "Relax, Dozer has this. He is a professional."

Darya melts into me as she lets out a deep breath. "I guess whatever happens, happens."

"Atlas is well behaved for a puppy. I'm impressed with how much progress he's made," I assure her.

Darya reaches back and places her hand on top of mine on her shoulder. "I wish I could say I had a lot to do with it, but it's mostly been Maya."

"She is very mature for her age. Most kids would be too busy running around to bother with something as tedious as training a puppy."

"I know! I am so proud of her. Still, you know from seeing her on the baseball field she's not always so on point."

"Yeah, she was cute. She said she couldn't catch the ball because she had to save a family of ladybugs crawling on the grass."

Darya snorts. "You're lucky it was during practice and not an actual game. Otherwise, there's a whole contingent of parents who would've come unglued."

"Yeah, I told Mr. Hollister if he didn't take it down a few notches, I would not allow him to attend his daughter's games."

"What did he say?" Darya asks.

"He threatened to send his mother-in-law to cheer for her. I understand from the other parents she's even more disruptive."

Our conversation is interrupted when Atlas notices Mitch has hot dogs and barks uncontrollably.

Maya and Darya start to step in but Mitch holds up a hand to stop them. "Normally, I would have you correct this kind of behavior, but I want the puppy to be excited about the food this time. I want to see how Dozer reacts to the frenzy."

"*Lass es,*" Mitch directs quietly as he hands Atlas a piece of hot dog. Of course, Atlas gobbles it down quickly as Dozer stays on command and looks at the morsel wistfully.

Moving over to look directly at Atlas, Mitch commands sit. As soon as the puppy's bottom hits the deck, Mitch tells him to leave it. Atlas looks a bit dejected but stays put as Mitch feeds the hot dog to Dozer. He glances up at Maya in surprise. "We haven't covered this in class yet."

Maya grins a bit smugly. "I was planning to surprise you. I went on YouTube and figured out what was next. I was right, huh?"

"You were. I guess it won't be too much longer before you can teach my classes."

"I'm just a kid!" Maya protests. "I think you have to be a grown-up to be a teacher."

"You may have a point. Maybe I'll wait a couple of years before I retire."

"What's the last test?" Darya asks.

"This one's easy. I need Maya to give Dozer a tight hug for me."

Dozer holds stoically still during the hug, but he does not appear to be bothered by Maya's presence.

"Okay, clearly Dozer would make a great family pet, but how does that help me?"

I walk over to Maya and squat down in front of her. "Do you want to watch a movie with Mitch and Jessica? I'm going on a walk with your mom."

"Do they have *Air Bud*?" Maya asks.

Jessica grins as she grabs a big tray of food. "We sure do! It's one of my favorite movies. Come on, let's go. We can bring the hot dogs inside and have a picnic on the front room floor."

Maya starts to skip away as she follows Jessica into the house with Atlas following behind, at the last minute she turns to Darya. "Bye Mom, be careful."

I grab a lead off the hook on the post on Mitch's deck. Using a hand gesture for the command to come, I signal to Dozer. He immediately falls into a heel position. "Are you ready to show your stuff?" I whisper as I attach the lead to his collar.

I reach out for Darya's hand as we walk through the gate. As soon as we hit the sidewalk, I put Dozer on duty with a softly uttered phrase. His body language immediately becomes more alert as he walks between Darya and the curb.

"What just happened?" Darya asks as she watches Dozer.

"I gave him the command to guard you. It's basically like putting bullets in the chamber. Nothing will happen until a triggering event occurs. I wanted to show you — play mode and work mode are distinctly different things."

"Are you sure he won't want to go after Maya if he's working?"

"No, he won't see her as a threat. Mitch works hard to make sure protection dogs are family dogs."

"Oh, I'm relieved to hear that. I have to admit, I was a little nervous to get a big dog, but there is something about Dozer that is very comforting. Dozer looks like a big shaggy teddy bear."

"Don't let appearances fool you, if anyone tries to hurt you, the teddy bear will disappear."

"I find that hard to believe. He looks quite laid-back. Are you sure he won't be a big couch potato?"

"Oh, I'm certain he will be a couch potato, but he'll also be a heckuva protection dog. This dog is crazy smart."

Darya shrugs. "Okay, I'll take your word for it. Color me skeptical though."

I squeeze her hand as we walk around a fire hydrant. As we pass by an abandoned building, someone charges toward Darya. She cowers into my arms and hides her face. "Oh, *crap!*" she breathes as she starts to shake. Dozer is too busy to notice because he is trying to wake up the entire neighborhood. His bark sounds ferocious. The guy backs up and puts his hands up in the air as he screams, "Call the dog off!"

Darya looks up at me in panic. "How?"

I glance at Dozer as I command, "*Anhalten.*"

Dozer backs up and sits as the guy walks away shaking his head.

"Wow, I was not expecting that. I would definitely feel a lot safer with Dozer watching my back."

"That's the whole point of all this. Mitch dedicates a lot of his time to training service dogs and protection dogs."

"Jessica told me you used to work with Mitch when you were still in school."

"I did. Now I help him in other ways."

"What do you do?" Darya asks.

"At first when Mitch and Jessica ended up relocating in Kansas to help Walter and Wilma, I was scrambling with licensing stuff. But, before I could get all that straightened out, they elected to move to Gainesville so I relocated here too."

"I wondered how that happened. Isn't it weird we all ended up in Gainesville even though it wasn't planned?" Darya remarks with a crooked grin.

"I know. It's strange how that all worked out. Anyway, in honor of the work Nora, Mitch and I have done together I've tried to beef up my veterinary skills to cover the needs of search and rescue dogs. After I graduated from school, I took advanced training in orthopedics. I knew the search and rescue and service dogs Mitch worked with were prone to injuries and special stresses. I wanted to make sure I was prepared to treat the type of injuries his dogs would most likely encounter."

Darya snuggles up against my side. "You are a lethal combination of smart, nice, and handsome. I love the way you and Mitch work together to do good things in the world."

Conversations like this always make my stomach burn. I have to take a deep breath and swallow hard a few times before I can respond. "I consider myself blessed to be a veterinarian. I loved learning as a kid. Learning new things was an escape for me, and the order of science was the perfect anecdote to the mess at home. School was a respite from the chaos and disorder. I'm thankful I can accept cases for charity — it is my way to give back. Hope's Haven is part of that. I don't charge Mitch for routine vet care for the dogs he takes in."

Looking down at Dozer, I add, "I also try to find rescue dogs that would be good candidates for service animals. Sometimes, Mitch uses them for service animals and other times for protection or search and rescue. He has quite an army of trainers out at Hope's Haven now."

"Do you have much luck finding good rescue dogs?"

"You'd be surprised. Today, somebody surrendered three dogs which were about six months old. They're very sweet Golden Retrievers, but the owners decided they didn't want the hair all over their home. I was happy to take them off their hands for Mitch."

"I am so glad you could save them. Do you think Mitch will train a few more guide dogs? Tuffy is remarkable."

"John and Tuffy make a solid team. That's the rewarding part of the job. Mitch takes dogs other people have thrown away and gives them a mission in life. He doesn't care what they look like or if they're purebreds."

"Dozer here is such an unusual breed, I've never seen one before. I take it dogs like him aren't a dime a dozen?"

"True. Dozer was like hitting the lottery."

Suddenly, we're charged at from the street. The guy has a baseball bat.

Dozer vaults straight in the air and hits the guy dead center in his torso. Our assailant falls to the ground. Dozer bites at his arms. The guy looks at me with pleading eyes.

"*Achtung*," I shout.

Dozer gives a small whine of frustration as he backs off and stands protectively in front of Darya.

After a few deep breaths, Darya walks around Dozer and helps the guy up. "I don't know what short straw you drew today to pull this kind of duty. However, you did your job very well; I was scared to death for a second. Are you okay?" Darya says as she tries to look under the young man's protective suit.

The guy rubs his arm. "Ahh, that was nothing. At least Dozer has manners. I was working with Mitch to help train another dog who was seriously lacking an off switch. I had bruises for weeks."

Darya looks at me with wide eyes. "Okay, I'm convinced. Dozer does have what it takes to watch my back. Are you done trying to give me a heart attack?"

I shrug. "In truth, I don't know what Mitch has planned. All of these incidents are as big a surprise to me as to you."

"I'm not sure I should ever trust you to plan our activities after this."

"I don't blame you. Still, if we hadn't shown you, you wouldn't have had complete faith in Dozer."

"I can see where you're coming from — but, geez, I think you took ten years off my life."

I wish Mitch hadn't put me in this position. I want Darya to trust me. I try to explain as best I can, "Sorry. I'm trying to keep you safe."

"I know; I just can't decide whether I'm angry or ecstatic."

A little girl passes us on a bicycle and then stops and turns around. She throws her bike to the ground and runs up to Dozer. Darya and I both cringe as the little girl sticks her hand in Dozer's face. To his credit, Dozer just sits at Darya's feet observing the antics of the child. "Can I pet your dog?" Darya kneels down beside the child. "I would rather you didn't. Dozer is working right now."

"He doesn't have a vest," the little girl observes.

"You're right. He doesn't, but he's still on the job. Thank you for asking if you can pet him."

"I love dogs. I just want to give him a hug. Is that all right?"

I glance over at Darya. "It might tell you how well Dozer deals with unexpected interruptions. A lot of people don't understand working dogs should not be handled."

"All right, you can pet Dozer for a couple minutes," I concede.

The little girl throws her arms around Dozer's neck and hangs on for all she's worth. The only part of Dozer that breaks protocol is his tail, which is rapidly cleaning off a spot on the sidewalk.

"This is an awesome dog. I'm going to ask my mom if I can have one too. Okay … bye!" She runs to her bike and takes off.

With a confused look, Darya asks, "Do you think that was planned?"

"I have no idea, but Dozer was a rock star."

"He was. Now, I need to go back and make my own little rockstar enormously happy and tell her she was right. We do need a big dog. *This* big dog."

CHAPTER TEN

DARYA

"I CAN'T BELIEVE YOU not only brought me dinner, but you're cooking it as well." When I curl up on the couch, Dozer tries to be stealthy and climb on the other side of the couch and lay his head in my lap. I swear, if I hadn't seen him act as a protection dog, I would've never believed he was capable of it. He's a big old baby.

"It's not impressive; I'm making macaroni and cheese and apple crisp. It's not rocket science," Stuart protests.

"You don't understand how much I've been craving macaroni and cheese which doesn't come from a well-known box. It's about all Maya likes to eat. She's even figured out a way to make it in the microwave."

"Mitch could tell you stories. When we were growing up, I went through a stage where all I wanted to eat were those nasty frozen burritos. Mitch and Nora were so grossed out. Admittedly, I stayed in that phase a lot longer than I should've."

I chuckle. "I guess I don't have much room to talk. My food obsession was peanut butter and jelly sandwiches. They had to have the crusts cut off and be cut diagonally — otherwise, I treated them as if they were poison."

Stuart grins. "I'm sure glad we've outgrown our food obsessions we had as kids. I bet Maya will eventually shed hers too."

"I'm glad your food tastes have changed, because your cooking smells delicious. Aside from a few cookouts at Jessica and Mitch's place, people rarely ever cook for me. It's a luxury I usually don't have as a single mom." I pause for a moment. "I guess that's not right. Maya makes me eggs and toast and she managed to learn to make French toast by watching a YouTube video. Occasionally, she whips up a batch for me. She can be so sweet."

Stuart walks into the living room with a handful of hot pads in his apron pocket. He is carrying my large casserole dish. "Be forewarned: I can't guarantee these will be any match for Maya's culinary excellence." He sets the food on the coffee table.

"Don't sell yourself short. This looks restaurant-worthy," I compliment as he serves me.

"Where's Maya tonight?" Stuart asks me, looking around my apartment.

"Get this … Jessica took her to the mall and is having an old-fashioned slumber-party. I was told in no uncertain terms I couldn't attend because I'm the 'mom'. Jessica informed me the other day since she is an only child, she won't get the chance to be an aunt, so she's using Maya as a stand-in niece. I thought she was kidding, but she was here bright and early to take Maya for the weekend."

"You have to keep in mind Jessica completely adores children. Remember, she works with the children's program at the library. She is very passionate about her cause."

"Jessica will make a wonderful mother, won't she?"

"I think so. Mitch and Jessica will be the cool parents on the block. I can see it now."

"I'm excited for her — and not just because we get to go shopping for adorable clothes."

I lean back against Stuart's chest as he flips through the channels to find a game he wants to watch. When he reaches the beginning of my channels again, he groans. "The last time I saw this few channels, I was at my grandparents' house."

I chuckle. "Have you been talking to my daughter? That's what she says. But, I'm not here much to watch TV, and most of the stuff Maya watches is available online."

"I guess I'm spoiled. I've got virtually every channel under the sun."

Dozer scoots closer and plops his head in the middle of my lap. Stuart looks down. "How's it going with him?"

"Better than I expected. When I told Captain Allegheny about all of Dozer's training at the TSA and Hope's Haven, he suggested I bring him to work. It wasn't until the captain told me how much it costs to get protection animals that I realized what a gift Mitch had given me. I had no idea these dogs go for tens of thousands of dollars."

"Mitch has a 'pay it forward' system. You went out of your way to rescue Atlas and give him a home. So, under Mitch's karma-math, you were due for some kindness."

"If he does that all the time, how does he keep the

training center open?"

"Fortunately for Mitch, most of his staff is as dedicated to his cause as he is. He has several corporate clients who pay full price."

"Good; I feel guilty I'm not in a position to pay."

Stuart strokes my arms as he looks over my shoulder at Dozer. "It seems like you two need each other. Sometimes, things happen for a reason even when we don't know why."

I rest my head against Stuart's chest as I sigh. "I'm afraid you'll think I'm crazy. But, something about Dozer is familiar to me. When he looks into my eyes, it's almost as if I see Sergio's warm brown eyes and quick smile. Nobody knows this but me — but for Sergio and me, a red bandanna signified love shared. Sergio would keep them in his back pocket. Whenever he thought of me, he would tie a bandanna onto something of mine. I never knew whether I'd find the bandanna on my steering wheel or on my purse handle. I would repay the favor by returning it to him. I hid it in his gym bag or tied it to his desk drawer. It was our silent way of communicating how much we love each other." I draw in a shaky breath as I cope with the rush of memories. "When I saw a red bandanna on Dozer, I couldn't help but think it was a sign from Sergio."

Stuart wraps his arms around me. "Beautiful. I miss doing sweet random things. Nora had a tattoo of a butterfly on her hip. She got it when she turned eighteen. She told me the butterfly signified freedom and life for her. It was her emancipation from a childhood that would make any reasonable person cringe."

"Oh, I'm sorry. Having a past like that can make it

hard to look forward to the future."

"Things were tough on all three of us in different ways. But, together we were stronger. Anyway, I used to get her something with a butterfly every single week. Whether she was home or away. Her search and rescue work could make it incredibly difficult for me to give her gifts, but I tried, even if it was just a letter with a sticker or a small charm for her necklace. I would go out in search for butterflies and film them. I would set the footage to music and tell her how much I loved her. She would play those little mini movies over and over again. She was planning to decorate the nursery with butterflies as a tribute to our friendship turned to love."

I wipe my eyes with the heel of my hand. "You guys must've been incredible together. As sad as it is that she is gone, I'm so glad you had the opportunity to love like I loved my Sergio. It is the most comforting thing in the world, isn't it?"

Stuart nods against my head. "It is. I never thought I would find the same sort of connection again. Yet, every time I hold you in my arms, it's as if my heart has found its home. That strange feeling of longing that has plagued me since the day Nora died is quiet."

I gently push Dozer's head off my lap so I can turn around and face Stuart. I'm almost afraid I misheard what he said while I was lost in my cloud of memories about Sergio.

Facing Stuart, I reach out and grab both of his hands and squeeze. I hold on for dear life as I search for the perfect words. Deciding there aren't any, I take a deep breath and forge ahead. "I'm not even sure what to say. I don't want to hurt you — you've been the best thing to happen to Maya and me since I can't remember when.

But —"

Stuart groans and looks profoundly sad. "Why is there always a 'but'?"

I cringe at the look of devastation on his face. I wish I could soften the blow. "I'm sorry. It's not anything you did."

"Funny, I've heard that line before," he replies in a shaky voice.

"I know it sounds like a line, but it's not. There is an active threat against my life and I have to do everything I can to protect my daughter. Having Dozer helps a lot, but he could be hurt too. I'm not in a good space to be in a serious relationship right now. I can't introduce Maya to a situation like that and then have to bail. It's not fair for you, and it's cruel to her."

"So, don't bail," Stuart challenges.

"I don't know if it's that easy. I'm physically in danger — and mentally, I'm still hung up on my dead husband — and I bring an energetic, inquisitive eight-year-old to the mix. I'm sure you could find someone else who doesn't have these issues."

"What if I don't want someone else? I have been doing the solo thing since I was twenty-one years old. You are the first person to understand what it's like to live life this way. I didn't expect anything to develop between us, but I like you — a lot. I want to see where this goes. I understand it's risky to date a police detective who's a single mom. Even so, I'm willing to take all that on. You're important to me."

"I care about you enough not to put you at risk. You do important work with your practice. I don't want to stand in the way of that."

"Darya, I have been a risk taker ever since I was a kid. I have been a search and rescue volunteer for almost half my life. Although I'm not technically law enforcement, I've picked up skills that will help me protect you along the way. Let me help you watch your back."

"Why are you willing to go out on the limb for me?"

Stuart leans forward and kisses me. His lips are soft, but his kiss is thorough. It stirs desires in me I haven't felt for years. "I thought I've made it abundantly clear. You are strong, beautiful and an amazing mother. Having you in my life challenges me to leave my comfort zone and become a better person. You even get my off-the-wall jokes and think they're funny. What more can a guy ask for?"

Resting my forehead against his, I admit, "This is a big, scary step for me."

Stuart places his hands around my waist and pulls me closer. "If anyone can understand that, it's me. I'll try to protect your heart and everything else."

"The same goes for you." I embrace him tightly and kiss him with a passion I never thought I would feel again.

"Mom?" Maya tries to get my attention. I'm going over old case reports to prep for court. I've noticed the last few weeks she has gone from calling me Mommy to plain old Mom. I guess it was inevitable, but it still stings. My baby girl is growing up far too fast.

After I tuck the pencil behind my ear and close the trial folder, I turn to Maya. "What's up?"

"Is Doctor Stuart your boyfriend?"

I shrug. "I suppose you could call him that."

"Have we had a boyfriend before?"

I smother a grin over her use of the word we. However, there's truth to it. Stuart has been incredibly attentive to both of us. When Maya broke the strap on her backpack the other day, Stuart stepped up and took her to the mall for me so I could attend a briefing at work.

I shake my head. "No, I haven't had a boyfriend since your dad died. This dating thing is new."

"Doctor Stuart is nice and all, but would Daddy be mad at you?"

Maya's innocent question makes me pause for a moment before I answer candidly, "No, your dad wouldn't be angry I've found another guy who thinks I am smart and beautiful. Sergio used to tell me how much he loved me every single day. So, I think he would be thrilled I have found a spot of happiness in my life."

"So, Daddy wouldn't be mad if I like Stuart too? He is kinda like a daddy. He teaches me to play baseball and takes me to McDonald's for French fries. The other day, he even let me paint his toenails a sparkly purple color."

"Cool," I answer with a smile. "It sounds like the kind of thing your daddy would've done. I think Sergio would be happy you made a good friend. He would have been thrilled you play baseball. Sergio used to play baseball as a kid and he was a gargantuan sports fan. He would watch the baseball playoffs and World Cup soccer. It was like his obsession."

"Do you think that's why I'm so good at sports? Do I take after my dad?"

I smile softly as I concede, "I wasn't a very good athlete. I'm sure you got your coordination genes from your dad."

"Stuart says I'm a great ball player. Maybe he can teach you how to play baseball too. He is a good coach. He doesn't yell at us like the other coach did."

"So, are you okay with sharing me with Stuart?" I ask tentatively. I'm not sure what I'll do if she's not on board.

Maya rolls her eyes. "Mom, have you looked in the mirror recently? You smile all the time. I think it's because Stuart is your boyfriend. What did you think I would say? It's like a total no-brainer."

I guess I should have learned long before now not to underestimate my daughter's observational skills.

I grin at her as I tighten my ponytail holder. "You know, I never thought about it, but you're right. I am happy these days and you and Stuart are the two reasons."

CHAPTER ELEVEN

STUART

THE TEENAGER STANDING IN a slouched position with his hands in his pockets looks at me with wide eyes. "I won't get in trouble for doing this or anything, will I?"

I shake my head. "No, I don't think so. You did the right thing here, man. What's your name?"

"Dashonte Greeley," he mumbles.

"Hey, Dashonte, didn't I meet you a few years ago in Tampa? I used to talk about careers in veterinary medicine during career day at local schools. You were at one of those, right?"

"Dude! How did you figure that out? I was a kid back then."

"I have a memory for faces. How did you find me?"

He shrugs. "What do you think? I Googled you like every other teenager."

I cringe as the little terrier mix puppy I'm holding cries out in pain. No matter how careful I am as I cut off the duct tape, it seems to cause him excruciating pain.

I look up at Dashonte. "Can you tell me again what you saw?"

Dashonte shifts uncomfortably. "This ain't gonna make me any friends. Still, I had to do something. I work at that new trampoline place in town, you know, the one where all the kids play? Anyway, I was putting boxes out back to be recycled, and I noticed some kids. I don't know who they are, but I've seen them in my neighborhood. I heard terrible sounds coming from their direction. They seemed to be spraying an animal with something. I seen 'em light it on fire. I went back and slammed the door as hard as I could. It's metal and the hinges are freakin' loud. I was planning to scare them away. I didn't want to take them all on, but they were hurting something."

"Did they come after you?" I ask as I examine the teenager for injuries.

He shakes his head. "Nah, they scattered like ants when they heard the door. I was shocked when they dropped all their crap right there. After they left, I went over to see what they were doing. I about threw up when I found this little dog. The jerks taped his feet together so he couldn't run away. They covered him in Axe and set him on fire. It's like the dare from the Internet."

I roll my eyes in disgust. "I saw the news mention that kind of garbage. I can't believe anybody is stupid enough to do it."

"Yeah, if you want to be crazy and hurt yourself, that's your problem, but to take it out on a poor, defenseless animal is low. Do you think the puppy will live?"

"I do. Thanks to you. You intervened before they could do more damage."

Dashonte looks embarrassed. "Not all teenagers are bad news."

"I know. I have several high school students who work at my clinic."

"You need another one? I don't get enough hours at Bounce. I'm trying to save money to get a car."

I smile sympathetically. "I remember that struggle. Unfortunately, I don't have anything right now. Most of the kids who work for me are volunteers."

"I might be down with that if you ever have room. I like all sorts of animals, but our landlord won't let us have them."

"I understand. Hey, can you give me a hand here? I need you to hold his back leg still while I cut some of this tape away. He's squirming too much."

"Sure thing. What'll happen to those kids if they ever get busted?"

"I don't know. It's not my area of expertise. That's why I've been taking pictures. Would you be willing to tell a friend of mine what happened? She's a detective. If anyone can help us figure out who did this, it's probably Detective Vick."

"I don't know, man. I'm all about saving the dog, but I don't know about snitching. Sometimes, it's
best to pretend you saw nothing."

"I get it. I really do, but if these guys aren't stopped, how many other dogs will they hurt?"

A look of indecision crosses Dashonte's face. "Can I file one of those anonymous reports? I wouldn't even have to give my name, right?"

"I can tell Detective Vick you'd like to protect your identity. I don't want you to feel like standing up for the dog will put you in danger."

"I already crossed that line when I got involved. You should've heard this thing cry. It was one of the worst sounds I've ever heard. These scumbags need to be caught, so I guess I need to step up and finish the job."

Since my home is in a historic neighborhood and quite old, my vet clinic always seems even more disturbing after dark. Dashonte is apparently running late and time seems to be crawling by. He asked me to be here while he meets with Darya. Honestly, I think we are all a little nervous. While we wait, I trim Dozer's toenails.

"Is everything going all right with Dozer?"

Darya smirks at me. "Better than all right. There's a guy who works in the arson unit who has no idea about appropriate workplace etiquette. I've had to put up with his crap for years. With Dozer around, he is keeping a wide berth. I didn't expect that, but it's been a happy little bonus."

I give Dozer a scratch behind the ears as I praise, "Way to go, buddy. It can be hard to tell who the bad guys are."

"I don't know if Glaser is actually a bad guy or just a jerk. Either way, I'm happy he's avoiding me. It cracks me up because he likes to be the intimidator and crowd into everyone else's space — but he doesn't like it so much when the shoe is on the other foot. I thought he would pee his pants the other day when Dozer and I joined him on the elevator."

"Sounds like poetic justice."

When there is a knock on the back door, Dozer hops

off the table and stands protectively in front of Darya.

"Be right back. That should be Dashonte now."

When I answer the back door, Dashonte is covered in sweat. As we walk by the kitchen, I toss a can of soda at him. "Are you okay?" I ask as he collapses on a chair in the waiting room.

"Some dweeb stole my bike," he huffs with an angry scowl on his face.

"That sucks man, I'm sorry."

"You don't get it. My mom's car is broke down and I've been using my bike to get groceries. Now I got nothin'. My mom is going to kill me."

"Why? Was it your fault?"

"No, they cut my lock," he insists indignantly.

"That sucks," I comment. "Do you think it has anything to do with Ranger?"

Dashonte rolls his eyes. "In my neighborhood, who knows? We've got skinheads fighting the gangs. There is no shortage of lowlifes."

"Well, Darya is here. Hopefully, you guys can work together and take a few criminals off the street."

Before I can finish my sentence, Darya comes into the waiting room carrying a water dish for Dozer.

"Righteous dog!" Dashonte exclaims when he sees Dozer.

Darya grins widely. "Isn't he? His name is Dozer." Darya mumbles something to her dog. Dozer relaxes and walks over to Dashonte and sticks his head in the teenager's lap.

"Is this thing going to tear into me?" Dashonte looks

startled.

I shake my head. "Only if you pose a threat to Detective Vick."

Dashonte looks to Darya for confirmation. She nods. "Doctor Stuart is right. Dozer is a big teddy bear. He plays with my little girl all the time."

"I know you," Dashonte blurts, as he looks closer at Darya. "Usually you wear a tie with comic book characters."

Darya raises an eyebrow. "That's me. I'm sorry — I don't remember who you are."

"I don't know if we ever met face-to-face, but you helped my uncle when his landlord was stealing stuff from his store."

"How is D'Angelo doing?"

"Much better thanks to you — it's a lot easier to make money when your stuff isn't walking out the door."

Darya turns toward me. "Come to think of it, D'Angelo could probably fix the fret on your guitar. His shop is a hidden gem. He's one of the nicest guys I have ever worked with."

"I'm too busy to play these days, but I'll keep that in mind," I pledge.

Darya turns to Dashonte. "I understand you have information for me?"

"I could. But you have to do something for me —"

"I can try, but I don't know if I'll be able to."

"They do it all the time on television shows," Dashonte argues stubbornly.

"That's TV, this is reality. My answer depends on

what you want me to do. Sometimes, my hands are tied, but I like to work with witnesses when I can."

"I want to tell you what I know, but I don't want to let anyone know I've been talking to you. It would be dangerous to my health, if you know what I mean."

"At the moment, I don't see where that would be a problem. As long as we can determine you weren't part of the problem, we should be able to shield your identity. I understand why you don't want to broadcast to the world you're speaking with people like me."

"It's hard for me to know who to trust. I know you did my uncle a solid, so I trust you to keep your word."

Darya lets out a small sigh. "Okay, why don't you start from the beginning. Tell me what happened in your own words. The little details count. If you remember anything, let me know. I'll sort out what is important from what isn't."

"This might not make a lot of sense because I was upset when it happened. My heart was racing, and I felt a little lightheaded. I was afraid they would turn on me."

"Completely understandable. Thank you again for stepping forward."

"I was doing my regular garbage duty. We get these huge boxes full of foam or balls for the ball pit. I broke them down and was on my way to put them in the recycling bin. Then, I noticed an animal making a screeching sound. I couldn't even tell what it was. I knew it was in terrible pain. The door to our business, you know, the one we use to get big shipments? It is heavy and metal. When we open and close it, it makes a very loud sound. So, I removed the doorstop and shoved it closed with a loud bang. That was enough to scare the kids off."

"Kids? How old do you think they were?"

"They looked younger than me. A couple of them looked little — like nine or ten years old."

"Did you recognize any of them?"

"A couple of them looked like they could be from my neighborhood. They probably go to school with my little brother. But, I don't know their names."

"What did you see once they ran away?"

"It almost made me throw up because it was so disgusting and evil. I went over and looked in this plastic tote box and found Ranger. His tiny legs were taped together and you could smell the burning fur. There was a bottle of Axe and a couple of lighters on the ground. The poor puppy was crying in pain."

"What did you do next?" Darya asks as she continues to write notes.

"I knew my mom was still at work and my brother had practice. It was up to me to figure out what to do. So, I looked on my phone to see if there was an animal clinic around. Dr. Stuart's was the closest. When I looked up his website, he looked a little familiar. I figured I knew him from the neighborhood."

I glance over at Darya and explain, "It turns out to be an even weirder coincidence. I spoke to Dashonte's class when Mitch and I lived in Tampa."

"I was stupid happy when I figured out Dr. Stuart has late hours at his clinic. There was no way I would've been able to figure out what to do for the puppy on my own," Dashonte replies.

"I'm so glad you brought him in; you couldn't treat

this at home. Ranger needs intravenous support and pain medication. Ranger has terrier hair. It was a little tricky to trim it away from all the areas without causing him more pain."

"Ranger? You know whose dog this is?"

Dashonte shrugs. "I got no clue. But, I named him Ranger for a forest ranger. You know, like Smokey the Bear?"

"Cute!" Darya responds with a smile.

"I also figured he was tough. Kinda like my older brother who is in the Army Rangers."

"Well, I think it's a great name," I add.

"Were Ranger's injuries similar to the ones on Atlas?" Darya asks me.

"Remarkably so. It makes me wonder about the case I had a few months ago where I thought it was a chemical burn. If so, we have a group of serial animal abusers — not good."

Dashonte looks down at the ground. "I might know why these kids are doing this —"

"Yeah? What's your theory?" Darya questions conversationally, as if this information is not crucial to her case. I've learned this is her interview style. She applies no pressure; she just gives you permission to tell what you already know.

"I might be wrong, but there is this guy in our neighborhood. He lives with his brother. He goes by the street name, Kilo Monster. I don't know his real name. His brother's name is Little C. They say they are from Chicago. Anyway, these guys claim to have ties to The Gangster Disciples. Kilo says it's one of the most powerful gangs in prison."

Darya nods. "I've heard of them."

"Kilo is trying to get a bunch of kids in our neighborhood to work for the gang, you know, like as lookouts and to be diversions if there's a fight. To join, you have to prove you're tough. Since one of the kids was filming the others lighting Ranger on fire, I bet they were trying to get initiated."

Darya grimaces. "Makes sense. It's sick, but I've heard of stuff like that happening before. They also have jump-ins and the kids end up shooting each other instead."

A strange look passes over Dashonte's face. Playing a hunch, I ask, "Have Kilo and his brother approached you?"

Dashonte nods slowly. "Yeah, I told him I wasn't interested. My brother is part of the most powerful gang of warriors there is. I want to follow in his footsteps. I don't need that kind of crap to mess me up. Besides, I know what they do. My mom is sick. She doesn't need to worry about that kind of stuff moving into our neighborhood. She's got enough problems."

"I'm sorry your mom isn't doing well. Is there anything I can do?"

"Can you make her take her medicine? She's got high blood pressure. The doctor said if she doesn't take her pills, she could get much worse. But, she doesn't like to take them because they cost money. I've been payin' for 'em from my paycheck. She doesn't know. My mom thinks I got a scholarship from the drug company. So, don't tell her, okay? She'd be upset. I'm supposed to be saving money for my schooling and a car."

"We won't tell her," I promise as I leave the room.

I hear Darya add, "I've got a friend who is tied into all the resources available in our community, do you mind if I connect the two of you?"

"I don't know, I'll ask. My mom is kinda touchy about all that. She knows you helped my uncle, maybe if you came to talk to her she would be okay with it."

"I can do that," Darya pledges.

Scooping the white and gray terrier mix out of his kennel, I carry him to the waiting room.

"Dude! Are you sure that's the same dog? He looks like he belongs in a dog food commercial."

"Believe it or not, this is Ranger. With your permission, I'd like to have my friend Mitch evaluate him. Breeds like Ranger make fantastic hearing dogs for the deaf."

"That would be righteous! He should have a good life after what he's been through," Dashonte exclaims.

Darya smiles. "I know several professional working dogs. Although they work hard, most of them are spoiled rotten."

"Sounds perfect for Ranger."

Ranger practically leaps out of my arms when he sees Dashonte. Darya's eyes mist up. "Look, Ranger knows you were the hero of the day."

"Honestly, I was terrified, but I'm glad I could help him."

"We are too. Hopefully, what you told me will give me a place to start. I'll have Francine, our sketch artist work with you to help identify the juvenile offenders."

Dashonte slumps and hugs Ranger close to him. "I don't want to be anywhere near where you work. Nothing personal, but it's bad for a guy's reputation."

"Don't worry about it, we'll take care of you," Darya assures him as she hands him a nondescript business card. "Put my number in your phone and call me if you need me."

Dashonte frowns as he flips the card around in his hand. "I hope I'm not making the biggest mistake of my life."

"I don't think you are. Who knows whose life you will change by doing the right thing? We are proud to have you on our team. Your brother would be proud too."

"I'm counting on it, Doc. I've got big shoes to fill."

CHAPTER TWELVE

DARYA

I THROW MY PURSE in the bottom drawer of my desk as I stop to take a deep breath. This morning has been absolutely crazy, and my day hasn't even started yet. Maya's shoelace broke as I was trying to get her out the door to go to summer camp. She fell and scraped her knee and then decided she didn't even want to go. By the time I got her all cleaned up and calmed down enough to get on the bus, the line at the coffee shop was a-mile-and-a-half long. I can already tell this is not the kind of day I want to face without copious amounts of caffeine.

Captain Allegheny looks over the rims of his reading glasses as he walks past my desk. "It's nice of you to make an appearance, Vick. I need you at this meeting. We're in the conference room. Clear your schedule."

His tone sends a shiver up my spine. I don't think caffeine and a scone will help.

I call the front desk and tell Tori to reschedule my upcoming interview with a witness. I grab a legal pad and a fresh ink pen as I head toward the large conference room. It is disconcerting to join a meeting I wasn't planning to attend.

I'm not sure what to expect as Captain Allegheny opens the door for me. I recognize several of the law enforcement officers in the room. They come from a variety of backgrounds. I nod at Cody when he smiles at me. Dozer wags his tail before he crawls under the table to take a nap.

"I hope you'll all welcome Detective Vick to our task force. She has worked in this capacity before and, if I say so myself, was pretty stellar."

I flush as I take a seat. "I hope you'll pardon my ignorance, but I'm not exactly sure why I'm here. Can someone fill me in?"

"Do you want the PC answer or do you want the unvarnished truth?"

The atmosphere in the room is practically vibrating with tension. Many people don't understand the type of friendship Cody and I have developed over the last few years. We can basically share anything with the other without fear of judgment. He is one of the coolest police officers I've ever met in all my years on the force. I take a deep breath and expel it. "Why don't we save time? Tell me what I need to know."

Joe Mannington shuffles a few papers in a file. "I'm sorry we didn't get a chance to do this the nice polite way, but this situation abruptly landed in our lap. There has been chatter online and through our CIs that Klar Nation United is holding a big meeting in Jacksonville this weekend."

I flinch when I hear the name. This is not the first time I've encountered this group. They are one of the most violent groups of white supremacists I've run across in a while. I raise an eyebrow. "In case no one has noticed, I'm not their target demographic. If you want me to go undercover, it'll be a little tricky."

Cody points to his dark forearm as he grimaces. "Sorry to break it to you, Detective, we are the perfect operatives for this assignment."

A feeling of dread washes over me as the implications of what Cody is suggesting fully hits me.

I look up at Captain Allegheny. "I thought we were keeping me on low-profile assignments and out of the limelight for a while until the danger passes?"

He looks chagrined as he clears his throat nervously. "I've been overruled. Apparently, they want you and Officer Erickson to help beat the bad guys out of the bushes."

I glance over at Cody. "Are you on board with this? You've been following this case since the beginning, I presume. Does this seem like a good bet to you?"

Cody shrugs. "It's either that or wait around for these guys to strike innocent civilians. I'm not okay with that, are you? This seems like the lesser of two evils. Besides, you and I have both done this before."

My stomach clenches painfully as I try to figure out what this will mean to my daily life.

"Setting myself up to be bait for a hate group doesn't seem like the smartest idea." I sigh.

"Don't forget, you've got back up," Dylan Palmer remarks.

"Yeah? Precisely how do I sneak a seventy-pound dog undercover?"

Joe Mannington smiles. "Meet Dusty — therapy dog extraordinaire. Two of the perps' wives work at the Lilies of Grace assisted living facility. You are going to pay them a visit."

"O-k-ay," I remark, drawing the simple word out into several syllables. "What will my distinguished colleague, Officer Erickson, be doing?"

"The op is set up for me to play an inspector who is in charge of renewing Dusty's certification as a therapy dog. You may or may not be playing a few footsie games with me; how is your flirting game these days?"

I smirk. "With you? A bit rusty. Making out with you is like kissing my brother."

Dylan Palmer laughs out loud. "It's too bad we can't trade places. Detective Vick doesn't have to pretend to like me," Palmer teases.

"You're jealous because she hasn't kissed you," Cody counters.

"Seriously, Dylan … you have a role in this operation?"

"Yeah, you're going to love this one. You get to boss me around. I am your trainee. The goal here is for you to be remarkably condescending. We want the perps to be told how awful you are to the poor white guy."

"Hey, Palmer, remember a few years ago when you decided to have anchovies and refried beans while we were on a stake out? I told you one day it would come back to haunt you. Apparently, this is it. Karma is interesting that way."

"Before you plot my demise, remember I'm watching your six," Dylan remarks.

"Point taken." I turn to Joe. "What's my lead time on this? I've got stuff I have to take care of before I'm free."

Joe looks at his watch. "As of now, you've got about ninety hours to get your ducks in a row."

"Oh … here I thought I would have to rush." I roll my eyes.

"I'm sorry, Stuart. I'd like to tell you more, but I can't. It's an ongoing, undercover operation." I tear up lettuce leaves for a salad.

"Just like that, huh? They want you to pick up stakes and put your life on the line even though you're a single parent? That's stupid."

"That's the way it works when you're part of a team. I'm better for certain tasks than other members of the force. I never wanted them to treat me differently because of Maya. I fight hard to fit in. I don't want to highlight what makes me different."

"Ordinarily, I get it, but they are putting you in the middle of a dangerous situation on purpose. How is that okay?" Stuart argues as he putters around the kitchen.

"The only way it wouldn't be okay is if I didn't carry my weight on the team. You know better than most people how it works. Everybody has to play their part."

"You're right. I do know better than most the sacrifices of charging headlong into a dangerous situation. I lost my fiancé, and you'll pardon me if I don't want that to happen to you. I love you too much to stand by on the sidelines when you're about to do something insanely reckless."

"I can't tell you all the details. I'm not allowed. But what I can say is I have a whole team of people supporting me, including Dozer. He makes this the safest operation I've ever been part of. How many people do you know who have their own protection watching their every move?"

"I feel a little better knowing Dozer will be with you. Still, I think this is an epically terrible idea."

I place my hands on my hips. "For the record, this was not my plan. It was my supervisor's idea."

"You went along with the plan. If I had to guess, I'd say you jumped in enthusiastically with both feet."

I roll my eyes at Stuart. "Actually, I had a healthy amount of skepticism about this operation. But, I got a full brief and I feel better now. I guess my only question to you is are you free to watch Maya or do I need to ask Mitch and Jessica?"

Stuart flops down in the recliner chair and sighs dramatically. "She's in day camp for the next month, right?"

"Yeah, I got four weeks scheduled. I like to give her a break before school starts up again."

Stuart's eyes widen. "You're not going to be gone the whole month, are you?"

"No, of course not. We don't have the type of operating budget required to run an operation with that kind of longevity. Hopefully, this will be a quick in and out — just a few days."

Stuart scrubs his hand down his face. "I'm coaching Maya anyway. As long as she's at day camp while I have office hours, I'd be happy to watch her. Better yet, I'd rather you stay home so I don't have to babysit her at all. It'll be incredibly difficult for me to watch you leave on this assignment. The last woman I loved never came back from what was supposed to be a quick, easy mission."

I set Maya's brush on the bathroom counter and tie the belt on her robe a little tighter. "You're all set. Stuart is waiting to read you a bedtime story."

"Mom, why does Stuart look so sad?"

I lead Maya over to the edge of my bed. I sit down and pull her into my lap. "I think Stuart is just worried about me. He is not used to me being away for my job."

"You have to go be like a spy, right?"

"I suppose you could say it like that," I concede.

"You'll have your gun there?"

"Yeah, you know me. I don't go anywhere without it."

"Dozer is going with you too, isn't he?"

"He is. I'll have a bunch of people I work with helping me do the job too."

"Okay, I'll watch out for Stuart while you're gone. I'll watch lots of movies with him like Grandma does with me."

"Thanks, Maya. I'll do my best to come home as quickly as I can."

"It's all right, Mom. You have lots of bad guys to catch."

I kiss the top of her head. "I love you, Maya."

Maya rolls her eyes at me. "No duh, Mom. You tell me every day."

I hug her tightly as I remark, "I don't want you to ever forget it."

"Mom, I'm smart. I'm not about to forget, and neither is Doctor Stuart."

I swallow hard as I remember the anger on Stuart's face when we last discussed my impending assignment. He seemed like he'd just a soon forget he ever met me.

"I hope so. I'll be home soon. Be good for Stuart."

"Atlas and I are always good. Mitch says we are the smartest dog training team he's ever seen."

"So you are," I agree as I surreptitiously wipe away tears.

I squint as I try to gauge the accuracy of the cluster of holes in my target from downrange. I tuck the loose piece of vinyl back under my ear protection as it tickles my neck. As I wait for the mechanical feed to bring the target closer I hear the door to the gun range open.

I hear a familiar voice over my left shoulder. "*¡Buen trabajo!* Detective Vick, are you sure you don't want to abandon ship and work for Identity Bank?"

I chuckle softly. "Isaac, come on now. I know you play poker with my captain. Don't stick me in the middle. You and I have had this discussion many times. Although I am woefully underpaid, my heart is set on being a public servant."

Isaac studies me closely. "Is the budget so tight they don't provide you with proper equipment? Your ear protection is several years out of date."

I reach up to grab my dilapidated earmuffs. "Oh, I have newer ones, I can't bring myself to use them. Sergio got these for me when I graduated from the police academy, and they are my favorite pair."

"I know it's hard, but it is better to move on from the past. Better things can be in your future," Isaac responds carefully.

"Why do I get the feeling we're talking about more than my broken ear protection?"

"I'm making an observation, that's all," Isaac insists with a mysterious smile.

"It's so hard to move on. With Sergio, I never had to explain why my job was important or why I was called in for an operation at the very last moment, but Stuart seems to be having a hard time understanding the team has to function together even though I have outside commitments. I don't know how this will play out. He might not accept the dangers of my job. I don't know how to handle that. This is why I've allowed no one to get close in all these years. I was afraid whoever came into my life could not accept the risks of being involved with me. Now all of my nightmares seem to be coming true."

"When you allow new people in your life, it's always an adjustment. Remember Stuart has his own demons to deal with. It is not easy for him to let go of all of his fears and face a new reality — especially when his new reality means you face danger every day in your job. That's the definition of a living nightmare for him, don't you think?"

I rest against a shooting station as I ponder Isaac's words. "You're right. He has to replay his darkest fears every time I walk out the door. How can that possibly be healthy for us? Do you think we can overcome our pasts and be a normal family?"

"I have no great answers. I almost threw away everything that matters to me to try to keep my world safe and in balance. I guess the secret is your love has to be stronger than your fear."

"I'm working on it, Isaac. I wish Stuart could understand."

"I'm sure he will. Your young man is a very bright and compassionate soul. Eventually, he'll figure out you guys are fighting on the same team."

"I hope so. I like not having to fly solo. In the meantime, I need to get in more practice because I don't want the bad guys getting the drop on me."

"The low-lifes don't have a snowball's chance in you-know-where against you."

"From your lips to God's ears, that's all I have to say."

CHAPTER THIRTEEN

STUART

THE STACK OF FOLDING chairs comes precariously close to tumbling as I slam several chairs on top with more force than necessary.

"Problem here?" Mitch pointedly removes the other stack of chairs from my hands.

"At the moment, my whole life is a problem," I grouse.

"What's going on?" Mitch flops down on the old leather couch in the corner of the training room. He motions for me to join him.

Reluctantly, I grab a bottle of water and sit on the couch. Unlike Mitch, I am not the picture of relaxation.

"Darya is leaving for an undercover assignment."

Mitch grins. "I feel sorry for the criminals. Darya is scary good at acting."

"I don't understand why she volunteered to go. She has Maya to consider. What is she thinking?" I the amount of heat in my voice.

He raises an eyebrow. "I don't know. Maybe she figures she's doing her job — you know, the one she was hired to do?"

"Yeah, but it's dangerous," I protest.

Mitch sighs. "Her job is dangerous every day of the week. Some people hate police officers just because they exist and they are on a mission to eliminate them."

"Don't remind me. This seems even more dangerous than usual. I can't believe she volunteered to go on this assignment. She is a mom. How can she forget?"

"Darya is a careful and dedicated mother. If she had any choice in the matter, I'm sure she would've made other arrangements. She has worked hard to make it to where she is. If she turned down assignments because it was inconvenient for her personal life, it would screw up her career."

I practically growl as I run my hands through my hair. "Well, you'd think her supervisor would take all that into account before assigning Darya to an undercover mission. What if she's walking into an ambush? She can't even tell me what she's doing. I've been watching her get ready to go on this assignment. I can tell she's nervous. If she's freaked out, there has to be a good reason. I can't believe she is doing this to me — to us. More importantly, I can't believe she's doing it to Maya."

Mitch shakes his head. "What exactly is she doing to you? She is doing her job like every other professional. Darya is showing Maya she can grow up to be anything she wants to be. I don't understand how this is bad."

"She is a mother —" I protest, even though it's evident Mitch isn't siding with me.

"So? If things continue to go well with you and Darya, you'll be Maya's stepdad. Does that mean you need to give up your large animal practice? After all, it could be dangerous. You could get kicked in the head and go into a coma and die. What about those risks?"

I openly scoff at Mitch. "Come on! You know that's very unlikely. I've worked around animals my whole life. I know how to protect myself."

"You think Darya can't? Have you looked at her desk at work? Her whole cubicle is decorated with commendations and awards she's received from her department. Face it, Eastwood, your girlfriend is a kick-butt cop. There's a reason they want her in on whatever this is."

"What you're telling me is I'm being an idiot here? Is that the long and short of it?"

"You and I have been through a lot together. I know what you loved and lost. I loved Nora too. But Darya is not Nora. Just because she is going on a mission, it doesn't mean the outcome will be the same. Darya is not an adrenaline seeker. She does her job carefully and with intention."

"You had to go there, didn't you?" I snap, letting my agitation show.

"Why not? I like to call a spade a spade. It's always hard to see Darya put herself on the line for her job, but that's not what this is really about, is it?" Mitch presses.

A wave of nausea settles over me as I break out in a cold sweat. I get up and pace around the room. My knees feel shaky and weak. "*Geez!* I want you to be wrong. But you're not. I am judging Darya through the filter of my past with Nora. It's like a bad horror movie. The only difference is Maya will be safe and sound here in Gainesville with me. Unfortunately, my baby died with Nora."

Mitch's face contorts with emotion as he processes what I said. Nora and I always planned to share our news with our best friend, but we never got the chance before her death. This was not the way I wanted to tell Mitch, but it's too late now.

When Mitch regains the ability to speak, he looks at me with a stunned expression. "Nora was pregnant and nobody said anything?"

I nod slowly and then take a drink of my water before I answer, "We were still digesting the news ourselves when she decided to go on one last mission because the world needed her more than I did."

"That explains a lot of what happened back then. Before Nora took off, she told me she needed to have a conversation with me. Of course, because I was half in love with your fiancé, I convinced myself it was because she was going to break up with you and get together with me," Mitch admits.

"Nora never told me," I whisper.

"That's funny, I had visions of the two of you having a big old laugh about my fruitless hang up over Nora. I guess I see the whole interaction differently now. She was probably about to tell me to grow up and get over my adolescent crush so the two of you could move on with your lives."

"Nora probably wouldn't have been as blunt," I interject.

"I'm sorry Nora died. I feel bad. I didn't realize it was as painful to you as it was for me. Now that I know, I understand why it threw you for such a loop. I'd be devastated if anything happened to our little one. Heck, I worry Jessica is doing too much or if she feels lightheaded. I can't imagine what you must have been feeling knowing your son or daughter was on that search and rescue mission with Nora."

I walk back over to the couch and sink into it, laying my head on the back of the couch. "I never, ever want to relive getting that notification again. It was excruciating to find out long distance my fiancé and child had died and I couldn't do anything to fix it and make it better."

"I can't even imagine. Now, I know why you took it upon yourself to tell all of Nora's family in person what happened."

"Yeah, I felt like I owed it to them. They lost more than their daughter in that earthquake. I didn't know how to tell everyone after we had been keeping it a secret for so long."

Mitch reaches over and puts his hand on my knee. "I'm sorry, Stu. If I'd known what was going on, I might've been a little less self-absorbed in my own loss."

I shrug. "You know I forgave you a long time ago for being in love with my fiancé? Nora was imminently lovable. As a mom to be, she was nearly perfect."

"You know who else you need to forgive?" Mitch asks.

I look at him blankly.

"You need to forgive yourself. If Nora felt like she needed to be part of the earthquake rescue team, she was going regardless of anything you said. Remember, Nora didn't have any reason to think that rescue mission would be her last. After all, she had done dozens and dozens of similar missions over the years."

"I know. Still, 20/20 hindsight can be painful."

"What happened to Nora isn't going to happen to Darya. The situations are completely different. Darya doesn't charge into things without thinking. She is methodical and precise."

"Intellectually, I know all that. My heart isn't ready to get on board yet."

"You better get your brain wrapped around what's really going on, otherwise you'll damage your relationship with Darya. I went through something similar with Jessica. I was so hung up on my past with Nora I almost didn't see the best thing to ever happen to my future."

I nod. "I'll work on it. Driving Darya to her assignment will be one of the most difficult things I've ever done. Honestly, I don't know if I'll be able to keep it together."

"I know you can. You've been through tougher stuff and Maya is counting on you."

"I hope you're right. Maya will have a hard enough time without me adding to her distress."

Darya tucks her hair behind her ear as she gratefully accepts a cup of coffee from me. "Sorry it took so long. Maya decided she wanted to preemptively tell me everything that will happen in her life while I'm gone."

"Strangely, I have the same compulsion. There isn't enough time for me to say everything I'd like to say before you leave."

Darya tucks her foot under her other leg and sits down on the couch. She sets her coffee down on the coffee table and reaches out for my hands. "I know this is the first time you've encountered this situation, but I *am* coming back. It might be a week or two, but this operation will conclude, and I'll be home to see all of you soon."

"I am trying hard to believe in that scenario, but the last time I faced the prospect of the woman I love going on a work-related trip, it didn't end so well. What you are doing is dangerous — even you can't deny that. I'm trying to put that out of my mind."

"I know this has to be hard for you because of Nora, but the rest of my team and I will do everything in our power to make sure everyone makes it home safely. I am not the only person with family and loved ones."

"I wish we had a magic wand to make everything miraculously safe," I comment with a sigh. "Now that I have finally found you, I'm more than a little terrified something is going to happen to you."

"Stuart, I am a police officer. It's not only my job, it's a huge part of who I am. I can't guarantee you I won't get hurt on this assignment or another one in the future. I can only promise you I will do my best to stay safe. That's all I have ever been able to do."

I look down at the floor where Dozer is sleeping comfortably. Finally, I drag my gaze back to Darya. "I know. I also get that I am being hypocritical. I still work search and rescue scenes, not as many as I used to, but I still do."

"So if you —" Darya starts.

"I'm *not* proud of my double standards," I interrupt. "I am working on them. It seems like my head and heart are in two different places. I want to trust everything will be okay, but I still struggle with it every time I see you walk out the door."

Darya sighs. "I remember the feeling well. I used to feel that way every time Sergio went on a call. I drove myself crazy for years until I finally decided all my worry was taking the focus off of my own work. That wasn't healthy for either one of us. So, I tried to have faith in Sergio's ability to make everything right in my world. It was working well up until the day a terrorist killed my husband."

"I can't fathom how betrayed you must've felt," I remark.

"Betrayed is a good word for it, I always figured his expertise would save him. He was one of the smartest men I've ever met. However, all of his training couldn't fix the fact he didn't know the device was present on his car. You know, I always laugh when I see bomb scenes depicted on TV. The bombs always have brightly colored lights or wires to identify themselves. The technicians at the FBI told me whoever made the bomb that blew up Sergio made it so it would purposefully blend in with all the rest of the routine parts on Sergio's car."

"That is beyond evil; I'm sorry it happened to you. I will try to buck up and deal with my fear. If I'm being honest, I know I'm being selfish when I tell you I don't want you to do this mission."

"Although I can understand your fear, you have to understand I am doing what I do so people like Dashonte can go to work or school and come home without fearing they'll be ambushed by criminals. I knew going in I would have to make sacrifices to keep other families safe."

"That's what's keeping me sane. I know what you do is important. I'll have to put the lid on my fears and hope this assignment is over quickly."

"I hope so too. I miss Maya already and I'm not even gone yet. I can't imagine how it will be without both of you. As the old musical used to say, 'I've grown quite accustomed to your face.'."

I raise an eyebrow. "Only my face?"

In a move worthy of any Olympic gymnast, Darya pivots around on the couch and throws her arms around my neck. She kisses me deeply. Pulling away, she buries her face in my neck. "Oh, trust me I will miss far more than your face. I will miss the way you smell when we dress up to go out. I'll miss the sound of your beating heart, which helps melt away my stress at the end of every day. I'll miss your quick irreverent sense of humor and the way you laugh at all my jokes — even the ones that aren't funny. I'll miss the way you spin Maya around in circles to make her giggle. I'll miss the look of contentment on your face when you help an animal find a new home. Most of all, I'll miss the way you hug me. When I am in your arms, I feel as if no evil can ever touch my life again."

I didn't realize I was holding my breath until she finished her monologue. I take a gulp of air. "Wow! I meant that as a joke, but I'm so glad you didn't take it as one. Your words blow me away."

"They are all true," she insists as she snuggles closer.

"My words might not be as eloquent as yours, but I have my own list of things I'll miss about you."

"This should be interesting." Darya flushes a deep shade of red.

"Relax, turnabout is fair play. You might learn a thing or two."

"We'll see," Darya comments as she hides her face in my chest.

"I will miss the love notes you leave in random places for me to find. I've still never figured out how you do that without getting caught. I will miss you touching me every time you are within arm's reach, even if it's just to brush your fingertips across my shoulders. Those little gestures make me feel connected to you even when we both work insane hours. I will miss how hard you try not to laugh when Maya is too mischievous for her own good."

"I always figured that made me a bad mom because I can't help but laugh at her antics — even when I know she's in the wrong."

"Nah, it makes you human. I love the fact you allow Maya to make her own mistakes and learn from them. I love that you brought me Atlas cradled in a soft towel while you were wearing a bulletproof vest and your sidearm. I will miss the sound of your laughter. Most of all, I will miss the knowledge you are simply a phone call away if I need a shoulder to cry on or someone to see the humor in a dark and tragic situation."

"I thought you said you didn't have a way with words. Those were powerful words." Darya wipes a tear away.

She snuggles closer and rests her cheek against my chest. "Do you ever stop to think how unlikely it is that we are a pair?"

"Mm-hmm," I respond with a rumble of laughter. "I could've saved myself a world of hurt if I had listened to Mitch. He kept telling me about this cool police officer he knew. I was still nursing my broken heart, and I was not interested in anything serious. For a long time I dated women I knew were not remotely right for me so I could avoid the awkwardness of talking about a future I was not ready for."

"Oh my gosh! I thought I was the only person who did that. I dated a bunch of nice guys who I knew would never hold my interest for more than a couple minutes. I felt pressure to date for the sake of saying I had moved on. But, my heart was never in it."

"Is your heart in it now?" I ask, afraid of the answer.

Darya looks up and kisses the bottom of my chin. "It is. I never thought I would be in a position to utter those words, but with you, I don't need to be ashamed of the fact Sergio left this planet holding my heart in his hands. I have spent several years trying to build a world where I didn't need anything or anybody. Having you in my life has shown me the only person I was hurting was myself. I need you and my daughter needs you."

I tilt Darya's chin up and kiss her gently. "I need you too," I whisper. "Please don't go. There must be someone else who could go in your place."

Darya pulls away from me abruptly. "Wait a minute! I'm confused. One minute you tell me how much you love me in beautiful, eloquent words and the very next second you're asking me to give up a huge part of who I am. It can't be both. Either you love me, as in all of me, or you don't."

"Are you saying I can't be in love with you if I'm not in love with your job? That's not fair," I counter.

"You don't have to be in love with my job, but I expect you to understand my need to do it when you're professing you love me." Her eyes flash angrily.

"Well, that street goes both ways. If you loved me, you would understand how difficult this is for me. You wouldn't ask me to relive my pain."

Darya crosses her arms and studies me for a moment before she says, "I've always understood it's difficult. Hello? Did you forget I lost my husband in the line of duty? I have not only been figuratively in your shoes; I've literally been in your shoes. I spent years watching my husband go out the door and wondering if he would come home because of the intrinsic dangers of his job. But, you know what? I let him do his job."

"Good for you. I guess I'm not as noble as you are. I want you here with me and Maya," I insist.

Darya's eyes grow dark as she gets right in my face. "The ball is in your court now. You need to decide whether you are determined to relive your past and hope for a different ending or whether you can put the pain and fear behind you and live for today."

"But —" I start to protest.

Darya flicks tears away as she continues to pack her duffel bag. "I don't know what to say. I've explained it to you in as many ways as I know how. If you don't understand that, you don't understand me and if you don't understand me, you can't possibly love me. I hope you're still here when I finish the mission, but if you can't be, at least be honest with yourself about the reasons."

With a grim look and tears flowing down her face, Darya zips up her duffel bag and throws it over her shoulder. My heart breaks when I hear her whisper under her breath, "This is not how I wanted to say goodbye."

CHAPTER FOURTEEN

DARYA

AS THE FRONT DESK person leaves the waiting area, I receive a call from Dylan. This cracks me up since he is literally eighteen inches from me. There is a solid reason behind his call. We don't want to be caught on any security cameras whispering secrets to each other.

"No, I'm not interested. I just upgraded my cable. My boyfriend was unhappy with what I had before," I answer.

Dylan smirks. "Good to know. Umm… I thought it might be easier for me to portray a bumbling trainer if the dog I'm working with couldn't read my mind and always do exactly what I'm thinking — never mind what I actually ask him to do."

"I understand. But Lexicon comes in at a different frequency than most channels. You might need to use a different signal system if you want better service."

"Clever. I'll try that, thanks."

I let Dylan hang up first while I pretend to talk on the phone a little while longer before I hang up and tuck it into my purse.

After a while, an administrator comes out and looks at us with dismay. "Oh, I don't know if we were expecting

155

two dogs —"

I stand up and shake the administrator's hand. "I'm so sorry. You didn't get notified of the new arrangements? This is my new employee, Dudley. I'm showing him the ropes. I hope you don't mind I've decided to use your exemplary facility. From what I've heard, people in my organization have had a positive working relationship with Lilies of Grace. I guess your residents adore our animals."

The administrator looks slightly confused. "You're not the same person who was here the last time."

"No, sir, my name is Lacey Samuels. My predecessor had to take time off for personal issues. I guess that means I'll get a promotion and finally have a chance to leave the office every once in a while."

"I'm Mr. Pearson, the facility administrator." He reaches out to shake Dylan's hand. "Dudley? Like Dudley Do-Right? That was my favorite cartoon when I was a kid. Call me Billy."

Dylan drops Lexicon's leash as he clumsily stands up and shakes the guy's hand. "N-n-no," he says, "It's just Dudley White."

The administrator groans. "You know I will never remember that. The memory is the first to go," he adds with a hearty chuckle.

"No one ever does," Dylan mumbles.

I turn to address my colleague. "Mr. White, I've told you repeatedly you need to speak up when interacting with clients. To do otherwise is rude," I chastise abruptly.

Mr. Pearson's eyes are wide with shock as he watches our interaction carefully.

"Sorry, ma'am," Dylan stammers. "I'll try to do better."

"See that you do. Otherwise, I'll have to report to the director of our program."

"Oh, please don't. I count on this job to support my family."

"Well, if you want the job, you need to perform it like you care."

"I'm sorry, sir, he's new," I apologize to the director while Dylan flashes a hidden signal to Lexicon. Lexicon is Mitch's demonstration dog. He often takes Lexicon on the road as he visits different schools and other organizations for charity appearances. He has a whole comedy act based on Lexicon and his special talent makes him perfect for this assignment.

"Lexicon, come," Dylan directs as he gives the hand signal for stay. Lexicon has been trained to respond to hand signals first. His butt stays planted beside the chairs in the waiting room.

"I thought you said your dogs were trained," the administrator comments skeptically.

"Some handlers don't seem to be able to catch on."

Mr. Pearson raises an eyebrow at Dylan. "You don't have to put up with her bullcrap."

Dylan looks up at the guy in shock. "Sir? The woman is my supervisor."

"Well, I see two problems with that equation. First, she's a woman and secondly, look at her — she probably came off the boat yesterday. You don't have to take orders from a person like that. America was made for true patriots."

I have to take a deep breath and remember I'm only playing a role in this situation. His words cut close to home. I have heard similar things in real life more times than I'd like to count.

"I hear what you're saying," Dylan responds. "My grandpa used to say the only way to get a job done right was to hire your own kind."

"Exactly! You're preaching to the choir, son," Mr. Pearson says, as he puffs up his chest and glares at me. "It's hard to know who speaks our language. Come talk to me after you have visited with the patients. I have information you might find helpful in dealing with your little situation here," he offers as he rolls his eyes at me. "Some people get promotions who shouldn't, if you know what I mean." He all but winks at Dylan.

It looks like our Intel wasn't entirely complete. We thought we would be interacting with medical assistants whose spouses were involved in Klar. I didn't expect to encounter a supporter right at first. I am surprised he's so upfront about his beliefs at work.

I struggle to put on my game face as we walk into a patient's room. The administrator raises his annoyingly perky voice. "Mr. Fleckman, I brought you visitors."

Dylan looks over at me and winks as he whispers under his breath, "Let the games begin."

As soon as we enter the bed-and-breakfast that is serving as our safe house, Cody takes my briefcase from my hand. "You're probably ready for a shower or two — or ten after that ordeal. I'm amazed at your composure. I half expected you to deck the guy into next week. Was it the camera angle or did that pervert give you a full on grope from your neck to your knees?"

I shudder. "No, your cameras caught about all there was to catch. I've actually never run across anyone with hands as quick as Mr. Pearson's. The guy is like Houdini. One minute he's four feet from me, and the next minute he knows about my choice of lingerie this morning. It's probably a good thing I was shocked into silence, who knows what I would've said if I'd had my wits about me. I might've blown the whole operation before it even got started."

"Well, based on the audio we received, Dylan is well on his way to infiltrating this group for us. Mr. Pearson wasn't exactly shy about connecting Dudley here with all of his supremacist buddies."

Dylan shrugs. "Yeah, I expected them to be far more cautious. Maybe having the dogs around dulled his usual defenses. Any way you slice it, the man was downright chatty."

Dylan shoots a cross look in my direction. "Vick, did you really have to name me Dudley?"

I choke on a snort of laughter. "Consider it payback for the time you made me play a hooker named Candy Barr whose bubblegum had a higher IQ than she did."

"I only did that because you always beat the pants off of me when we play trivia. I figured if I made you dumb for a week, I might actually have a chance to win."

I grimace as I recall the op. "Don't remind me. That was a killer operation. We never got to break character the whole time we were under."

"Good times, Vick, good times. Who knew there were all these perks? When do you ever get a chance to play a character who isn't smarter than plankton?"

I sigh as I admit, "It was fun to play someone who wasn't expected to have every answer to every problem."

"Speaking of characters, how do I approach this meeting? It's not as if either one of you would fit in well to back me up."

"I'm not sure you were read into this because you got to the meeting late. Captain Allegheny told me we have someone already on the inside. She works for ATF," I explain as I go over to my purse to fish out my notebook. "Here it is. Your informant's name is Melody Joy Johnson. She knows we're on the inside and she needs to pose as being interested in you."

Dylan sticks his tongue out at me. "See? You're not the only person who can have an undercover significant other."

"For your sake, I hope your attraction to the ATF agent is a little stronger than my attraction to Cody."

"I should hope so too. Most of the time you guys act as if you can't stand each other."

"That's not true," protests Cody. "I like Detective Vick just fine. In fact, I was thinking of making my move, before she found the animal doc. I knew I couldn't compete. He's got cute animals on his side."

I grin to myself as I concede, "You're right. Stuart has all of his bases covered."

"Oh man! I recognize that look. Don't tell me, I've lost another one of my favorite law enforcement officers to the lure of love. First it was Katie… now you. I know we don't work together very often, but I like having you on the interagency task force with me," Cody laments. "Now, you will probably move away to God-knows-where like my former partner did."

"Relax, Cody," I respond as I strip off my thigh holster. "In love or not, I'm not moving. My daughter has friends and a school she loves. Besides, Stuart has a thriving practice that caters to local charities. He has no plans to relocate."

Cody turns to Dylan and asks, "Have you been to the Doc's house? It's sweet."

Dylan shrugs. "I haven't been invited. I figure maybe Vick doesn't want us to check out her newest squeeze."

"Not true!" I protest. "We've been busy."

Cody winks at Dylan. "I remember what it's like to be in a new relationship. You're always busy."

I stick my tongue out at Cody. "Funny and not entirely wrong. I was referring to Maya's school schedule, baseball, and all the work we've been doing with the dogs."

"It's been a while since I've had any good reason to be 'busy'," Cody complains.

"You never know. These things can sneak up on you when you least expect them. I wasn't looking for a relationship with Stuart when it happened. We had been friends for years, but things between us gradually changed. I woke up one morning and decided I didn't want to think about what life would be like without him."

"How does he do with Maya?" Dylan asks.

"You know when you play the slot machines, and there is a whole row of trinkets you need to match up? I feel like Stuart is the missing piece. He makes me feel like I've won the jackpot. I thought Maya and I were functioning well as a unit before, but Stuart has strengthened us."

"Cool. I dated this one chick who introduced me to all of her kids and then got angry with me when we got along. It was so awkward."

"Wow! I can't imagine. Stuart is coaching Maya's ball team. I couldn't be happier. I love the fact she looks up to him. He is such a great role model."

"Yeah, I tried to teach my ex's kid how to shoot a basket, but she went ballistic. She said if she wanted her kids to hang around with a guy, she would've stuck with their father."

"Man, you should be happy that one took a hike. It sounds like you dodged the proverbial bullet," Cody remarks.

"Most of the time, I am, but then I run into somebody like Vick here who is blissfully happy in her relationship, and I wonder where I missed the boat."

I frown. "Look, I have to level with you. Things are not always blissful between Stuart and me. He doesn't like what I do for a living. I've tried to tell him police work is more than an occupation to me. I am a cop through and through. I don't know how I'd exist if I wasn't in law enforcement."

"Talk about your impossible choice. I thought you and Stuart had the perfect relationship. If you guys are struggling, how am I ever supposed to find anyone?" Dylan asks.

"I'm sorry, I didn't mean to be such a downer. Most of the time, being in a relationship is great," I insist. "If you're interested, I have an idea."

"I can't wait to hear this. Before you met the Doc, you barely dated. I'm not sure I should trust you for advice," Cody teases.

I wrinkle my nose at Cody. "Okay, whatever… you guys know Mitch and Marcus, right?"

"Yeah, we went to Mitch and Jessica's wedding reception. Marcus was there. Why?"

"Well, both Mitch and Marcus met their spouses through an online dating service, maybe you should try it," I suggest.

"Nah, I'm too big of a skeptic. I have arrested far too many perps who use those kinds of services to lure their victims. I'd always wonder which scam my potential date is getting ready to pull. It wouldn't be a pretty scene," Dylan admits.

"I still think it's better than meeting someone in the produce aisle of the grocery store. I had one sleaze-ball come up to me and ask me if he could squeeze my breasts to see how they compare to the firmness of the melon he was holding. I turned around and left the store. I was utterly speechless."

"Geez, no wonder you didn't date much before Stuart." Dylan rolls his eyes.

"Speaking of prizes, we ought to get busy working on our plan for tomorrow. I'm sure Ms. Lovebug here would like to get back to her life so she can salvage her relationship," Cody says as he tries to redirect our conversation.

"Give me a few moments to get cleaned up and regroup," I plead. "I need to scrub the day off my body and out of my mind."

"I'm taking Lexicon to do his business. Want me to take Dozer out? We can start after you take a shower. Did any of the other task members have any luck with the facial recognition software? I'd like to know who we're dealing with. I doubt this guy's name is really John Johnson."

"No, Dozer's good. We took care of that already. I feel better with him around. I'm more than unnerved after today." Giving myself a mental shake, I try to focus on his other question. "You never know. I have come across suspects with odd names during my career. I had a victim of an armed bank robbery who was named Rob Banks. I couldn't even make that up."

Dylan sighs. "Okay, point taken. It's not necessarily an alias, but I'd still bet my lunch money on it."

"I'll take that bet," I respond, knowing I'll probably end up buying lunch either way.

"Regardless of what his name is, we have to figure out what role he plays in the organization. I want to know what I'm going into tomorrow."

"If I had to guess, I'd say they'll try to indoctrinate you into the world of bigotry and hate."

"Yeah, that's probably one of the hardest things about this assignment," Dylan admits. He glances over at me. "Did I ever tell you my little sister is from Nairobi?"

"Really? I didn't know," I answer as I try to remember the pictures he has posted in his cubicle.

"All this racist crap doesn't fly with me. This acting job is one of the toughest I've ever been asked to do."

I nod. "Trust me. I totally understand. Let's pull together and get these creeps off the street, shall we?"

"That's the plan," Cody says as he pulls out his computer.

"I'll be right out so we can start our planning

session." I grab a set of sweats from my suitcase and head toward the bathroom.

"You do remember I told you I have a sister?" Dylan asks with an amused smile. "I know better. Cody and I could probably take a nap in the amount of time you'll take to get ready."

"You might think you know women, but you don't know me. I take shorter showers than my boyfriend or my daughter."

Cody comically plugs his ears. "TMI! I totally didn't need to know that."

"If you guys didn't want me to set you straight, you shouldn't have used it for your comedy routine."

"Yep, and that's why they call you The Guru," Cody teases.

"Someone has to be the brains of this op and keep the two of you in line," I tease as I call Dozer to follow me.

CHAPTER FIFTEEN

STUART

"Do you have homework every day — even during the summer?" Maya asks, as she colors next to me at the kitchen table.

"Pretty much. I have to keep a record of the things I do at the clinic so I can remember all the important details. The charting always takes more time than I think it will."

"It'd be easier just to remember it all," Maya suggests.

"You're right. It would be, but I see lots of different animals at my clinic. I'd hate to get mixed up and administer the wrong medicine to one of my patients. That would be dangerous."

"So, do you have those chart thingies for Atlas and Dozer?"

"Yep, Atlas' file is thick, for sure. He went through a lot before you adopted him. I'm super proud of you guys. You make a fantastic pet parent."

"Thanks. I don't know much about being a parent. I only have a mom. I wish I had a dad like you, but I don't think I should wish for that."

"Why not?" I ask, curious about her reasoning.

"Well, I think my mom still loves my dad. I don't want to hurt her feelings."

"Good thinking. I don't want to hurt your mom either. But, it's all right if she still loves your dad. Sergio was an important part of your mom's life for a long time."

"Do you have somebody you loved who is dead?" Maya asked shrewdly.

"Actually, I do. I was engaged to a very beautiful woman. Nora was brave and fearless, so she did her job as a search and rescue worker and got killed during an earthquake."

"I bet that makes your heart hurt." Maya replies in a somber tone.

"Yeah, it does. I still wonder what my life would be like if Nora had lived. Nora would be a mom. Thinking back, my child would be just a little older than you if Nora hadn't died while she was pregnant."

"Oh, that's sad. I bet you cry a lot."

"I still cry, but not nearly as often as I used to right after it happened."

"Why?" Maya asks with an intensely curious expression on her face

I shift uncomfortably in my chair as I ponder her question. Even after all of these years, talking about Nora's death is difficult for me. "Oh, lots of reasons I suppose. Sometimes, I panic and I forget what she looked like."

"Oh ... My mom would understand that. She made a big picture of my dad and she put it on my nightstand so I can kiss him goodnight every night before I go to bed. You know what?" she whispers. "I even tell him about stuff that's going on in school."

"I think that's great. Everyone needs someone to talk to, even if the person can't really hear you."

"My mom told me God listens to our prayers. I figure daddies and mommies who died and disappeared are the same."

I shrug. "That's a great idea, but I guess no one knows for sure."

Maya puts her head down and colors for a couple of minutes while I go back to writing notes in each chart. After a bit, I start to feel as if I'm being watched, so I look up from my task and notice Maya is intently staring at me.

"Do you need something, sweetie?"

Hesitantly, she asks, "Can I ask you a question?"

I smile and nod. "Go ahead."

"I'm confused. Sergio López is my dad, but I remember nothing about him. My mom tells me stories, but it's not the same. Do you think he'll be mad at me if I sometimes forget and think of you as my dad?"

Her question catches me off guard. I'm not even sure how to answer it. I'm desperately trying to remember the Psych classes I took as an undergraduate, but nothing is coming to mind.

"Maya, I think you should do whatever makes you feel comfortable. I'm sure your dad would want you to do whatever makes you happiest. Just because I am doing a bunch of daddy kind of things, doesn't mean I don't want you to have good thoughts about Sergio. I know your mom loved your dad. It's not a surprise. I'm glad they were so happy. Because they loved each other so much, they had you — you are one of my favorite people ever."

Maya blushes. "You're choosing a kid as your favorite person? Not President Lincoln or Helen Keller?"

"You're right; those people were very cool. I still think you're just as cool — look how well you work with animals."

"You mean like in class this week when I took over for the woman who was scared of her dog? Lefty paid attention to me just like he did for Mitch. The lady was so surprised. She never thought a kid could control her dog because he's so big. But guess what? I got him to do almost everything Atlas can do. The only thing I couldn't teach him was to roll over. We ran out of time. If I would've had longer, I would've gotten him to roll over too."

"I have no doubt. You are great with dogs."

"I think I've decided I want to grow up and be a vet like you," Maya says with a solemn look. "Without you, I wouldn't have a puppy."

"Thanks. That means a lot. I try to save as many animals as I can and I'm glad Atlas was one of them."

My dreams have been fluctuating between beautiful, romantic vignettes with Darya to downright horrifying depictions of the violence she could face on her assignment. I have been consciously avoiding sleep for as long as I possibly can. Finally, I drift off to sleep at about two-thirty in the morning, unable to stay awake any longer.

When a cold hand touches me on the cheek, I practically jump out of bed. When I finally calm down enough to focus my eyes, I see Maya in her Princess Belle nightgown staring at me intently with tears rolling down her face.

I take a deep breath to slow my heart, which is pounding out of my chest. Sitting up on the edge of my bed, I ask her in a sleep-roughened voice, "Maya, what's wrong?"

She holds her hand out, palm up. I am half expecting to see a grisly dog bite. Puzzled, I see nothing.

"Let me put my glasses on," I instruct as I reach over and grab my glasses off the nightstand.

I inspect her hand again. This time, I see a tiny white tooth. "Wow! *Cha-ching* — the tooth fairy will pay pretty good for this one; there are no fillings in it."

"I don't think so. My mom always tells the tooth fairy when I lose a tooth, and she isn't here to say anything. Besides, the tooth fairy doesn't know I'm here. She thinks I live with my mom."

I place my arm around her shoulders and try to cover my amusement over her quandary. "I think tooth fairies have a GPS system that tells them where you are when you lose your tooth. I lost one of my teeth while I was at summer camp and the tooth fairy still figured it out."

"There's more!" she wails. "My mom puts it in a special box and takes my picture. She's not here. I miss her so much." Maya's shoulders shake as she sobs.

I give Maya a brief hug. "I know it's not the same, honey. but we can try our best to make it special." I stand up and walk over to my dresser. I open the drawer and I remove a box I haven't touched in years. Carefully, I lift it out of the drawer and set it on top of the dresser. "I know it's not your mom's box, but this box is special to me. Maybe we can keep it in here until your mom comes back."

Maya walks over slowly with suspicion in her eyes. When she sees the box, she shoots me a quizzical look. "Your box has butterflies on it."

"I know, that's part of what makes it so special. My girlfriend, Nora and I were planning to get married, and she was planning to keep her wedding ring in this box. She picked it out because she loved butterflies and stained glass."

"It's a pretty box. My mom would like something like this too. 'Cept my mom likes birds."

Maya stands on her tiptoes to get a better look. I bring the box down to her level and show her the inside. When I open the lid, the box makes a musical noise. Closing the lid, I turn it over and wind it up.

"Oh my Gosh! It's a music box. I love music boxes … but it's too pretty for my tooth. There's blood on my tooth."

I gingerly take the tooth out of Maya's hand as I explain, "That won't be a problem. I have special soap that helps get rid of blood and other nasty stuff. We'll make it squeaky clean for the box. Besides, you don't want an icky tooth in your picture."

Maya lowers her head and slumps her shoulders. "It won't make any difference. My mom can't be in the picture with me."

"How about this? I will take a picture of us together, and you can show your tooth and where it fell out. I will send it to your mom's boss. I bet you her captain can get her the picture without blowing her cover."

Maya stands outside of my scrub room as she watches me carefully clean her tooth. I dry it off with gauze and place it on a clean gauze pad.

"Can I write a letter to my mom and tell her how much I love and miss her?" Maya asks as she wipes her tears away with the sleeve of her nightgown.

"I think she would love it. It would probably make her smile."

"Should we do it with your computer or mine?" Maya's eyes brim with excitement.

"Since I have the captain's email address on my computer, let's use mine. We can even use my WebCam to take the picture."

"Let me go brush my hair. I'll be right back," Maya shouts over her shoulder as she runs from the room.

After she leaves, I breathe a sigh of relief. Maya seems happier now. I feel strangely exhausted as I boot up my computer.

Maya comes back into my bedroom wearing a different nightgown with her hair up in a ponytail, reminiscent of how Darya frequently wears hers.

"Okay, I'm ready," she announces.

I place my laptop on my desk, which is chaotically covered with junk mail of indeterminate age.

I sit in the chair and pat my knee. "Come on, let's get our picture taken."

Maya sits on my knee and grins at the camera as she shows the tooth. I take a series of pictures before I proclaim, "I think I've got it."

I open an email and ask Maya, "So, what do you want to say to your mom?"

Maya rolls her eyes at me. "I'm old enough to type on my own. It's my private business. No boys allowed."

I lift her off my knee and stand up before I place her back in my beat-up leather office chair. I walk over to an overflowing laundry basket of clean laundry I haven't had a chance to put away and make myself conspicuously busy folding clothes.

Looking back over my shoulder, I comment, "Okay, I get it. Make sure you tell your mom how much I miss her, okay?"

Maya grins slowly. "This is weird. It's kinda like passing notes in class for grown-ups."

I chuckle. "I suppose you're right. Don't say anything to embarrass me."

"You mean like when you stare out the window while you hold my mom's picture?"

"Exactly. I would much rather you tell her we are doing well and even managed to bake cookies the other day."

"Should I tell her about how you set off the smoke alarm with the first batch and just about gave Sol and Atlas a heart attack?"

"You can if you want. Your mom knows me well enough to know she could predict something like that would happen. I can be a little absent-minded."

"Yeah, but you're always there when we need you — that's awesome. I know I'm not the same as having a baby, but I think you are a great dad. I'm so glad you love my mom."

Unexpected emotion washes over me as I process Maya's unabashed acceptance. "Thank you, Maya. I can't go back and change the past, but you and your mom have made my future so much better." I walk over and kiss Maya on the top of her head. "Loving you guys is a very awesome thing. I can't think of anything better."

Chapter Sixteen

Darya

I FIGHT THE URGE to pull on the burning IV in my hand. Scowling, I look up at Cody. "Is this necessary? It wasn't a big deal."

"Sorry, Vick. You gotta suck it up. It's for your own good."

Looking down, I wince. Wonderful. It's already bruising. "I don't understand why I have an IV for a concussion. It seems like a bit of overkill."

"Well, for one thing, the doctor says you're incredibly dehydrated. Did you forget to drink the whole time you were in the surveillance van?" Dylan chastises.

"No… Maybe … So sue me. I was busy watching our perps. I still can't wrap my head around what I saw. Can you believe they were holding that teen hostage? What did they have to gain?"

"I'm not exactly sure. We followed you here so we don't have any updates. I guess that kid was from Michigan."

I whistle through my teeth. "That's a way away from here."

"This is just the scuttlebutt, but from what I understand, the victim had been missing from his family for several months and they had given him up for dead."

"I don't get what a group of white supremacists would be doing with a seventeen-year-old African-American skateboarder," I wonder as I move the ice pack to a different goose egg on my head.

"I was just on the perimeter, but I heard one of the agents who spoke to the kidnapping victim telling his supervisor they threatened to identify him as a member of ISIS and strap a bomb on him. They were planning to send him to a sporting event at a high school and cause chaos they could then blame on immigrants."

"That's deranged." I flinch at the pain in my head. "So they carted him around from state to state?"

"One of the Klar members was a long-haul trucker. The sucker would blindfold, bind and gag the teenager and throw him in the back of his rig."

"It's a wonder they didn't get caught."

Cody grins at me. "Thanks to you and your wonder dog, they did. No one else on the team saw what they were doing."

"Where is Dozer?" I ask.

"He is at a vet clinic about a block away getting his own stitches. He'll be fine, but some lunatic went after him with a pocket knife."

I practically growl in frustration. "It's too bad Dozer isn't a designated canine with our department. If he was, that jerk could face serious jail time."

Dylan chuckles wryly. "I think our perps will have enough charges to worry about with their human victims."

"I hope so. It would be a pain in the butt to go through all this for nothing. I'm bummed our team won't get credit for the takedown."

"Who says we won't?" Cody asks.

"Well, being unconscious and all sort of hurt my effectiveness during the takedown. I was the weak link on the team."

"Geez, Vick, it's not like you stepped out for a frappe. You were slammed in the back of the head with a metal pipe," Cody argues.

Dylan nods. "Cody is right. But, there's something more important than recognition. You are so lucky Dozer saw it coming — otherwise, it would've been much worse. Cody and I watched the replay on surveillance. Dozer took a chunk out of the guy's arm mid-swing."

I grimace as I gently touch an exceptionally sore spot on my head. "If this is the result of a partial swing, I would've been dead if he would've hit me full on."

"Dozer may not be an official police dog, but he more than stepped up. After he took your assailant down, he went after a perp who was fleeing the scene, which is when he got stabbed," Dylan explains.

"Not to change the subject or anything, but we're not talking about the elephant in the room. When our last op went south, and I sprained my ankle, you made me call both my mom and my girlfriend. Why are we not calling the doc?" Cody asks.

I throw my arm over my forehead and groan. "I guess I don't want to hear Stuart tell me 'I told you so'. He had a bad feeling about this whole thing from the beginning. He didn't want me to be part of this mission.

He had visions of me getting terribly injured, and I almost did. I'm not calling him because I don't know what to say. Besides, we haven't talked since the fight."

"I know you don't want to upset him, but the incident today is likely to generate rabid media interest. Do you want him to find out as he's flipping through the channels? What about Maya? You need to give them a heads up, even if it's hard," Dylan instructs firmly.

As I struggle to reach my cell phone, I turn to my coworkers and grouse, "I hate it when you guys are right. But, tell me how do I tell the guy I love that the job I love almost as much nearly got me killed today?"

"This is just me, but I'd start out with 'I'm fine' and 'I love you.' It seems to me those are the things the doc needs to hear first," Cody advises.

"True enough." I sigh as I dial Stuart's number. "Or at least I hope that's still true. We're not exactly talking right now."

At first, it seems like Stuart won't answer. Then I hear "The Critter Clinic" in Stuart's deep, businesslike voice.

I collapse against the bed as a rush of homesickness overtakes me. I've been pretending the separation hasn't been affecting me for several days. As soon as I hear his warm voice, all my hard-fought composure shatters.

"Darya?" he asks when I don't say anything.

All I can get out is an emotional "Hi," followed by a loud sniffle and a hiccup.

"*Oh crap!* What happened?"

"I'm good. Everyone is alive. We're just banged up."

"Define banged up," Stuart says curtly.

"Well … there was a tiny tussle. I am in the hospital

being treated for a concussion."

"*Dammit*!" Stuart spits.

"Wait, it's not as bad as it sounds. I got dehydrated, which is complicating things. So, they are giving me fluids. Hopefully, I'll get out of here in a few hours."

"I'm surprised Dozer let anyone get close enough to you to inflict injury. Usually, he is much more on the ball."

"Oh, trust me I have no problem with the way Dozer performed today. If he hadn't been there to take on my attackers, the ending could've been catastrophic. He was dealing with someone who was shouting at me from the front when someone came up behind me and hit me with something very hard. Fortunately, Dozer noticed what was happening and took a big long bite out of the guy's arm mid-swing."

"Where was the rest of your team?" Stuart demands, sounding furious.

"They were otherwise occupied rounding up bad guys. It was quite an intense situation."

"Where's Dozer now?" Stuart asks.

"Apparently, while I was unconscious, one of the perps decided he didn't like being chased by Dozer. The jerk attacked my dog with a pocket knife."

"Given the texture of Dozer's hair, I suspect it wasn't too effective unless it was the size of a machete," Stuart answers, sliding into professional mode.

"Cody has seen the tape. He says Dozer's wounds are mostly superficial. Dozer is at a vet a few miles away getting stitches."

"Do you need me to come to you? I need to get Jessica or Mitch to pick up Maya," Stuart offers. "*Crap!* I had such a bad feeling about this entire op. This is like my worst nightmare."

"No, it's not. You've already lived through your worst nightmare. This is just a speed bump. I got knocked in the head and didn't drink enough water. Dozer put his life on the line and came out with a few scrapes and bruises. I think all in all, we were lucky."

"I guess that depends on your definition of lucky. If Maya and I had a choice, we would choose for you not to be hurt at all."

"Yeah, that's the way it works in a perfect world, but you and I both know things are not perfect," I answer with a sigh.

"Are you sure you don't want me to come get you and take you home?"

I shake my head even though I know he can't see it over the phone. My world spins. "No, I don't need you to pick me up; it would upset Maya's routine. I have to wait until this bag of saline solution is empty and then the nurse said the doctor plans to release me."

"Okay, I guess I'll be here waiting with a drink and an ice pack for your head."

"Stuart …" I say quickly before he hangs up.

"Yeah?" he responds.

"I missed you more than I could've ever imagined, and I can't wait to get home. I love you."

"You took the words right out of my mouth. Hurry home, but be safe."

Six hours, thirty-four minutes, and thirty-seconds. That's how long it took me to get home.

It turns out it wasn't quite as easy as being released from the hospital. There was the commute home — that wasn't fun. I was so nauseous Cody had to pull over a few times so I could puke. After we got back to the station, I had to fill out reams of forms because I was injured during an op. For safety, they had me fill out the same stack of papers on behalf of Dozer. Captain Allegheny took mercy on me and let me go home as long as I promise to tackle the paperwork as soon as I get back to work. He ordered me to take three days off to recover. I wish I could feel bad, but at this point, I have a splitting headache and an upset stomach — so I don't. I feel like I haven't seen the people I love in months instead of days. I just want to go home and watch a marathon of silly TV shows and drink hot chocolate with Maya.

Cody squeezes my hand as he pulls up in front of Stuart's place. "I know it's hard, but remember what we do is important."

"I know it's important," I declare, shooting him a puzzled glance.

"Vick, listen to me. I'm saying it because you are about to be barraged with reasons you shouldn't have such a dangerous job. It's easy to forget what we do is important — especially if it seems like we've made no progress. I want to remind you that Jarel was glad you were on the job today. If you hadn't been, who knows how long he would've been missing and presumed dead."

"Thanks for the reminder," I say as Cody helps me out of the car. "I was feeling sorry for myself, but so many other people are worse off than I've ever thought of being."

As soon as Cody slams the door on his truck, Stuart's front door opens, and Maya comes barreling toward me. Stuart chases after her and reaches me first. "Whoa! Maya, you need to take it easy. Your mom is a little shaky on her feet. Why don't you let her sit down first?"

"Mom! Are you okay? Stuart told me you got hurt. Did someone try to shoot you?"

"No, this isn't like our friend, Katie. Someone was mad I caught them doing something they shouldn't be, so they tried to hit me with a long pipe. Dozer took care of them. We don't need to worry."

"Is Dozer hurt too?" Maya takes a moment to run her hands over Dozer's back.

I nod. "A bit. He chased after the bad guys, and one of them had a knife. So, Dozer has a few cuts on him. But, they are so small he doesn't even have to wear one of those funny looking collars."

Maya grabs my hand and walks me toward the house. "Remember when Atlas had to wear one of those collars? It was bigger than he was."

I take Stuart's hand as he helps me up the porch stairs. He pulls me close and puts his arm around my waist as he whispers in my ear, "I've waited more days than I care to count to tell you this. Darya Vick, I love you, and I am so glad you're safe. I don't know what I would've done if something happened to you."

"Mom, you had it handled, right? You weren't ever in any real danger, were you?" Maya asks in a distressed voice.

I promised myself I would never intentionally lie to my daughter, so this is a challenging conversation.

"I need to go sit in a chair and get a drink, then I'll

tell you what happened, okay?"

"Maya, go make sure Atlas isn't sitting in your mom's chair."

Dozer's ears perk up and his tail starts to wag vigorously when he hears Atlas' name. "I guess he's feeling better."

Maya lets go of my hand as she skips through the doorway and runs through the living room.

"It's going to be interesting to see how you explain this all away," Stuart challenges as worry is spelled out all over his face.

My back bristles and I stand up a little straighter. "I don't plan to explain anything away. My daughter is smart enough to know my job comes with risks."

"Knowing it's possible you might get hurt is different from seeing your injuries. You might get hurt worse the next time."

"Well, I don't lie to her. She needs to know how it really is."

"I wasn't suggesting you lie to her, I was thinking you might want to consider a safer line of work since Maya has already lost a parent."

I feel as if I have been hit in the chest with a medicine ball. I thought Stuart was worried about me going on this undercover op. I didn't realize he thinks I shouldn't be a law enforcement officer. That changes things. I don't want to have to choose between Stuart and my job.

"Low blow," I hiss as I walk over to a rocking chair and sit down. "We'll talk about this later." I mutter half under my breath. I don't need Maya to know I am being torn apart syllable by syllable and by the look of disapproval on Stuart's face.

Maya walks in slowly from the kitchen. At first, I can't see what's happening, but eventually, she gets close enough that I can see she is carrying a very full glass of soda.

Stuart sees the catastrophe waiting to happen at the same time I do. He swoops in and offers to take the glass. "Why don't you go get your mom an ice pack? They are in the bottom drawer of the freezer. You can wrap it in a dish towel to make it more comfortable for your mom."

As Stuart cautiously takes the soda out of Maya's hands, she turns toward me. "Are you sure you're all right? You only get me the ice pack if I'm hurt really bad. Are you hurt bad?"

I look at Stuart helplessly as I search for the right words. As hard as I try, nothing sage or magical is coming to mind. How do I break the news to them I love a job that may kill me?

CHAPTER SEVENTEEN

STUART

I draw in a deep breath and try to calm down as I watch Darya freeze and look to me for guidance before she speaks to Maya. It's probably a good thing I'm not doing the talking right now. My nerves are frayed, and I'm shaken by the small line of sutures on Darya's forehead. You would think I'd be used to seeing stitches. It's so different when they are in someone you love. My compulsion is to remind Darya I don't want her to work in law enforcement anymore. It's too dangerous.

Darya scoots over in the rocking chair to make space for Maya. Instinctively, she straightens Maya's ponytail before she speaks, "Maya, I can't guarantee you I won't get hurt while I do my job. I might even get shot, but if I'm going into a dangerous situation, I always wear a bulletproof vest."

"That didn't stop you from having to go to the hospital," Maya argues.

Darya sighs. "I know. Today was very unusual. You've come to work with me before. You know most of my job involves sitting at my desk and putting facts together about a case like they are puzzle pieces. I rarely do dangerous stuff anymore."

"But you still do sometimes, right?" Maya presses.

"I do," Darya confirms. "But I always have a team backing me up and keeping me safe. I even have Dozer to help me now. I'm pretty much the safest person in my whole department."

"I saw on YouTube that people hate police officers now, is that true?"

Darya's eyes widen in surprise. "What are you watching on YouTube?"

Maya shrugs. "Lots of stuff. I was looking for hints about how to play my video game. This guy was doing a 'let's play' video of the game and he said all policemen should die because they are all bad people. He used a bunch of cuss words too."

"Maybe you should stop watching this guy's videos," I suggest, shaking my head in disbelief.

"I did. I unsubscribed from his channel and I don't go there anymore. He scared me a lot. Mom, what if everyone feels like him?"

Darya swallows hard. "Sweetie, not everyone hates police officers. I help a lot of people. Sometimes, they come back and say thank you and give me a hug."

"How do you know who the bad guys are?" Maya asks.

I slump against the back of the couch as this conversation unfolds. I am grateful for Maya's questions. They are the same ones I have been trying to figure out for myself. I think Maya is spot on. I want to ask those same questions every time Darya walks out the door. We usually don't let Maya watch the news, but privately I still monitor it. What I see there on a nightly basis are like shards of glass in my soul. While all the things Darya said about her current duties as a detective are technically correct, she still faces danger every single day in her job. That does not even account for whether there is still someone after her related to her husband's death.

Darya brushes the hair out of Maya's face. "It's true, I don't always know who the bad guys are. Usually, we have a good idea though. We like to keep track of them down at the police department. If anything seems out of place or wrong, my coworkers will tell me we need to watch out for a particular suspect."

"Dozer will take care of all the rest, right?" Maya asks.

"He will. You should've seen how he took on several people at once to protect me. He was a hero."

"Okay, I feel better. Mom, can you ask your boss to give you more stuff to do at your desk? I don't want you to get hurt."

"I'll see what I can do. I'll talk to Captain Allegheny and it'll be a while before I feel up to doing anything dangerous. In fact, I have three days off. What would you like to do?"

"I want to go to Disney World!" Maya answers enthusiastically.

"I suppose you would. Unfortunately, that takes a little more advanced planning. We want Stuart to come with us, and he has to work."

"When is your birthday, Maya?" I ask as an idea forms.

"My birthday is on December fourteenth."

"You'll be nine?" I ask with a smile.

"Okay, let's think about going to Disney World for your birthday. Does that seem like a good plan?"

"That doesn't sound good; it sounds awesome! One of my friends went there for her birthday, and she got to meet the princesses and everything."

"That does sound special," I answer.

"I know it's not quite as cool as Disney World, but do you want to go to Build-a-Bear in the next couple of days?" Darya takes a sip of her soda.

"Yes, yes, yes!" Maya jumps up and down. "I was mad because one of the puppies got to my favorite teddy bear. Now, I can make him again."

"Okay, we've got a date. If you don't mind, I've had an incredibly long day, and I'd like to take a shower and crawl into my favorite jammies. I need to get some sleep."

"Are you allowed to do that? I thought you said the doctor diagnosed you with a concussion," I counter.

Darya glares at me. "Trust you to know that. But, you're right. You're supposed to wake me up periodically to make sure everything looks good."

I chuckle at her annoyance. "You may be an animal on two legs, but a concussion is a concussion. I did graduate."

"Yes, I know. Most of the time I think that's a good thing, but at this very moment, I find it truly annoying," Darya admits as she rubs her temple and heads toward the bathroom.

When I go to check up on Darya, I find her propped up against my headboard looking weary. She is writing on a tablet of yellow paper.

"I checked out Dozer and gave him a dose of antibiotics. Whoever stitched him up did a bang up job," I say as I hand Darya a mug of hot chocolate topped with whipped cream.

"You are so good to me," she says as she reaches out for the mug.

She takes a small sip, then sets the mug of hot chocolate down on the bedside table before she continues to write.

"What are you working on? I thought you were planning to take a nap."

Darya shrugs. "I will need to document what happened today anyway. I thought I would get a head start on writing all my contemporaneous notes so my memories will be fresher. I worry about my concussion impacting my ability to remember things. I mean, I know I can't remember what happened when I was passed out, but I remember all the things that happened before I was struck. I need to record them before they slip my mind."

"Sounds like a good strategy, but I don't want you to overdo it."

Darya raises her eyebrow. "I've been a grown-up for quite a while now; I can figure this all out."

"I don't want to tell you how to live your life, but your body went through a major trauma; you have to take care of yourself," I reply, letting my frustration leak through.

"If you don't want to tell me how to live my life, then don't. I know you're trying to take care of me, but I can handle this."

"I lied." I feel my stomach clench.

Darya looks up from her writing with a startled expression on her face. "Lied about what?"

"I lied because I do want to tell you what to do with your life. I want to tell you to go find a job in a mall selling perfume or shoes or anything else. I don't want you to be in the line of fire. I love you too much. Maya *needs* you too much," I blurt as I gesture emphatically.

Several moments pass before Darya speaks. When she does, it is in an emotionless, flat tone. "I thought we've already had this conversation more than once. Were you not listening? Let me ask you something: do you work with livestock?"

I nod and say, "Of course."

"Even the really big bulls, like Holsteins?"

I shrug. "I have."

"And you help out with the wild horse rescue at the Paynes Prairie Preserve?"

"It's one of my favorite things to do."

"You work with reptiles, including poisonous snakes? How about big dogs with powerful jaws?"

"You know I do," I snap. I know Darya is backing me into a corner.

"Being a veterinarian is more than a job to you, right? It's part of who you are."

I gesture around the room. "I live at my vet clinic; what do you think?"

"You do, and I am glad you are so committed to your job. But, you can't deny your job isn't dangerous. Something could go very, very wrong."

"The odds are slim," I argue.

"Maybe so, but something still could happen. How would you feel if I told you I was worried about your well-being and you could no longer be a veterinarian despite all the time effort, and money you put into becoming one?"

"It would feel crappy!" I admit as I raise my voice. "My risk isn't the same as yours. You put yourself on the line every single day."

"You do too. It just looks different," Darya argues. "If you think I can separate out being a member of law enforcement from who I am, you don't know me well enough. I am dedicated to this job. I have been for years, even after my husband was killed in the line of duty."

I rub my temples as a headache looms large. "Okay, fine; you want me to tell the whole truth? I don't know if I can handle the thought of losing another person I love. It about killed me the first time. I almost didn't finish school I was so devastated. It would destroy me to have to go through it all again. If you truly loved me, you would understand. You would not put me through the mental torture every single day."

Darya shakes her head and glares at me. "And if you truly loved me, you'd understand that what you're asking me to do is impossible. It would be like denying part of who I am. You want to sweep my whole identity away because a crazy nut bonked me over the head."

"I'm sorry, I can't change how I feel," I say as a sense of dread gathers in my stomach.

"I guess we are at an impasse then because I can't help the way I feel either," Darya says stubbornly. "I'm not willing to give up part of myself to be who you wish I was. Maya and I have been alone for many years. I can deal with the challenges. I love being with you, but if you are trying to change me, I guess we have to go our separate ways."

Darya gets up and gathers her things. I watch in stunned silence for a while and then I object, "You can't leave tonight. I need to make sure you're okay."

A tear slides down her face. "Honestly, I don't know if I'll ever be okay after this. I thought we had something special built on mutual respect, but now I don't know," Darya puts down her legal pad and rolls away from me. She pulls her blankets up around her neck. "If you won't let me go, please leave. You can check on me whenever you need to, but I am too exhausted and hyped up on adrenaline to trust myself not to say something I'll regret later."

I get off the bed, feeling dazed. "As you wish. I hope you are okay, I really do." I slowly walk out of my bedroom, turn out the light and shut the door.

Turning around, I lean against it. My hands are shaking and my heart is racing. I never expected what should have been a happy homecoming to go so far off the rails. I guess I need to do some serious soul-searching. Eventually, I have to figure out whether I even want to put our relationship back on track.

CHAPTER EIGHTEEN

DARYA

"Hold still, Miss Squirmy Pants! If you don't, I'll never get this braid in."

"You have to! Did I tell you Megan's mom is a picture taker? She is going to take pictures of us all dressed up as princesses. Isn't that cool?"

"Sounds cool. After you go to the movies?"

Maya's brow furrows. "Mrs. Appleton says we have to get it done before because we might get food on ourselves at the movies. Did you pack my favorite pillow?"

"Of course I did. I saw the list you put on the refrigerator. You've been checking it a million times. I put your pillow and your toothbrush in your suitcase this morning."

I barely get the rubber band into Maya's braid before the doorbell rings. Maya takes off running. "See you later, Mom," she calls as she opens the front door.

I watch her leave with total wonderment. I'm not sure where my shy, timid child went, but what I just saw is mind-boggling. It wasn't long ago I had to take Maya to new places and stay there with her while she acclimated. Now, she is ready to do a two-night sleepover without batting an eyelash. It's nothing less than stunning. "Wait!" I call after her. "Didn't you forget something?"

She dumps her bags down on the front stoop, turns around and runs back toward me. She throws her arms around my neck and pulls my head down so she can kiss my cheek. "Sorry, Mom, I'm just so excited. I love you."

Squeezing her tightly for a moment, I relish her closeness. "I know you do, sweetie. I love you too. Have a wonderful time."

"You won't be lonely without me here?" she asks as an afterthought.

"No, I'll be fine. I'm going out with friends too."

"It's more fun if you dress up like a princess," Maya says as she does a twirl and a curtsy.

I chuckle. "I'll keep that in mind. But I don't think we're doing that today."

"Whatever," Maya rolls her eyes. "If you're bored, don't blame me."

I ruffle her hair as I walk her to the front door. "I won't, I promise. I'll see you in a couple of days."

"You look grumpier than Jess does when she doesn't get to eat. What's up?" Jade asks, as I take a seat in the corner booth where Jade, Rogue and Jessica are sitting.

I put my purse on the bench beside me. "I might as well tell you because everyone is tight as ticks around here, but I'm afraid Stuart and I might be over."

Rogue looks at me in shock. "You guys seemed fine

last month when we all played pool together. What happened?"

I shrug. "I guess life happened … or more specifically my job got in the way. Stuart doesn't like the fact I work in a dangerous field. He wants me to go do something safer like sales in a mall or a corporate office."

Jade arches an eyebrow. "Has your otherwise-smart boyfriend checked the news recently? Working in a mall or an office isn't necessarily safer. I don't see you as the corporate type either. You like to get your hands dirty and do the tough stuff."

"See? I don't understand why everyone else in my world can get it except him. Even my daughter comprehends the fact that even though the job is hard, it still needs to be done." I take a gulp of red wine.

"You guys have been dating a while. Did it just occur to him you're a police officer?" Jessica asks as she sits in her chair and rubs her belly.

"No, I had a bizarre confrontation with members of a white supremacy gang. I think he's worried about the anti-police bias that's been floating around in the atmosphere recently. Still, he doesn't seem to acknowledge my training. It is so frustrating."

Rogue clears her throat. "I know this probably isn't what you want hear, but I'll give you another perspective. As someone who loves two men who love to rush in and save the world, I can tell you it's tough to be the one left waiting for news. I worry about my husband and my dad all the time."

I take another sip of my wine before I admit, "I can imagine. Tristan and Isaac do a lot behind the scenes. I'm sure most of it's dangerous."

"I try to ignore that part of their job and focus on the good they are doing in the world. Still, at night before I close my eyes to go to sleep, my heart pounds and my stomach turns when I consider the realities of their line of work."

"What am I supposed to do? Give up the job I love — and spent years building — so the man I love can be more comfortable? Doesn't seem fair."

Jade speaks up as she hands me an appetizer. "When I first dated Declan, he had just been attacked on a shuttle bus. After he recovered and went back to busking, I about had a stroke every time he went out the front door. I was afraid he would end up like he did the last time or worse. It took a long time, but I learned to balance my fear against the knowledge he'd been doing this for many years before I ever came into his life and he will probably continue it for as long as he lives. That's the kind of person Declan is. He's a free spirit and doesn't want to be tied down by much."

"Doesn't he have a contract with Aidan O'Brien?" I ask. I don't know Jade very well. Even though we often find ourselves at the same events, I usually hear things secondhand about most of Jessica's friends.

"He does now, but that still doesn't cure him of his need for an audience and his drive to bring music to everyone, whether or not they can afford a ticket. So, whenever he is out, especially in dicey parts of town, I still hold my breath."

"This is very interesting, but all I know is I can't change who I am to make myself into the perfect Barbie Stuart would like me to be. I don't need him to run my life. I've been doing that for many years on my own. I am not a dress-up doll he can push around."

"I think he knows, Darya," Jessica responds. "That's probably part of why Stuart is so afraid. He knows you don't back down from a challenge — any challenge — even if it puts your life at risk. I think it is hard for many men to understand some of us can go toe to toe with our male counterparts and completely dominate."

"Are Stuart and I doomed? Do I have to hide who I really am to make the man in my life happy?"

Jessica butters a slice of French bread and nibbles on it for a moment before she says, "I don't want to hurt you when I say this, but I think we might be ignoring the biggest elephant in the room."

"I've laid it all out, I don't know what you're talking about." I tear my French bread in tiny pieces as my agitation grows.

"You forget my husband and your boyfriend were both in love with the same woman in their lives. If Stuart is anything like Mitch, he still feels the loss. Nora was more than Stuart's girlfriend; they were best friends forever before they dated. To hear Mitch tell it, Nora was the glue that held them all together and helped them all through very rough childhoods. I know the guys don't like to talk about it much, but I guess they each suffered in their own ways — even Nora. I don't suppose it was easy for her to choose between two men who loved her. When she was killed, it affected Mitch and Stuart profoundly."

I nod at Jessica. "I think you might be on to something. Stuart has told me Nora's death makes him more afraid to lose me to an incident at my workplace. I think half the time we're together, he forgets I am not Nora. He must feel the same way about Sergio and me. I mention Sergio's name with Stuart more than I ever have with anyone else."

"Have you ever stopped to consider why?" Jade asks.

"I don't know if it's due to the shared sense of loss, or if I'm just more comfortable and open with Stuart."

"I don't know about your situation, but I do know when I got together with Declan, it was almost as if he opened up my ability to process my feelings and work through the death of my brother. I don't know if you know this, but my brother committed suicide while he was away at college."

"Oh, I'm so sorry. Are you okay now?" I ask as I try to imagine the pain.

Jade rolls her shoulder. "It's been many years now, although the pain will never go away, it is more manageable as time goes on."

"I feel guilty because I've forgotten many of the little things about Sergio. It haunts me that sometimes it's easier to remember the hard times with my husband than all the casual, loving times. Although I know both men loved me fiercely, with every step in my relationship with Stuart, I seem to compare it to what I felt like when I was with Sergio. It's almost automatic and I know it's not fair to him. Still, I can't stop doing it."

Rogue glances over at me with a sympathetic look. "Is that why you reacted so strongly to Stuart's discomfort about your career? Sergio was probably more accepting of the risks. Even though Stuart volunteers in search and rescue, it's not exactly the same."

I straighten the napkin out so it covers my lap before I address Rogue's question, "As much as I hate to admit this, there is an element of truth to what you say. I probably reacted more harshly than I should've, given the circumstances. Stuart wasn't intentionally trying to hurt me. Even so, I don't know how to reconcile our differences. They seem pretty fundamental."

Rogue pins me with a direct gaze. "I know it might seem like that. When push comes to shove, a healthy relationship has lots of flexibility. It takes a while to figure that all out. I know you didn't know us when Tristan and I first started dating, but we were like oil and water. I don't even know how we got together. I grew up poor, and he owns a plane. I was profoundly uncomfortable with his wealth for a long time. I judged him too harshly for being different. I thought being rich was the same as being shallow. So, Tristan and I both had to adjust our expectations. He had to learn that letting me struggle and do things my way — although hard for him to watch — was for the best. Tristan wanted to make everything better in my life all at once. I felt judged. I was working hard to make it on my own, and I didn't want him to come in and change everything in my life."

"That's exactly how I'm feeling!" I exclaim. "As much as I love him, Maya and I were doing fine as our own little family. I feel like he is questioning my ability to be a good mom and a good role model."

"Knowing him as well as I do, I suspect that was never his intent," Rogue replies.

"I hope not!" My voice chokes as I wipe away tears. "If you and Tristan were so different, how did you end up together?"

Rogue laughs softly. "It wasn't easy for me; I had to give up a lot of my preconceived notions about who I deserved to have in my life and how I wanted that person to behave. I had to get to know Tristan below the facade he puts on for everyone else."

"I don't get the sense Tristan is pretending with anyone," I counter.

Rogue winces as she clarifies, "I don't mean that exactly. What I mean is Tristan is not as tough and impervious to criticism as you might think, given his success. Underneath all his money, before Ivy and I came into his life, he was lonely and isolated."

"Yeah, we kind of adopted him and made him our own personal kabillionaire," Jade quips.

Jessica glances up at me as she winks. "You know how it is with this group, you're just sort of adopted in — once you're in, you're in. It's like the Mafia of niceness."

I look around at the collection of smart, accomplished women at the table as a new wave of pain washes over me. I have to swallow hard and take a couple of deep breaths before I can talk. "I'm glad it's all worked out for all of you, but I don't know if Stuart and I can weather this storm. He seems adamant he doesn't want me to be in law enforcement and I am equally sure I want to stay there. I don't know how we can meet in the middle when we are so far apart."

"I don't know a lot about this, Katie is my only other friend who has been in law enforcement. Is it possible for you to still be awesome at your job but not take as many chances with your life? That seems to be where Stuart is having difficulty, right?" Jessica asks.

"It's not quite as simple as that. People judge female officers against a different standard. We not only have to be as good as our counterparts, but we have to be better — much better. We always have to put ourselves out there more assertively than the men and do a flawless job," I explain as I take another drink of wine.

"Totally not fair," Rogue mouths at me when I catch her eye.

I shrug before I continue, "If we fail, people judge all female officers against our performance. If I suddenly decide I won't put myself in the most dangerous situations, I'd be completely ostracized and marginalized. I would hate my job because I've worked hard to earn the respect of my colleagues."

"It's worth a shot if you think Stuart is the one for you. I think you should talk to your supervisor and see if there's a happy medium. I agree. You shouldn't have to give up all of who you are, but you could remove the parts that Stuart finds the most painful, right?"

I sigh and rub my eyes with the heels of my hands as I try to process everyone's suggestions. "My honest answer is I don't know. I've never tried to change the role I play within our department. I never figured I'd have to. After I recovered from Sergio's death, I threw myself into my career because I knew I was the only support for Maya. I wanted to advance as far in the department as I possibly could. That has been my track for years. I don't know if I even know how to change directions at this point."

"Remember what I said about flexibility? I never said it was easy; I just said it was worth it," Rogue says. "You never know what's possible until you try."

"I thought the bad guys were tough, but they've got nothing on you guys. You pull no punches. I thought I would get sympathy — not a reality check," I admit.

"It's only because we respect you so much. We won't BS you and make it sound easy. Still, we are all proof that if you work hard enough together, you and Stuart can overcome anything," Jessica explains as she comes over to my side of the booth and gives me a hug.

"Jess is right, we stand with you as women. Stuart's

reaction was a little high and to the right, as my father would say. But, it was an emotional situation. You need to cut yourself some slack. Then again, I've been married a lot less time than these two. You can take my advice with a grain of salt," Jade adds.

"All of this is a little hard for me to figure out right now. My gut tells me you guys are right. It'll probably be okay between us, but it may take us a while to get there."

CHAPTER NINETEEN

STUART

MITCH STANDS IN FRONT of me as I am examining one of the golden retriever pups I rescued and turned over to Hope's Haven. As I draw up the vaccine, he scowls at me. "I thought I told you not to mess things up. Darya has enough crap going on in her life without you adding to it. At this moment, if I had to choose between you and Darya, I'd have to think hard."

I glance up at Mitch. "Look, I didn't mean to bust us up. I was just telling Darya I'd rather she didn't put herself in the line of fire every day. I'm sorry. It's the way I feel. I don't know if I can handle the loss of another woman. You know how Nora's death turned both of our lives upside down."

I give the puppy his shots and hand the squirming bundle back to Mitch.

"I shouldn't have to remind you of this, but I will anyway. Darya is *not* Nora."

Feeling stung, I cross my arms and glare at Mitch. "Think I don't know that?" I ask as I wash my hands. When I finish, I address Mitch sarcastically, "I know, it's awful. Our breakup probably hurts your feelings and puts you and Jess in an awkward situation, but things were said that should've never been said. I'm not sure if we can come back from that."

Mitch scoops the puppy up in one arm and grabs the bag of flea medicine as he heads toward the door. He turns around before he leaves the room. "Okay … I understand. I've been there too. That's how I know you need to ask yourself one simple question. Can you live with yourself if you don't try?"

After Mitch leaves, I lean on the exam table as I hang my head. I don't know if I've ever lost so much sleep in such a short period — at least not since Nora died. If there are simple solutions to my problem, I haven't been able to find them.

Dashonte walks around the corner as he brings antibacterial wipes to clean the table. "Doc, that was harsh. You okay?"

"How much did you overhear?" I ask, startled by his question.

"Pretty much all of it. Walls around here are thin. What in the hell did you do?"

"Language, Dashonte. Language. We are in a place of business, remember?"

"Sorry, boss. So, what really happened? Your lady seems like she's chill."

I hide a grin at Dashonte's question. As responsible as Dashonte is, his professional vocabulary could use work.

"To tell you the truth, it wasn't Darya who lost her chill. It was me. I freaked out."

"Why?" Dashonte wipes down the table.

I sigh. "Good question. I guess I let my past impact

my future. In the end, Darya and I might pay the price for my stupidity."

"So… don't be stupid," suggests Dashonte with a shrug.

"I'm trying to figure out how to make that happen, but it's not so easy. We have a ton of issues to sort through. I don't know if it'll ever work out."

"You know I've learned lots of hard lessons from my mom, right?" Dashonte asks.

I nod.

"Well, one thing I've learned is if you screw up, the best thing you can do is apologize."

"You're right. 'I am sorry' may not be enough to fix all that's wrong between us, though."

"You won't know until you try," Dashonte advises.

I clap him on the shoulder as I walk by, "Solid advice. I'll see how it goes."

I wait impatiently for Darya to answer the phone. I've turned this conversation over and over in my head so many times. I'm anxious to get it all over with and move on with our lives, if that's what I have to do.

Finally, she answers her phone in a breathless tone. "Detective Vick, how can I help you?"

"Do you have a few minutes to talk?" I ask.

"Umm … actually, no," she answers. "I have to go help Dylan with an interrogation. I can't get into all of this at work. I'm sorry. I just ran back to my desk to grab a file."

"Look, I called to say I'm sorry," I blurt.

"That's nice to hear, but we have so much more to talk about. In case you haven't noticed, we're on opposite ends of the spectrum. *Crap!* I've got to go, Dylan is waiting for me."

"Can I call you later?" I ask with more emotion than I would've liked.

"I'm sorry, Stuart, it's a crazy week. Call me back in a few days."

When I call Darya the next day, she sounds ill. When she hears it's me, she blurts, "I'm not in a good place to talk right now."

"Relax, no personal stuff. I called for business reasons. We had two kittens come in with the same issue as the dogs."

Darya sighs. "Freakin'-fantastic. It's not as if half our force is out with the flu or anything. I'll be right over."

My hands are full when Dashonte escorts Darya to the surgery room. I am trying to do CPR on a tiny, badly burned kitten. His long hair indicates he was once a beautiful creature, but now he is lifeless.

I call Dashonte over and show him how to do chest compressions. "I need you to do this while I draw up atropine."

Dashonte looks up at me with wide eyes as he asks, "Seriously? You trust me to do this? I got fired from my last job."

I look around the surgery room. "Is there anyone

else here who works at The Critter Clinic?"

"No, but man —" Dashonte gasps as he continues to gently and quickly push on the tiny kitten's chest.

"Besides, you weren't fired. You were let go in a reduction in force. I talked to your supervisor; they had nothing but great things to say about you — especially your ability to manage a crisis," I respond as I get the injection ready.

"Not feeling so calm now, Doc. I gotta be honest with you."

"That's completely natural. An animal this critical sends every vet or vet tech, no matter how experienced, into an adrenaline frenzy."

"Will the kitten make it?" Darya asks from her perch in the corner.

I jump when I hear her voice. I've been so focused on saving the cat, I forgot she was there. I shake my head. "It's unlikely. This one is too far gone. I've been doing CPR for a while now. It's not working," I remark as I reach down to the kitten's thigh area and try to find a pulse. I look at my watch again. I put my hand over Dashonte's hand to still it. "I think I need to call this one. He's not responding."

"Are you kidding me? We're giving up?" Dashonte exclaims. "This cat was burned to death! I hope they fry in hell."

I take off my paper clothing protector and throw it in the biohazard bin as I get a paper towel wet and wipe down my face and wash my hands.

"I'm sorry, Dashonte, we can't save them all. Trust me; I feel the same way about all of this as you do."

"I am so sorry you couldn't help that little baby,"

Darya says softly. "How is the other kitten doing?"

Her comment focuses me again as I cover the deceased kitten with a sterile towel. I know as sad as it is, Darya will have to take pictures. The kitten presents a tragic picture with a tiny intubation tube hanging out of his mouth.

"Luckily, that kitten seems to have escaped before they could do serious damage. I may have to amputate her tail because it's badly burned and the skin may not regenerate. At least she is in stable condition for now."

"I'll do everything in my power to help find these creeps. This torture needs to stop. Every time I look at the patch of baldness on Atlas' back, it serves as a reminder we still have work to do in this case."

"Who's Atlas?" Dashonte asks, trying to follow the conversation.

"Atlas is one of the first victims. He is a tiny Chihuahua mix. Darya was the one who brought him in. They bonded so well she adopted him."

"Mad respect," Dashonte nods at Darya. "I hope he wasn't hurt too bad."

"It was touch and go there for a bit, but he seems to be a normal puppy now. Actually, I can't say that. My daughter is a whiz at dog training, so he is smarter than your average dog."

"A truer statement has never been said," I add. "What she has done with Atlas is downright amazing. I think she should do agility with him."

"I was talking to Mitch the other day. He says that's the next step in their training regime. Maya has blown through all the basic stuff."

"Rad. I wish I could have a pet, but they're not

allowed where I live."

"I'm sorry; pets are great," Darya says to Dashonte. Looking down at the exam table where the kitten lies, she adds, "At least most people think so. Because there was a death in this case, I have to call in forensics to take formal pictures. We have a serial animal abuser on our hands. I want to document everything by the book."

Darya picks up her cell phone and dials a series of numbers. As she is talking, I have the luxury of studying her for a few moments. I don't think I'll ever get used to the impact she has on me. I have to fight the urge to interrupt everything she's doing to give her a long, thorough kiss. Unfortunately, this isn't the time or place and I'm not even sure I have the right to do that anymore. I hate being in this limbo. It's as if part of my soul is gone.

As I am taking in the simple beauty of her, she catches me staring.

Darya clears her throat and looks away for a second. "What?"

"Nothing, I was thinking how beautiful you look. I miss you."

"I appreciate the compliment, but your eyes must be lying to you. I am fighting off a wicked bug that has been going around the station and I haven't slept well in over a week."

"Funny, I haven't slept well since we split either."

Darya blows her bangs out of her eyes. It is a clear sign she is irritated. "I didn't say that's why I'm not sleeping."

I grin. "You didn't say it wasn't either. Just sayin'."

Darya shrugs. "Honestly, you're not wrong. It's a

harder adjustment than I expected it to be. But we can't talk about it here. The forensic team will be here in a few minutes and we have to focus on catching the jerks that did this. I can't have my brain in two places at once."

"Fair enough, but can we please settle all of this soon? It's funny, I've spent many years alone and I've never been as lonely as I am right now."

Darya squeezes her eyes shut and a tear escapes as she says in a broken voice, "It's weird how that works. I feel the same way. Truthfully, it kinda sucks."

"I'd like to go back to the way it was, when it *didn't* suck."

"Unfortunately, I don't know if we can get there," Darya admits.

"Please don't give up on us quite yet."

"I'll do my best to change that, I promise."

Before I have a chance to say anything else, my doorbell rings, putting the brakes on any further efforts to put my life back together.

CHAPTER TWENTY

DARYA

"Mom, the strap on my sandal broke and all my other shoes are too tight. What are we going to do?" Maya holds up her broken shoe.

I put down the laundry I'm folding. "I guess we'll have to go to the mall and get you a new pair. We need to hurry though. I have a date with Stuart tonight."

Maya grins. "Oh, goody! I hope Stuart comes back. He has been gone a long time. I don't like only seeing him at baseball practice. He makes great pancakes."

My daughter is not wrong. Stuart does make seriously delicious pancakes. Admittedly, Maya probably considers them a luxury. She is almost nine years old, and I still haven't gotten the knack of making pancakes. I always burn the edges.

"I know that's what you hope for, but I'm not sure if it will happen tonight. We're just planning to talk. Stuart and I have a lot of grown-up problems to solve."

With laser-sharp insight, Maya answers, "Grown-up problems are dumb. I don't know what's so hard. Either you are Stuart's best friend, or you're not."

It's funny how my child can drill down on my issues

better than I can. Sometimes, I wish I could go back to the same black and white naïveté I once had. Unfortunately, life has taught me some bitter lessons and I now see the world in shades of gray.

Opening my junk drawer in the kitchen, I locate duct tape. Maya holds up her foot as I put the sandal on and tape it closed.

"That's ugly!" Maya says as she examines her foot.

"It will have to do until we can get to the mall. Should we call Jessica and ask her if she can come with us? She probably needs stuff for the baby. We might as well make it fun."

"Yeah! She cracks me up. I bet she can help me pick out rad sandals."

While Jessica and Maya walk hand-in-hand down the breezeway in the mall, I follow behind with Dozer in his typical relaxed heel pattern. Jessica suddenly turns a little green. She stops in her tracks and puts her hand over her mouth.

Maya stares at her with open curiosity. "Are you okay, Jessica?" Maya asks. "Are you going to throw up?"

Jessica shrugs. "Being pregnant is harder than I expected it to be. I thought my morning sickness would disappear after the first trimester. Every once in a while it still gets set off. The guy who just walked by bathed in cologne was enough to make me want to lose my breakfast."

"Oh, I was the same way. You know what triggered my nausea with Maya? Coffee. Do you know how much coffee is served at a police department? It is insane. I was trying not to let anyone know I was expecting, but it was more challenging to hide it by the day. Every time somebody had a cup of coffee, I wanted to toss my cookies. I am so surprised no one guessed."

Jessica pats her growing baby bump. "Isn't it weird that when you're pregnant, perfect strangers come up and tell you the most awful story they've ever heard about having a baby?"

"I didn't get much of that while I was pregnant because hardly anyone could tell. I'm tall enough I was able to hide most of it under big jackets. Breast-feeding was another story. Everyone and their dog had an opinion about how I should do it or how long I should continue. It was insane."

Jessica rolls her eyes. "Thanks for the heads up that it's not going to get better anytime soon. I was hoping people would lighten up."

"I know it's tough, but you'll love being a parent. It is the highlight of my life."

"I'm the highlight of your life?" Maya asks. "That sounds weird. Am I yellow, orange or pink?"

"You're so funny," I tease. I look down at Maya's fingernails and joke, "I don't know. These days, I think you could probably be all three."

Jessica holds up their hands and looks. "I didn't even notice you have fluorescent nail polish on too. We match. Epic!"

I choke on my laughter as I look at Jessica. She has her hair in braids tied off with brightly colored ribbons, and she is wearing an Ariana Grande T-shirt she got at a recent concert. "Let's face it; you are a nine-year-old trapped in the body of a grown-up, Jess."

She laughs out loud. "I don't think that's a secret from anyone. It's part of what makes me such a good children's librarian."

Maya drops back and pulls on my shirt. "Is this the store, Mom?"

I look up at the sign. "Yes, I have coupons for this store; we should be able to —"

I am interrupted as Dozer growls and lunges at one of the other patrons of the mall. I can tell by the hair standing up on the back of his neck this is serious. "Maya, Strategy Two! Take Jess," I shout.

Out of the corner of my eye, I see Maya dragging Jessica into the store. "Come on; we have to hide," Maya instructs. My attention is diverted by Dozer, I can't take the time to watch them further. I have to trust my daughter's training during our drills will pay off.

I draw my sidearm from my ankle holster and turn to where the suspect is and command, "Freeze! Police. If you don't comply, I will release the dog."

The guy drops his backpack and puts his hands in the air. Suddenly, Dozer spins around to address something going on behind me. As I whirl around to face the threat, the guy's arm comes down against my shooting hand. He hits me so hard the gun goes flying.

Shaking off the pain, I use my martial arts training to wrestle him into an inescapable hold. He seems shocked I'm able to get the upper hand. As I'm holding him, I'm breathing heavily. The guy is big and strong. A crowd is gathering. I look up at a teenage girl who has her cell phone out taking pictures. "Stop and call 9-1-1 please. I need backup like, yesterday."

Eventually, mall security shows up and calls the police with their radios. One guard jumps on the guy's legs and helps me control him. As I take a breath of relief, I notice Dozer is sitting in a very odd position. A feeling of dread comes over me as I see the abandoned backpack and Dozer's alert.

As I take in a deep breath and tighten my grip on the suspect, I hiss, "*Crap!* Call in the bomb disposal unit too." Addressing the security guard, I ask, "Do you have an evacuation plan? If so, you might want to use it."

The guard looks at me skeptically. "Why? What do you know?"

"I know my dog was trained by the TSA to work as an explosive detection canine. All I can tell you is he is alerting strongly on that backpack. I've worked with this dog long enough to know he does not overreact to threats. If Dozer says there's something in the bag, I'd be willing to bet my life savings there is. You might want to start evacuating now."

"Who are you to tell us how to do our jobs?"

Okay, that was the last straw. I look up at the guy and growl, "I am a detective. I work with the local police department. If my hands were free, I would show you my badge. But, I'm a little busy here. If you don't believe me, call my boss, Captain Allegheny."

A person from the crowd adds, "I know Detective Vick. She is a detective. She helped solve a burglary at my shop. Call the darn police."

The customer gathers several people up and marches them out the front door. Finally, a group of street cops comes in and relieves me from having to hold this jerk down. As soon as they have the suspect in custody with zip ties, I pivot to them. "I need to go. I'm here with my daughter, and I'm off duty. I will come to the station and fill out whatever paperwork, but I have to make sure my daughter and my friend are safe."

"Understood, Detective Vick," the younger cop says with a brisk nod. As I turn to leave, Doug from the bomb disposal unit walks up to me and gives me a brief hug. "Long time no see. But … how do you always find yourself in the middle of these things?"

I shrug. "I guess it's my special talent. I've got to go. I will talk to you in a minute. Check the backpack. I don't know what substance Dozer found, but there's something in there."

"10-4. We've got it from here."

"I know you do. I count on you guys to be the best."

As I walk away to find my daughter and Jess, I can't make the shaking in my knees stop. This is the scariest thing I've encountered in a long time. Even though I was injured in the last op, it wasn't as frightening because my family wasn't involved.

One of my first thoughts is Stuart is going to go absolutely ballistic when he hears what happened today. On the other hand, it underscores the fact there really isn't any safe environment anywhere. This isn't about being a police officer, it's about being an American family in dangerous times.

I run into the store and ask the clerk where the restroom is. She points me to the back of the store. When I reach the bathroom door, I hold my breath for a moment before I announce, "The code word is pickle juice."

From the other side of the bathroom door, I hear

Maya answer in a shaky voice, "We are okay, Mom. Are you?"

"Dozer and I are fine. The bad guy is caught. We need to go. You can unlock the door now."

I hear the reassuring metal clank of the lock. A second later, Maya launches herself at me. She hangs off of me like a little monkey and twines her arms around my neck. She squeezes me tight. "Mommy! I am so glad you're okay; I was so scared."

"I know you were, sweetie, but you did exactly the right thing."

Jessica emerges from the stall. She is wiping her eyes with a piece of toilet paper. "Darya, you have the most levelheaded kid I have ever seen in my life. If it were up to me, I would've still been sitting there. Maya got me to safety like a seasoned pro."

"I hate to tell you guys this, but the threat is not over. I have friends from the BDU coming to check out a suspicious backpack."

Maya draws in a quick, startled breath.

"BDU?" Jessica asks as I hustle her and Maya out of the bathroom and toward the mall exit doors.

"That's where my dad used to work. It means they think there is a bomb," Maya explains.

"Oh, wow! They made that determination quickly. We were only in the restroom for a few minutes."

I smile as I look down at Dozer. "They had a little help from a very talented law enforcement agent who isn't really an agent."

"They should give Dozer a paycheck if he keeps rescuing people," quips Jessica.

"No kidding!" I open the doors of the SUV for Jessica and Maya. "I'm taking us all to the station. They will probably want to talk to you guys too because you were witnesses. You can take my rig home after you've spoken to them. I have to stick around and talk to people because I drew my weapon. It'll be a long night."

"What about your date with Stuart?" Maya asks from the backseat.

"Oh, shoot! In all the craziness, I completely forgot," I admit. "I don't even know how to begin to explain all of this."

"I don't think the news you've been involved in another incident will go over very well," Jessica comments.

"Oh no! I like Stuart. I don't want him to be mad at you," Maya exclaims in a worried voice.

I heave out a sigh. "I know, sweetie. You know how some people are afraid of spiders and snakes? Stuart is afraid like that about me. He's frightened I'll get hurt; it is his biggest fear."

"Does he know you kick the bad guys' butts?" Maya asks. She looks up into the rearview mirror and grins at me. That girl owns my heart. The fact she is still supportive after what she's just been through means the world to me.

"Your daughter might be on to something. Maybe Stuart doesn't understand what a warrior you are," Jessica agrees.

"Maybe not, unfortunately, I have a hunch tonight might not be the greatest time to tell him," I roll my eyes and grimace.

CHAPTER TWENTY-ONE

STUART

As I place my instruments into the autoclave, I'm startled by the sound of the doorbell because I am not expecting anyone. That's the downside to working out of your home. I hope it's not a grisly emergency because I still need to get ready for my date with Darya. This one dinner may decide my entire future. I don't want to mess it up.

When I open the door, I'm surprised to see Mitch and Isaac standing on the other side. They don't even wait for me to invite them in before they come in and sit down on my couch. "It was like I thought," Mitch says to Isaac. "He hasn't been watching the news."

"No, I just finished a tooth cleaning and extraction on a bull mastiff with a severe case of halitosis. Why? Should I be watching the news?"

"At this point, it's probably better if you don't," Isaac advises with a somber look.

I curse under my breath. "Something happened to Darya, didn't it? I thought she had today off."

"She did. We need to go," Mitch urges with a sense of desperation. "She was at the mall with Jessica and Maya. One of the news stations is reporting an officer-involved shooting, and another one says the bomb squad has been called. Jessica sent me a text about some of the specifics, but there are still a lot of missing details. All I know is we need to get out of here."

I glance down. "I've got to ditch these scrubs."

"Hurry your butt up," Mitch says impatiently. "My pregnant wife is currently in the middle of a meltdown at the police station."

"I hear you. Going now!" I sprint upstairs.

I haven't changed clothes this fast since I was caught in a hurricane on the edge of a jetty during my days as an active member of the team at Search and Rescue of Central Florida.

I run downstairs and grab my keys and cell phone off the coffee table. "I'm good to go now," I announce as I jam all my stuff in my pockets.

After I climb in the front seat with Isaac, I turn to him and ask, "What do you know? You and your sources are usually more up to date than the news stations. Identity Bank is always in-the-know."

"Tristan is on his way there. He is trying to help several of the stores retrieve their surveillance footage to give to the police. Beyond that, I know no one is hurt, not even the suspect. That tells me Darya did not discharge her weapon. She has precision aim, if she meant to shoot someone, they'd be dead."

"Jessica told me they were evacuated from the mall. Apparently, the guy who tried to attack Darya dropped a backpack and Dozer alerted to it," Mitch adds.

"That's big. I've done drills with Dozer to keep his skills sharp. He does *not* false alert on things. If Dozer alerted to the backpack, there *is* something there." I pivot to look back at Mitch in the backseat.

"That's what I'm afraid of," Mitch says. "It's a crazy world we live in. The girls just went to buy a pair of shoes and all heck broke loose."

"I am not even sure Darya will want to see me. We still haven't settled things between us."

"I've known Darya a long time, whether or not she tells you she needs support, she does," Isaac advises.

"I hope so," I respond as Isaac pulls into the station parking lot.

After they both bolt from the car, I take a moment to collect myself. Even though my adrenaline is ratcheted up, I don't want to say anything to make things between Darya and me worse. I stand outside the car and take deep breaths to calm down and focus. Honestly, I don't know if I remember what it's like to be centered. Life with Darya is turning out to be much more of a roller coaster than I ever anticipated. After Nora died, I thought I'd given up the drama in my life. I try to remember Mitch's admonition that Darya is not Nora. Although I know this logically, my fear response doesn't seem to understand the difference.

Mitch comes out of the building to check on me. "Did you get lost on your way to the door?" he asks.

"No, I'm trying to pull it together so I don't unload on Darya. I jumped the gun last time and went off half-cocked. I need a moment to chill so I don't make the same mistake twice."

Mitch claps me on the shoulder. "Good for you. You mucked it up the last time."

I scowl at him. "Did you come out here for a particular reason or just to harass me?"

"Sorry, bad timing. I came out to tell you Jessica and Maya are almost ready to go. Unfortunately, Darya will be tied up a few more hours. Do you want one of us to drop off your car after we get everyone settled?"

"Yeah, that would be great. I think I'll stick around here for a while until she is finished."

"Sounds like a plan. By the way, you might want to get your butt inside. Your absence is pretty conspicuous."

"On it." I stick my cell phone back into my pocket and tuck in my shirt.

Mitch sees my pensive expression and adds, "I wouldn't worry quite so much if I were you. It seems like Darya was visibly disappointed when you didn't follow us through the doors."

"I guess that's something," I concede.

"I've got one word of advice for you —"

"Oh, I can't wait to hear this," I answer sarcastically.

"Roll your eyes if you want to, but I was going to tell you to remember it's not always all about you."

I blush and look away. "As usual, you're right. Darya needs my love, not my fear. My paranoia can wait."

"Agreed. I wish you the best of luck," Mitch says, as he turns around to walk into the building.

A young policeman escorts me to Darya's new office space. When I see her, I am struck by how exhausted she looks. She has enough paperwork in front of her to kill a tree or two. She is busy typing up notes on her computer and doesn't appear to see me come into her office.

I was wrong. As soon as Darya finishes the sentence she is typing, she looks up at me. Her eyes are red as if she's been crying. Quietly, she comes over and shuts the door behind me. "I guess it's about time for me to take advantage of one of the perks of being promoted to an actual office space instead of a cubicle."

I look over at Dozer who is sleeping in a dog bed embroidered with his name. "He looks exceptionally comfortable in your office."

"As he should, he was a hero again today. Right now, I don't want to tell the story again. I just want you to hold me. I know we haven't sorted everything out between us, but I need you."

"I can do that." I hold my arms open wide for her.

"Please don't let go," she asks in a broken whisper. "I came close to dying today. Closer than I ever want to be again." She walks into my arms and kisses me soundly.

Holding her in my arms fills the cracks in my soul. I feel as if I can breathe easier. It is almost as if the shattered parts of me begin to mend. I could stay like this forever.

After several moments, I pull away. I release a deep shuddering breath. "Thank goodness, you're okay. All I could think about on my way over here was how I left you with angry, bitter words. It would've been horrible if it was the last conversation we ever had."

"I know. After the adrenaline rush passed, that's exactly how I felt. I'm sorry we won't get a chance to go to dinner and talk about all of this. Sadly, I'll be filling out reports for half my natural life."

"That's annoying. Though, according to Isaac, you stepped up and saved a lot of people."

Darya shrugs. "I was implementing my years of training. It was all instinct. Well, instinct and Dozer. He saw the threats first."

"Maybe but if you hadn't paid attention to Dozer's reactions, things could have been so much worse."

"Dozer deserves the credit in this situation; I heard from Doug over at the BDU. He says their forensic analysis showed there were liquid explosives in the backpack. That kid was planning to use himself as a suicide bomber."

"I almost wish I didn't know that. On the other hand, I'm glad you told me. It's another sign of how rock solid your instincts and nerves are. I'm so proud of you," I murmur against her hair as I continue to embrace her.

"I know you don't want to hear about all this stuff, but this is the reality of my job. If I hide this from you, it's not an honest relationship."

"I guess I have to put my big boy undies on and deal with it. I spent a lot of time thinking during the last few days. After a while, I concluded my issues are not your issues. You've got your own stuff to deal with."

Darya's computer beeps, and she looks back toward the screen. She sighs. "I am so relieved. Your words make me want to cry. I've been so frustrated because every time we start to talk about this, it seems like life intervenes. I have to get to these reports. I had to draw my weapon, so there is a bucket load of paperwork I need to finish as quickly as possible."

Darya's stomach growls, and she places her hand over it. "You have no idea how much I wish we were having Chinese food right now. I'm so sorry our dinner plans were interrupted."

"Hey, don't blame yourself. This one is on a group of teenagers with too much access to the Internet and not enough brains."

Darya shudders. "Yeah, we came precariously close to having at least one less teenager on the planet. I wonder if those kids understand what could've happened."

"Do they know what these kids hoped to do?" I ask.

Darya looks up at the clock. "*Crap!* I have a briefing on this in a few minutes. I've got to get back to work so I'm prepared. I'll know more after the briefing."

"Okay, I'm out of here. But, I'll be around if you need me. Send me a text message."

"Stuart, I don't think you understand. It could be hours before I get home," Darya cautions.

"Mitch and Jessica have Maya. If you need me to, I can take her to my house tonight after Isaac and Mitch bring back my car."

Darya pulls her hair up into a ponytail and tightens the hairband as she weighs her options. "I don't know what to do. Jessica is recovering from the incident as well. She doesn't need the burden of a child hanging around. Jess doesn't need any more stress in her life. It's hard on the baby."

"Or, Maya could be just the person Jessica needs. It's impossible to be serious around Maya," I counter. "I'll tell you what … I'll keep in touch with Mitch. We'll figure it out from there and let you know. Either way, I am a phone call away if you need me."

"You'll never know how much I appreciate that. I've missed your calmness in the middle of my chaos."

"I'm happy to do it," I answer with a smile. For the first time in several days, I'm hopeful Darya and I might have a fighting chance.

As I walk into Darya's office, my arms are so full I have to stabilize her drink with my chin to prevent it from falling. I figure if she doesn't have the time to go to dinner, I will bring dinner to her. I got all of her favorite foods as well as mine. We'll be eating Chinese food for days.

I set the food down and look up at Darya. Since I brought her food from her favorite place, I thought she'd be showering me with kisses. Instead, I encounter a woman who looks like she is shell-shocked. Perhaps the adrenaline from the day has caught up with her.

Rushing over to her, I pull her up into a tight embrace as I murmur in her ear, "What's wrong?"

Darya gives me a brief hug and then sits back down. "I'm still processing all of it. Allegedly, when they arrested the juvenile, they found a note in his possession, which names me and every other minority police officer as a target. When confronted with this information, he sang like a bird. As if that's not bad enough, it's not just minority personnel at our agency at risk. It is every fire department, ambulance driver, EMT and medical provider in our region."

I whistle quietly between my teeth. "Must be some list."

She shakes her head sadly. "Unfortunately, it's not as large as it should be. Minority hires are too uncommon. Even so, it's long enough. Everyone is on edge."

"So, how does a kid get a hit list of people across that many agencies?" I struggle to keep my voice even. I can feel the tension in my arms and hands as I try to stay relaxed. I don't want this to be a repeat of our last conversation about the dangers of her job.

"Welcome to the sixty-four-thousand-dollar question. He claims he was getting paid in both cash and weed. At the moment, he's asserting he knows nothing more about who's behind this. Who knows whether we should believe him? The good news is he named his accomplices. The street cops are out searching for them as we speak."

"Hopefully, they'll come up with something soon," I reply, feeling inadequate and unprepared to deal with the situation.

Darya hides her face in her hands. "I don't even know how I'll protect myself and my daughter. Dozer is great, but he can't fight systemic discrimination. Someone deliberately set out to kill me. I was shocked to find out it has nothing to do with Sergio. It has to do with the color of my skin. My God, we are almost a quarter of the way through this century. How in the world does that kind of stuff still happen? I half expect to see men in white robes burning crosses in front of the police station. I'm not ashamed to tell you I'm completely freaked out by this."

"With all due respect, why are you still here? You need time to absorb this information in private. This is not where you need to be at the moment."

"I can still help them put the puzzle pieces together," Darya protests as she wipes away a tear. "I know it may not seem like it, but I'm tough."

I walk up behind her and massage her shoulders. "Those same puzzle pieces will still be there tomorrow, or maybe there'll be different ones, but the whole weight of the case does not rest on your shoulders. You know it doesn't take away your toughness to take a break, right?"

"I'm afraid the bombing that killed Sergio is at the root of all this. I need to be the one to solve it to avenge his death."

"I know Sergio was a hero, but I think this is bigger than him. It might even be bigger than the whole state of Florida. Who knows? This could be a nationwide movement," I suggest.

Darya draws in a shaky breath as she sags back against her office chair. "You're right; all the evidence points that way. How do we fight hate this large?"

"All you can do is take it one suspect at a time, but you need to rest and catch your breath. Do you have to be here? Or are you choosing to be?" I ask gently.

A tear slides down Darya's face. "At this point, it's a choice. I can't let these guys get away with this. There are so many lives at stake. If that bomb had gone off today, who knows how many people would've been killed."

"I understand. But, at this point, you are going to collapse from exhaustion. You need to call it a day and come back tomorrow with fresh eyes."

Darya rolls her neck and rubs her shoulder. "You're right, my eyes are so heavy I can barely focus. Besides, I need to check in with Maya to see how she's doing. She had the fright of her life today."

"Actually, she is having an impromptu slumber party with Megan Appleton. When I last talked to her, she was fine. She's proud of herself for being able to follow your safety plan. Maya thinks you are one super-hero of a woman. She wants to be just like you."

"Yesterday, I would've been so proud of her ambition. Today I'm scared for her."

"I know. In order to make the world a safer place, you must take care of yourself. Let's go home, eat and get real sleep for a change."

Darya takes a deep breath. "I know you're right. I hate to give up in the middle of things."

"You're not giving up. You're taking a step back to regroup. You will tackle this all tomorrow. I know you. You're incredibly smart and have a knack for finding things other people don't. You'll get there, but you can't do it all tonight."

Darya shuts down her computer, gets her purse out of her desk drawer and slings it over her shoulder. She reaches out and grabs my hand. "I'm ready to go home. I hope you don't mind, but I need industrial-strength cuddles tonight."

"Totally doable," I promise as I brush a light kiss across her lips.

This time, the guys don't even bother to ring the doorbell before they barge in my house. All the clamor makes it impossible for me to concentrate on my billing statements. I close my file and throw my pen on my desk before I stomp downstairs.

Mitch is standing at the bottom of the stairs with his friend. He pokes Tristan in the ribs with his elbow. "I don't know. It looks like his night didn't go so well. Look at the frown on his face."

"Shut up! You have no idea what happened." I glower at him.

"If it went so great, how come you look ready to wrestle a grizzly bear?"

"Not that it's any of your business, but I'm a bit on edge because Darya is back at work today. It was supposed to be her day off."

Tristan raises an eyebrow at me. "The way I heard it, no one is getting any time off anytime soon. They've got their hands full. It's all hands on deck."

"No freakin' kidding! Between teenage suicide bombers, people wielding lead pipes, and somebody who lights pets on fire, the world has gone mad. Darya thinks she has to solve all these problems by herself. She is working nearly around-the-clock. Even when she isn't officially working, her brain never shuts off to give her a break. She is falling asleep in the shower."

"I get it. It's hard to let go of the case once you start to unravel it," Tristan explains. "You're always afraid someone is going to drop the ball in your absence. I knew about the incident at the mall, and when Darya's op went south, but what's going on with the animals?"

"Remember meeting Dashonte? He used to work at the indoor gym with all that trampoline stuff. They say they let him go because revenue was down. I think it was related to the fact he became involved in something behind their business and they didn't want the police around to scare away customers."

"Yeah, I noticed you had a new kid. Is he one of your volunteers?"

"No, I gave him a job. I didn't want him to have to face repercussions for doing the right thing," I explain.

Looking at Tristan, I add, "Dashonte witnessed a group of teenagers or preteens lighting a puppy on fire. I've had four other cases recently with the same MO. Apparently, they use a spray cologne and then light it on fire."

"That's sadistic," Tristan shakes his head.

"I agree. So far, I've been lucky, only one animal involved has not made it. But, I don't want to play my odds much longer. I think these kids are getting bolder by the day."

Tristan looks at Mitch. "You've got a new batch of search and rescue dogs that need a bit of work out, don't you?"

Mitch nods. "I do. They are young, enthusiastic and looking for jobs."

"Things are slow around my shop at the moment. I propose a joint operation between Hope's Haven and Identity Bank."

"Won't that step on the toes of the local authorities?" I ask. "The last thing I want is Darya to feel like I don't trust her."

"Oh, don't get me wrong — the locals will be involved. We are going to give them a shot in the arm and a few more resources."

I pause for a moment. "I can't exactly speak for Darya, but I think she would be all about catching these guys sooner rather than later."

"Great, I'll set up a meeting with Captain Allegheny and Darya to see if we can set up an ad hoc task force to catch these kids before they graduate to harming human victims," Tristan offers.

"Thank you for offering to help. Hopefully, it will

relieve the pressure off of Darya."

Mitch rubs his hands together. "Now that we have a plan of attack, let's go eat pizza. There is no need to let it get cold."

At the mention of the word pizza, my stomach lets out a plaintive growl, reminding me I have been working so hard to ignore the fact Darya is gone that I forgot to eat.

"Sounds good to me. I could do with some decent food."

CHAPTER TWENTY-TWO

DARYA

I TRY NOT TO wrinkle my nose as I stand just inside the door of Captain Allegheny's office. I don't know how he can eat this stuff, but to each his own. I quietly set it on his desk as he concludes his phone call. Nervously, I take a seat as I try not to be overcome with emotion.

Captain Allegheny looks over his reading glasses at me. "Vick, what are you up to? You know bagels and lox are my favorite thing on the planet." He sniffs the air and adds, "Smells like you brought me my favorite vanilla roast coffee as well. I know from experience, you probably want something. Did I not make it clear during roll call no one would be awarded any vacation time for the foreseeable future?"

"You did, sir," I concede.

He leans back in his chair and loosens his tie. "So, tell me whatever life-shattering story you want to. I'm waiting to see how many people try to get around the vacation ban," he challenges.

What seemed like a good idea a few minutes ago suddenly seems like the worst thought I've ever had. My stomach plummets to my toes as I stammer, "This isn't about vacation time, it's about Maya."

His eyebrows almost reach his hairline. "Do you remember the conversation we had several years ago where you assured me your daughter would not interfere with your duties?"

I nod mutely.

Swallowing hard, I answer, "No… yes… maybe?"

"Which is it, Vick? It can't be all three," he counters, giving me a glimpse of the top-notch interrogator he is reputed to be.

"Look, I don't know. All I know is that since the two incidences, my daughter isn't sleeping. She has been in her own bed since she was a tiny toddler, but now she comes in to my room to sleep with me because she is terrified. She doesn't want me to leave her side even for a moment."

"Not to be a jerk, but how is this my problem? I've got much bigger issues going on in this station than the sleeping habits of your daughter."

"I understand. I wanted to talk to you about whether I could take an alternative assignment. I think I have enough experience to teach at the Academy."

"You could look into that, sure. But, I know you well enough to know you won't want to just teach. You'd always want to be in the middle of the action. That's the way you're built. You and I are both adrenaline junkies. Let me tell you, for people like us, desk duty is a pain in the butt."

"I know, sir. My daughter is getting old enough to understand the risks I face every day. She's very distressed about it. She panics every time I go to work. I need to do something. I thought perhaps I could still give back to this department if I moved my skills over to the teaching side of things."

"Oh yeah, they could probably use someone with your level of experience over at the Academy, but I don't think this is what this is about. I don't believe it's about your daughter at all. You're afraid. You don't work well backed up against a wall. I've watched your career over the past few years since you moved up here from Tampa. You want to be large and in charge. When you're not, you flounder. You're upset the white supremacists have gotten the upper hand. They are getting into your head. I think you are giving up."

Forgetting myself for a second, I stand up and yell in Captain Allegheny's face. "You are full of crap! I haven't given up on anything. I am trying to protect my family. In case you haven't noticed, I have a target on my back. For all I know, the same target is on Maya's back. That is unacceptable to me."

Captain Allegheny sighs. "I understand where you're coming from. Probably more than you think."

"Yeah? You could've fooled me," I answer sardonically as I take a seat. "We've been friends for a long time, but with all due respect, you're being a jerk."

"Maybe so. I'm trying to stop you from making a mistake because you're scared." The captain sits up straighter and runs his hand over his thigh. "I've been in your shoes. I wanted to throw it all in for a safer, more sedate and steady job. This was before your time, probably almost literally before your time. I was just a rookie cop, and I lost two people around me in the same week. My training officer was shot in the neck and passed away, and then the guy who recruited me to the force was killed in an MVA as he did a routine traffic stop. I spent a long time evaluating whether it was worth it for my family for me to wear the uniform."

"I'm sorry," I whisper softly.

"Thank you, it was many years ago, but I still appreciate the sentiment. I'm here to tell you you will eventually be able to put all of this in perspective. Someday, all this angst and fear will be a case collecting dust in a warehouse."

"That's difficult to imagine. Obviously, you're still here. So, what changed your mind?"

"Believe it or not, a buddy and I were at a little diner shooting the breeze about what I was planning to do. As crazy as it seems, we were drinking coffee and eating donuts. The waitress overheard what I was planning, and she begged me not to leave."

"Why?"

"It turns out I helped her brother find his missing boy. Everyone else had told him his son was nearly a teenager; therefore, he must be a runaway. I looked at everything in this kid's life, and he didn't seem like the type. So, I continued to search. I found him four blocks away in the home of a well-known pedophile."

"Wow, that must've been huge for you as a rookie officer."

"It was. It put me front and center with the media and made me realize without me on the force, the outcome could have been even worse. I knew then there was no way I could walk away from my job. There could've been other kids out there like him. So, I stayed. Eventually, my losses became outweighed by the positives in my career. I will always miss my friends, but they would've wanted me to stay on the force."

"Wow, that must've been quite the experience. Still, I don't know how your story fits my circumstances. Someone, or a group of someones are gunning for me. I don't know how to mitigate that danger."

"I can't make that decision for you, Vick. I can only say you are one of the most talented detectives I have ever worked with, and I would hate to see you be forced out of your job because of a wacky, self-important hate group. It seems wrong to me. Do me a favor — go talk to the people at the Academy and see what they can offer you. Also check in on cases you handled before. Talk to the people you've helped and see what you mean to them. I think it will give you perspective."

"I haven't made a final decision yet. I'm weighing my options. My career is having a devastating effect on my family and I'm struggling to find the right balance. Now that my life has been directly threatened, it's even more difficult for me to justify the danger. I'm not sure how all this will play out, but I wanted to let you know where my head is at."

"To tell you the truth, you are my best detective. You are a gifted interrogator, and you have great common sense that allows you to see the big picture. The bottom line is we'll catch the people who are threatening you faster if you stay involved in the case."

My eyes widen at his admission. Captain Allegheny is not a man who gives compliments out often.

He catches my look of surprise and adds, "Now, if you tell any of my other officers I said any of that, I will deny it. This is between you and me because I want to stop you from making a colossal mistake. The world needs you exactly where you are. Other people can teach, but you can't teach people to have instincts like yours."

"I appreciate your input, sir; I will take it into account when I make my decision. Understand my family is important to me too. If I lost them, I'm not sure I could cope. I've already lost one love of my life; I can't afford to lose anyone else."

"Understood. For now you still have a job to do. Go do it and bring these perps in, okay? I'm tired of people threatening this city. They need to be in jail." Captain Allegheny looks at his watch. "Oh, by the way I forgot to put this on the computerized schedule, but we have a meeting with Tristan Macklin and his group in about an hour. I expect you to be there. I'm putting you in charge of the task force."

"10-4," I respond with a salute. On shaky knees, I stand up and leave my boss's office. Unfortunately, things are cloudier for me now than they were when I went in.

I'm trying to balance my phone in the crook of my neck as I type on the computer. "Tristan, how in the world did you come up with all these images? My partner and I beat the bushes in that neighborhood trying to come up with security footage and came up almost empty handed."

Pressing the up arrow, I zoom in on anyone who looks like a teenager. I feel a bit voyeuristic, but it's crucial we find the perpetrators. "Someone dumped several carcasses off at The Critter Clinic the other day. That brings the total number of burned animals who didn't make it up to four. Whoever is doing this is picking up speed. Less and less time is elapsing between attacks as the weeks go on," I add.

"One of the advantages of installing surveillance systems all around town is that I maintain a constant flow of information with my clients. I've spent several years building up trust with them so they know I don't misuse anything they collect. When I ask them to turn over footage, they understand it's probably for a good cause. In past cases, I have been able to help find missing children through the use of surveillance footage from systems I've installed. My clients are usually aware of this when they hire me."

"To be honest, most of the time, that level of surveillance would give me the willies, but these days, I'm grateful for it. I know it makes me sound like a hypocrite, but I am desperate to find these kids. The attacks are getting worse."

"I'm running down leads as quickly as I can, but I ran across an anomaly in the data. I don't know if files got mixed up, or the cases are related. I ran the information on your suspects from the incident at the mall against local juveniles who have a record in the system. There seems to be a statistically significant amount of contact between your suspects in the attempted mall bombing and several members of Klar. I don't know if this trend holds true for adults, but I found it interesting, nonetheless. Kids put everything on social media and it makes confirming data a cinch."

For a few moments, I turn the new facts I've learned over in my brain. After a bit, Tristan asks, "Darya, are you still there?"

"Yeah, I'm putting the pieces together in my head. You know, what you're saying makes a lot of sense. I know it's a long shot, but it's possible. We've learned the threats against our city services like fire ambulance and police have been replicated in other cities too. It's always against minority employees. For them to figure all that out, they would have to have local contacts."

"Stands to reason. But, why young teenagers? Why wouldn't they target adults?"

"You said it yourself. Kids are usually invisible in the system and usually easily swayed by their peers. Not everyone has the resources or access to files and data Identity Bank does. It is possible the adult population are heavily involved, but the data may have been ignored."

"Do you want me to run the same analysis with the adult population?" Tristan asks.

"We can look, but I think these offenders are juveniles based on what Dashonte said. In fact, I believe they are younger than our typical offenders."

"I wonder how they're getting hooked up with a group like Klar?"

"Who knows? It could be YouTube or chat rooms. It could even be recruiters scouring the kids' neighborhood. According to Dashonte, there is an open gang war going on around where he lives. At least two gangs are fighting for new membership among the neighborhood kids. The person who tried to recruit him was dripping with jewelry and drove any teenager's dream car. The guy suggested all of his financial problems with his mom could be solved if only he joined the gang."

"According to the statement I read, Dashonte was able to specifically name the gang who tried to recruit him, correct?"

"Yeah, but it wasn't the Klar. Given the racial make up of the two groups, it is likely they are rival gangs."

"The implications of that are horrifying. If members

of the Klar are willing to blow themselves up as martyrs and the other gang members are willing to set live animals on fire, a gang war would be apocalyptic."

The light on my phone goes off indicating I need to go to my appointment. "On that cheery note, I have to go meet with a victim of a home invasion."

"Never a dull moment for you, is there?" Tristan quips.

"You know how this goes. You go where the case leads you. Sometimes it's easy, and other times it's complicated beyond belief. Hopefully, this one will be straightforward. I'll call you back after I've reviewed the footage."

"Sounds good. I may not be around. Rogue and I are going to Jessica's OB appointment. Mitch is stranded at the San Francisco airport because he was the keynote speaker at a service dog conference. He's totally ticked off he has to miss the last checkup before her due date."

"Poor guy. I know he wanted to be involved every step of the way. When is he coming home?"

"As soon as he can. At this point, he's considering simply driving up to Oregon."

"Jessica probably doesn't feel this way, but I can't believe how fast her pregnancy has progressed. It seems like yesterday they were breaking the news to us."

Tristan laughs. "Tell me about it. I had no idea she was this close, or I would've told him to keep his butt home."

"I've got to go, but if I find anything on the surveillance tapes, I'll leave you a message on your phone."

"What can I do for you today, Mrs. Wilcox?" I ask as I stand in the doorway of the older woman's home.

"Don't be silly, call me Rosemary. After all we've been through, I think we can treat each other as friends, am I right?"

I chuckle. "You have a good point. So, how can I help you today, Rosemary?" I repeat.

"Well, this may turn out to be nothing, but I thought maybe you should see this. I am a little befuddled, to tell you the truth."

"Okay, I'll be glad to take a look. What do you need to show me?"

"Well, it's a bit harder for me to do these days, but I still like a good spring cleaning. So, I was puttin' all the winter blankets away in the attic, and I came across all this stuff. There's a bunch of money and other stuff I don't recognize up there. Lord knows, I would know if I left a stack of money behind. It gets even stranger. There's all this men's perfume up there. You know, my Victor passed away a few years back. I got no need for that kind of stuff in the house anymore. Anyway, Victor — God rest his soul — wore Old Spice his whole life. That stuff ain't the red stuff."

"Oh, that is odd," I concede. "You can't think of any reason it would be in your house?" I press.

"Actually, wait … my grandson comes to stay with me and you know how teenagers can get an awful funk? I guess he could use that sorta stuff, but there's no reason that there should be money there. I can't even afford to pay him an allowance. Every once in a while, I pay Carver to mow the lawn, but not much."

"Why don't you show me where you found the stuff, Rosemary?"

"It's right here down at the end of the hallway. You have to pull down a ladder to climb, but it's not so bad. I don't understand how can-after-can of that stuff is in my attic. There were a bunch of lighters there too. I will kick Carver's butt if he is smoking. You know, those awful cigarettes are what killed my husband."

The hair on the back of my neck stands up as I listen to Rosemary's description of what she found. For her sake, I hope I'm wrong. As we walk down the long hallway, I notice pictures on both sides. I turn to Rosemary and ask, "Are these your kids?"

She laughs. "No, honey. My kids are all growed by now. These are my grandkids. See, there's Carver's graduation from the fifth grade." She points to a different picture. "Here he is startin' the seventh grade. He's such a smart boy. I hope he goes to college."

As I lean in to inspect it, my heart sinks. I know without even going into the attic I've likely identified the first teenager from the surveillance tape of the attack that killed the kitten.

I look at the hopeful face of Rosemary Wilcox, and my heart breaks a little. Apparently, I don't hide my expression well enough because Rosemary looks at me. "Please, please don't tell me my grand-baby Carver is up to no good. I knew the minute I saw all that money, things were going to be bad. I almost didn't tell you, but my Bible teaches me to tell the truth, even when it's hard."

"I appreciate that, Rosemary. I know nothing for sure at the moment. It's an educated guess. I could be totally off base. I have to speak to Carver to clear things up. Do you have any idea where he is?"

"I don't rightly know. He made a few friends from Georgia, and now he hangs out with them all the time. I know they play video games at the little market up the street. You might find him there," she answers. As she adjusts her glasses, her hands are trembling.

"Thank you for your help, Rosemary. Try not to worry; I just need to ask Carver some questions at the moment. Nothing terrible is happening today."

After Rosemary shows me the stash in the attic, I have even more doubts about whether I'll be able to keep my word to her. The cans of cologne up there are the same brand and size as the ones we recovered from the scene. This may be the break we need. Sadly, I'll probably shatter Rosemary's heart in the process. No one ever said police work was a picnic.

CHAPTER TWENTY-THREE

STUART

I CAREFULLY ROLL UP my sleeves and straighten my belt after I tuck in my shirt. "Are you sure I can't talk to you about this? It would be so much easier."

Darya shoots me a bemused smile. "Yes, I'm sure."

"But … you already know all the details of what's going on because you were part of it," I point out logically.

"Uh-huh, I do. That's precisely why I can't be the one to interview you. I'm too close to the case."

"Okay, but does your boss have to be the one to question me? I'm nervous. It's as if I'm the criminal instead of the witness."

"Captain Allegheny has a reputation of being a tough interrogator, but he's also very thorough and gets us the information we need in case all of this goes to court. You'll do fine. You keep meticulous notes," she assures me as she walks over and gives me a hug.

"When I treated the first kittens, I had no idea all of this would be so earth-shattering."

"I know how you feel. I thought I was rescuing one

puppy from a tragic situation. We're still figuring out the nation-wide ramifications."

"I guess it's time for me to go contribute to your case," I say as I get out of my truck.

"Don't worry about it. This isn't a test. You are merely adding layers of bricks to our case. We want these arrests to be rock solid so they will stand up in court. Every piece of information we get is helpful."

I grab my briefcase with all my files and glance up at her. "If you say so — all of this feels pretty life and death to me."

"You're good. Think of it this way: you're verbally charting the incidents in front of the captain."

"Good point. Let's do this."

Captain Allegheny must sense my discomfort because he moves our meeting from an interrogation room to a small conference room. I'm still being filmed, but it is less intimidating here. This whole process brings back far too many painful memories for me. Even though Nora died on a search and rescue mission, they still brought me in for questioning. I'll never forget how difficult it was to deal with my grief at the same time I was answering questions from the authorities. Since then, my heart races when anyone asks me a series of questions — especially when they aren't related to an animal's health.

Captain Allegheny takes a seat across from me and puts on his reading glasses. He studies me carefully before he says, "So, you're the guy who captured Detective Vick's heart. I hope you know what a treasure you have in that young woman. She reminds me of my wife. Strong, smart and dedicated. Gina was a school counselor for many years. She saw horrors she still dreams about even though she's been retired for a while now."

"You don't have to worry; I wake up every day amazed Darya is in love with me."

Captain Allegheny shuffles the papers in front of him. "Good to know."

"Darya says you have been instrumental in this case from the beginning. Thank you. Can you tell me how all this started for you?"

I pull out the files from my briefcase, and choose the earliest one. I take a moment to quickly review it. "Almost a year ago, on April ninth, one of my clients who works as a secretary at a small local church brought in a box containing two kittens. Both were about three months old and male; they had burns on them. The hair around the wounds had fallen out, and the skin lesions were healing, but they were infected. At the time, I assumed the kittens had gotten into some chemical, like lye. I treated their infection, and the church secretary adopted the stray kittens out to families within the congregation."

"It's good they had a happy ending, I suppose," Captain Allegheny comments.

"The next case was the tiny puppy Darya brought in. Because of his size, he was one of the more difficult to treat. As you know, Atlas pulled through. Based on the condition of his coat, I suspected fire may have been involved."

I pause as Captain Allegheny frantically writes. When he is finished, he instructs, "Continue, please."

"A couple of months later, a local teenager, Dashonte Greely was processing the recycling at his job when he stumbled across teenagers lighting a puppy on fire. He looked up my phone number online and brought him into my clinic. Dashonte was able to scare away the kids involved."

"Lucky for him. That could have ended badly."

"I successfully treated the puppy Dashonte affectionately calls Ranger. My staff placed him with an elderly client who recently lost her miniature schnauzer. I assume he is fat and happy. This client is well-known for spoiling her animals."

"What's next?" he asks me when he finishes writing. I switch files and review my notes.

"The next two were left on the doorstep of The Critter Clinic. There was nothing to identify them. Tragically, one of the kittens didn't make it because of the severity of his burns. Whoever is lighting these animals on fire is gaining skills at harming animals and is stepping up the pace."

"It often happens that way," Captain Allegheny replies as he shakes his head.

"The last group of animals was found by a delivery van at the end of my driveway. They were already beyond help. I performed necropsies on all of them. They died from smoke inhalation and blood loss created from the severe burns."

"I know I'm not supposed to have an opinion about all of this. Between you and me, this is sick," Captain Allegheny growls.

I nod and huff out a breath. "I have been a vet for several years and helped Mitch at a rescue center in Tampa before that. This is the worst case of animal torture I've seen in my whole career, especially when you consider Dashonte says most of the suspects he saw barely looked like teenagers."

Captain Allegheny flips back through his notes. He glances up at me. "I know Detective Vick already interviewed Mr. Greeley, but given the complexity of this case and its ramifications in the bigger picture, I'm going to re-interview him. Though, he appears genuine from what I've read."

"Yes, sir, I agree. After Dashonte lost his job at the kids' recreational facility, I hired him at the clinic; he has been one of my most enthusiastic new hires. I hope he pursues a career in veterinary medicine. He has a real affinity with the animals."

"I am glad. In this position, I tend to hear about the teenagers who are not doing well. It is nice to see one succeed." Captain Allegheny stares me down and asks pointedly, "Doctor Eastwood, do you have any idea who could be doing this to our animals?"

"No, sir, I do not. However, when they figure it out, I hope karma does a big number on them."

"You and me both, Eastwood. Thank you for taking the time to come in and answer my questions. I'll be in touch if I have anymore. Hopefully, with this information we'll be able to narrow our list of suspects."

"Glad to be of help," I say as I finally take a full breath. Both of us collect our belongings and stand up to leave.

As Captain Allegheny exits the room, he looks back over his shoulder. "Hey, Eastwood … Go take your girlfriend out to dinner. She works way too hard. She is the best detective I've got here, but she doesn't know when to cut herself a break."

"You know that steak place up the street with the

white tablecloths? I've been trying to take Darya on a date there for months, but life keeps getting in the way."

"It happens, especially when your partner is a cop, but it's worth the sacrifice. You fit your special moments in wherever they come."

"That's solid advice, Captain, I may take you up on it. Darya is off in a couple of hours, right?"

"To the best of my knowledge. I've been trying to convince her she doesn't have to solve every case in our office alone. We've got other officers and task forces working around the clock."

"Welcome to my reality," I answer with a grim smile. "It's hard not to be proud of Darya though. She treats every case as if it's the most important in the whole department."

Captain Allegheny reaches out to shake my hand. "I'm glad Detective Vick has finally found someone who understands what makes her tick. I wish you guys the best of luck. Lord knows if there is anyone who needs good karma in her life, it is Darya."

"Thank you, sir. I'll do my best to make her happy."

"That's all anyone can ask," he responds with a smile.

I have to suck in a deep breath as Darya walks in front of me with her long hair flowing down her back in soft curls. She peeks over her shoulder at me when we arrive at our table and smiles the first happy smile I've seen in weeks. My knees buckle at the dazzling sight — maybe this bold move was exactly perfect. The joy on her face is indescribable. I swear I'll make it my mission to put it there every single day.

Darya tucks the skirt of her flirty little dress under her as she sits on the lushly appointed seat. I carefully push the chair towards the table and take her purse and place it by her feet. Darya looks around the elegant restaurant. "I can't believe you arranged such a romantic date on short notice."

"I didn't do it by myself. Tristan and Rogue are babysitting Maya and your boss gave me a shove. Instead of waiting for the perfect time for all this to happen, I made it the perfect time. The rest of the pressing things in life can wait for us to actually have a life."

"During my early days in my department, I was scared to death of Captain Allegheny. I have since discovered although he is abrupt and to the point, the man has an incredibly gentle spirit. He'd like to retire, but he can't because his wife, Gina, is in an Alzheimer unit. It's so sad. She showed symptoms in her forties. She had to quit working for the school district. So, Captain goes over and talks to her every day to remind her of who they once were."

"Wow! He didn't say a word about that. Although, it's clear he loves his wife very much."

"For as much as he grumbles about his officers finding love or pairing off with each other, the man is a firm believer in happily-ever-after."

"I hope if anything happens to you, I am strong enough to handle it the way he has."

"Many lessons can be learned from their relationship. Even after all these years and all the hardships endured, they've never given up on each other."

"Speaking of ups and downs, how are you doing?"

Darya shrugs. "I've been better. It sucks to have to tell a beautiful, old soul of a grandmother that her young grandson may be at the center of an international conspiracy to commit hate crimes."

I lean back in my chair and scrub my hand down my face. "Really? Our rash of animal torture is all tied to the same group as the white supremacy suspects? Who would've thought?"

"As nearly as we can tell, the hate groups don't usually cross pollinate. It's more of a 'the enemy of my enemy is my friend' kind of deal. The Klar has been luring kids from other gangs to carry out their dirty work so the principles in the organization don't get nailed on the simple, petty stuff."

"I know you can't officially talk to me about what's going on in the investigation, but can you please tell me you guys are close to nailing the creeps?"

Darya stretches her shoulders out and rolls her neck. "We're working as fast as we can, but they always seem to be a step or two ahead of us."

"Good. I have every faith you'll be able to nail them."

Darya crosses her arms and raises an eyebrow at me. "*Every faith?* That's not how it seemed earlier. It was like you didn't even want to acknowledge my skills as a law enforcement professional."

I pick at my salad for a few moments while I gather my thoughts. Finally, I lift my eyes to meet her challenging gaze. "You're right. I've been less than supportive. That was my mistake. I was wrong."

Darya shakes her head. "I had doubts too. I even explored pursuing a different career path. As I was going through the process, I discovered something I'd forgotten about myself during the drama of being a target of someone's hate."

"Yeah? What?" I take a sip of water.

"I like being a cop and solving people's problems. When I took the opportunity to touch base with people I've served over the years, they helped me understand what I do is important."

"Of course it's important. I'm sorry I gave you the impression it wasn't."

"The constant danger made me seriously question my career choices. Talking to people who crossed paths with me in my job made the right choice easier to see. Every arrest I make may not make it to trial, or the jury might not agree with what we've found, but that didn't seem to matter to most people, everyone was glad I cared enough to listen to their stories about what happened to them."

"You're not the only one who spent some time soul-searching. After a giant — and blunt — push from Mitch, I started looking at why all of this is so hard for me."

"I've been on the receiving end of Mitch's 'helpful lectures' before. They can be thought-provoking at the very least."

I nod. "It was. For me to explain this, I have to tell you a bit about Nora. I've already shared that Mitch, Nora, and I were like the three musketeers. We did everything together for years. What I didn't tell you was Nora was the first one to charge into every situation. Recklessness was so typical of her, none of us were surprised when she chose an overtly dangerous occupation. It fit who she was."

"It certainly takes a certain mindset to do search and

rescue work," Darya remarks.

"It does. Even though Mitch and I both volunteer, we've never been as passionate about it as Nora was. She was driven to be in the middle of every incident. It made her good at her job, but it was difficult to sustain a relationship that way."

Darya's eyes tear up, and she nods. "I remember how that feels."

Now that I've started, I feel compelled to press on with my story. "I don't know what it was about that particular mission, but I had a feeling of dread. As soon as news of the quake hit, I wanted to hide any source of the news from Nora. I knew she would be on the next plane. I tried to stop her. In fact, I even threatened to break up with her over it. The love of my life and the mother of my child died alone with only the memory of my caustic words. I'd give anything to take them back. Sadly, I can't. Nora is dead and what was done was done."

"My heart breaks for you. I wish I could go back and fix it for you. I know what you mean because I have the same kind of guilt. The morning Sergio was killed, we argued about how to make coffee. It was so stupid. I was mad because Sergio liked to re-use coffee grounds and I thought it was gross. We had a big old kerfuffle about it. I'll always wonder if the reason he didn't notice something was amiss with his car was because he was distracted by our fight."

"That's so tough. I could never figure out whether I was angrier at myself for squabbling with Nora before she left or because she left me when I asked her not to. Truth be told, it was probably a bit of both."

"So, that's why you freaked out when I decided to

push through and work even though I was terrified?" Darya guesses.

"I wasn't sure until I took Mitch's advice and thought about the differences between you and Nora."

Darya groans. "I don't know how I'll fare in this comparison. Nora was your first love, and it's hard to compete with that."

"I think you'll be surprised. When I remember Nora, I think about the wild mustangs we help. They are majestic and beautiful, but also chaotic and untamed. Nora didn't want to take anyone's advice about anything. *Ever*. Our relationship was like a breathtaking roller coaster ride. We had a lot of high highs, but we had some devastating lows. Whenever she didn't like the input I gave, she'd pretend I didn't exist. It was so frustrating. The day before Nora went on her final rescue mission, it all came to a head."

I draw a shaky breath and take a sip of my beer.

"I was trying to keep my grades up to keep my scholarship and I couldn't deal with the simmering anger between us. Everything was so incredibly tense during that time. Nora was watching twenty-four-hour news coverage about the earthquake and freaking out more with each passing minute. She believed if she was there, she could find some living victims. Pregnancy wasn't making it any easier. Her emotions were all over the map. Even on a normal day, Nora was like a spitting firecracker of emotion. I never knew whether she would have an all-out explosion or a more sedate response."

Darya reaches her hand out to grab mine in a silent show of support.

I flinch as memories come flooding back like a

slideshow. "I can still remember our last conversation as if it were yesterday. Nora told me she had gone to the doctor and cleared the trip with him. After she told me that, there was a message on our answering machine. Out of habit, I picked it up thinking it was one of my study partners."

Darya grimaces. "I remember those days. You don't think logically during dead week. It's like being on autopilot."

"All logic went flying out the door when I heard the receptionist saying because Nora had missed her last two appointments, they would have to schedule her out another month."

Darya pulls in a sharp breath as she waits for me to finish the story.

"Nora insisted she had gone to the doctor, and the office messed up when they called her." I rake my hand through my hair and try to take a deep breath. "As I said, Nora never took anyone's advice about anything. Nora had a cousin who was big into natural medicine, and she believes Western doctors are the personification of evil. I was afraid Nora was listening to her cousin rather than her own doctor. In my mind, no circumstances would make it all right for Nora to face a chance of aftershocks and the real possibility she might encounter deceased victims. I argued she needed to take better care of herself and the baby."

"Your reaction was entirely legitimate. If Sergio had been in your shoes, he would have been livid with me."

"You saw how upset I got with you when you went to work when there was a target on your back. Now imagine a response about a hundred times more intense and angry. I was convinced Nora was lying to me and going on the trip to spite me."

"That must've been intense. I'm so sorry. I know from personal experience words can come back to haunt you."

"I know they did with you and me. I was treating you as if you were the same as Nora. I was wrong. You are much more methodical and cautious in your choices. You look at all the angles before you take action. You don't seek out an adrenaline thrill just so you can get a high. You don't do heroic things to bring attention to yourself."

"I know the way I handle things now is different from how I would've at twenty. When I was younger, I was much more impulsive. Time and heartbreak have taught me to be much more cautious."

"That's true. I've changed as well, or at least I'd like to think I have. However, my reaction to your situation shows maybe I haven't changed as much as I'd hoped."

"Actually, the fact you came to your senses so quickly and tried very hard to apologize shows you have changed a lot throughout the years."

"I want you to know I understand now. I get what you do and why you do it. There may never be a day I can completely breathe and let you go without a profound sense of worry," I concede. "Still, my fear does not outweigh the pain that comes from you being absent from my life. Before I fell in love with you, my heart and soul were being held hostage by my past, but now I feel like our hearts have been set free."

A tear slides down Darya's face. "I never expected to fall in love again. I thought I would be alone for the rest of my life. Then, you came in and changed everything and gave me a new perspective. I like your phrase—hearts set free—it perfectly sums up how I feel now that you're in my life. The rest of the issues between us are technicalities and semantics. Can we go back to being one of those ridiculously cute couples again? I've missed you so much."

"Absolutely, I would like nothing better. Let's go home," I suggest.

"But what about our food?" Darya protests.

"I'll have the waitress box it up. As nice as this restaurant is, it doesn't compete with the feeling of having you in my arms." I stand up, walk behind her and kiss her on her neck.

She arches into my touch. "Finally, we can agree. Let's go celebrate our victory."

Chapter Twenty-Four

Darya

Leaning over, I transfer an extra pat of butter to Stuart's plate of blueberry pancakes. "I can't believe how much you spoil me. Coffee, bacon, pancakes — it doesn't get much better than this."

Stuart reaches up and brushes my hair off my cheek. "My idea of heaven, for sure."

"It feels positively decadent to stay in bed this morning to do the crossword puzzle. It's not a luxury I have often. Maybe I should reach out to my friends more frequently and ask for babysitting services. This is nice."

Stuart grabs my hand and pulls me over to his lap. "Is it only nice because Maya is having a slumber party with Ivy and Marcus? What am I, chopped liver?"

He kisses me on the shoulder and then encourages me to relax against him. It's better this way; it's easier for me to say the words when I'm not looking directly at Stuart. "Don't worry. You are so much more than chopped liver.

You are the person who encouraged me to stop living in the past and live for the future.

You are the person who sees my deepest fears and

insecurities and loves me anyway.

You are the person who met a shy, timid little girl and turned her into a quick, agile athlete.

You are the person who saved my daughter's puppy and presented me with a dog who saved my life not once, but twice.

You are the person who thinks I'm beautiful, even when I'm brushing my teeth.

You are the person who cheers me on even though my job scares the crap out of you.

In short, you are about as close to perfect as anyone can be."

Stuart shakes his head. "Darya, I'm far from perfect. I tend to speak before I think, and I wear my heart on my sleeve. I don't always tell you what I'm thinking or why until it's far too late. I have a tendency to get angry when I'm scared and say things that hurt you."

"I have been your friend for years. You think I don't know this about you? The same passion that makes you lash out when you're hurt or scared allows you to care about everyone and everything around you and inspires you to make a difference in the world."

"I think that's probably the nicest thing anyone has ever said to me," Stuart admits as he runs his fingers through my hair.

I shift in Stuart's arms. Facing him, I insist, "It may be nice, but that doesn't mean it's not true. Having you in my corner helped me face down very real monsters in my life. Knowing you know everything about me — good, bad, and indifferent — and still love me empowers me. I love you for that. Even more importantly, you brought Maya into your world and made her feel at home in your life. I couldn't ask for anything more."

"You could ask for one more thing —" Stuart suggests with an odd expression on his face. Abruptly, he moves me off his lap, gets up and goes toward his dresser. He digs something out of his drawer and comes back to the bed. When he extends his hand toward me, I see a jewelry box with a tiny hummingbird on the top.

My heart beats faster when I see the beautifully crafted box. This man understands me inside and out. I may be tough and fast, but I'm still fragile. It's all I can do not to jump up and down on the bed like Maya.

When I shoot him a questioning look, he encourages, "Go ahead, open it."

Taking the box from his hand, I carefully open the lid, and the music box plays *You Are My Sunshine*. I turn into emotional mush. "My mom used to sing this song to me when I was little. I don't even know how you knew. It's beautiful," I gush tearfully.

"It's one of my favorite songs too, but that's not why I chose it. I chose this box because you've been the sunshine which warms my soul. Before I met you, I was lost in the darkness of the past. You have set me free to fly."

"Stop it. You're going to make me cry," I protest as I wipe my eyes.

"Oh, probably. In fact, I'm counting on it. Take another look at what's inside the box."

"There is something in the box? The music box is so gorgeous I thought it was the whole gift," I confess as I carefully examine the outside of the box.

Stuart grins and chuckles softly. "I can't believe I've pulled one over on the super detective."

As I turn the box around and open it again, I notice Stuart taking my picture with his cell phone. "Oh, knock it off! I still have bed head this morning. Besides, don't you have enough pictures of me on that thing?"

"I don't have a picture of this," Stuart answers mysteriously.

Holding the box up toward the window so I can see better, I finally notice the little black velvet on the bottom of the box is merely sitting in there. When I lift it up, I see a gold and silver ring. It is clever and unique. There are two metal bands, which contain a knot. I suck in a breath and quickly glance over at Stuart. I have a hunch I know what all this means, but I need to hear the words. One look at his stance and my heart flips over.

Stuart tilts his head as he takes the ring from my fingers. "You know, this isn't how I thought this would happen. I had a big dramatic, romantic date and a clever proposal planned for you, but I let my emotions run away with me last night and didn't get around to doing this before we left."

My hand shakes as I hold it out for him. "Darya Vick, will you please do me the honor of becoming my wife?"

I hold my breath as the man I never intended to love is down on one knee asking me a most important question. I try to focus on his words over the sound of my pounding heart.

As he holds up the ring to slide it on my finger, he explains, "I chose non-traditional engagement rings for us. To me, the gold and silver symbolizes that we are two very different people. The side-by-side knots are an acknowledgment we've both lost someone we loved deeply and our lives will always be impacted by their presence. It's welded together because the two of us, although strong on our own, are unbreakable together."

I can only nod as I swallow hard. Finally, I gain my ability to speak. "Yes, it would be my honor. My words aren't as poetic as yours, but this is the happiest I've been in years. I cannot wait for us to be an official family. I love you so much."

Stuart breathes a sigh of relief. "Oh, thank goodness. I didn't have a backup plan if you would've said no."

I can't disguise my ugly cry at the beauty of Stuart's words. It's a good thing he is not taking pictures right now, because I am a blubbering mess as he slides the ring on my finger.

"Maya will be so excited," I remark.

"I hope so. That little girl holds my heart in her hands."

"I know. Mine too." I wipe my eyes with the back of my hand and notice the ravages of my makeup from last night. Sighing, I take another look at my new ring. "I am blown away by this. I never expected this to happen. I love it. It's perfect."

"I'm glad you aren't offended I didn't buy you a huge rock. I looked at them, but they didn't seem to suit," Stuart says as his phone rings. Vaguely, I can hear the sound of my phone ringing as well. Unfortunately, I left my phone down in the kitchen while I was making pancakes.

As I rush past him, Stuart plugs his ear to try to hear better. The neighbor is mowing his lawn and making a terrible racket.

Jogging into the kitchen, I sit on the bar stool as I try to figure out whose call I missed. It's a number I don't recognize, but as I look closer, I'm dismayed to see I've missed a series of messages from Jessica.

Before I can finish reading the texts, I hear Stuart run down stairs and announce, "I guess our plans for the day

have changed."

We don't even need to step inside Jessica's room to know we're in the right place. I'd recognize her scream anywhere. When I look up at Stuart, he looks as if someone slugged him in the gut.

"I hope things aren't quite as intense as it sounds." He flinches.

"I think she's probably fine. I play video games with Jessica all the time. She is prone to being loud and dramatic. Remember, she has a background in theater. At least, I hope that's the explanation for her scream." I grab Stuart's hand.

Stuart reaches out and knocks on the door frame before we enter the room. As soon as Jessica sees me, she lets go of Mitch's hand and points at me. "I have new respect for you. I have no idea how you did this all by yourself. Pushing a baby out is so freaking scary. I thought I was prepared. I read tons and tons of books. They don't say how much it hurts." Jessica gasps again.

Stuart looks over at Mitch. "Have they placed an epidural or anything? How far dilated is she? Did she have to do Pitocin?"

"Jessica doesn't have any Pitocin on board; this is all natural," Mitch explains. "My little sprite decided she didn't want to spend very much time at the hospital, so she didn't tell me her contractions were less than two minutes apart until she couldn't stand it any longer. We've been here about an hour, and she is eight centimeters and fully effaced."

"Whoa! Jess, you could've been one of those women who had your baby in the car on the way to the delivery room," Stuart says with a chuckle.

"I was sure they were Braxton-Hicks contractions. I've always heard first babies come excruciatingly slow. I thought I'd be in labor for days before the baby moved into position. Mitch had a meeting about a grant for Hope's Haven. I figured I'd wait until he was done. I didn't see any need to keep him hanging around the hospital when he had important things to do."

"It can take several days for a first-time labor, but sometimes not," Stuart remarks.

Jessica rolls her eyes at Stuart. "Obviously not. Because here I am." She lets out a little shriek as a contraction hits. "Oh my Gosh! Is it supposed to feel like somebody is ripping my insides out? Maybe I was wrong to turn down an epidural. What if I screwed this whole thing up?" Panic is creeping into her voice.

"Relax, my patients give birth all the time without epidurals. We are born to do this kind of stuff without a lot of intervention."

"Stuart, you are not helping!" Jessica exclaims after the contraction passes. "What would you know about this? Your patients are animals. The only animal I resemble these days is a whale. I want this baby out of here."

I walk over and put ice chips in a rolled-up washcloth for Jessica. I place it gently on her brow. "I know it seems like it'll never be over, but it will be. I promise. You won't stay pregnant forever."

"At the moment, I suspect I'll probably never make love again. This is too high a price."

I chuckle. "You say that now. There'll come a day when one of your friends will have a baby and you'll sigh wistfully because your little one who was once that size is now not so little. We as mothers tend to forget how painful this is. If we didn't, society as we know it would cease to exist because women would never have more than one child."

The nurse comes in and leans over Jessica. "Less talking and more breathing, okay?"

She discreetly pulls back the blankets covering Jessica's legs as she studies the situation. The nurse's mouth forms a grim line.

Jessica looks at Stuart and blurts, "Mitch said it was okay if you accidentally saw my hoo-ha — with you being a doctor and all."

Stuart lurches back with his hands up in the air in front of him. "Look, you are not the right species to be my patient. I'm here to give my best friend support."

I elbow Stuart in the ribs. "Relax. I think she was kidding … mostly." Looking over at Jessica, I ask, "How are you feeling?"

Jessica lets out a string of curse words as she gasps, "I need to push!"

"Hold off for a moment, let me page Dr. Cox," the nurse cautions as she puts a code into her pager.

"I don't think this is something I'm in control of," Jessica replies with a low moan.

"The doctor will be here in a second," the nurse assures Jessica.

"Don't worry, Jess. Stuart delivers babies all the time. It can't be much different, right?" Mitch tells his wife.

"I don't know! I don't want to find out," Jessica screeches. She studies us for a second. "I changed my mind again. The only person I want here is Mitch. I can't let you guys see all this. If I do, you may never have another kid, Darya."

I laugh out loud. "Whoa, easy there. Stuart and I just got engaged this morning. We haven't even talked about having another child. As you know, Maya is precocious and takes a lot of energy to raise. I'm not sure I am young enough to have another one."

Wide-eyed, Stuart shoots me a questioning gaze as he asks, "Are you sure? Because I think Maya would make a phenomenal big sister."

"Honestly, I haven't ruled it in or out. We've been a little busy the last few months trying to catch criminals."

"You guys are *what?*" Jessica asks before she lets loose with another yell of pain. "I … can't … say I recommend this life plan to anyone right now. After all of this is over, I plan to be furious because you didn't send me pictures immediately. It's not every day my husband's best friend gets engaged to one of my other awesome friends. We should be celebrating, but I'm a little busy right now."

The doctor comes strolling through the door. He pauses for a moment to look at the readouts from the monitors. He looks directly at Stuart and me. "Decide if you are staying or going. It looks like it's show time."

"I'm willing to stay if you want me," I offer as I take Jessica's washcloth off her forehead and ring it out. I take a clean washcloth from the stack by the sink and wrap it around more ice and hand it to Jessica. I lean down and kiss her on the cheek. "Let me know how to help."

"You will probably hate me, but I think I want to do

this alone with just the doctor and Mitch. It sucks being so hormonal," Jessica grits between her teeth.

"Don't worry about it. When I was delivering Maya, I wasn't even sure I wanted the doctor in the room with me. I had a long, painful labor. Toward the end, I was so cranky people were avoiding me."

"That's kinda what I feel like right now," Jessica admits as she grits her teeth.

"Stuart and I will check on you later. We have to run some errands, and we'll be back."

"Don't be gone too long. Things are moving now!" Mitch advises Stuart.

"We'll be quick. Darya needs a caffeine fix, and we need to pick up a new USB drive," Stuart explains as he walks over to Jessica and squeezes her hand. "Stay strong; you have a little one counting on you now."

Jessica frowns as she mutters, "Don't remind me. I'm not even quite there yet, and I already feel like a failure as a mom."

"Jessica, nothing could be further from the truth. I am so proud of the way you handled the whole pregnancy. No one should have been sick as many months as you were," Mitch says.

"You can do this, Jess. I look forward to meeting your little one. We'll see you later." I grasp Stuart's hand and walk out the door.

When we reach the hallway, Stuart says, "It might just be me, but I'd like to be in Mitch's shoes. Maybe it's because I've never gotten to experience it firsthand, but I still think the whole process is akin to magic."

"You would make an excellent father, which is why I

haven't ruled it out entirely. There are risks after thirty that I don't know if I'm ready to cope with."

Stuart squeezes my hand reassuringly. "I guess we can leave it up to fate. As far as I'm concerned, fate has been unspeakably kind to us."

After the doors of the elevator to the parking garage close, I walk into his arms and give him a warm embrace. "I can't argue with you," I reply as I punctuate my remarks with small kisses leading to a long, thorough one.

Epilogue

Stuart

"Eww! Are you sure that will be done by the time everyone gets here?" Maya asks as she watches me put chicken on the grill.

"It'll be perfect." I close the grill lid. "Why?"

"I don't want the party to be lame. It's important."

"How is your mom feeling?" I ask, looking up toward our bedroom window.

"She said she's tired. She isn't used to wearing high heels and a dress. I'm glad she did though because there were TV cameras there and everything."

"I know. It's cool that your mom got an award from the Governor's office."

"Mom told me they wanted her to give a speech, but she didn't want to do it because it wasn't just her who found the bad guys. She said it wasn't fair for her to take all the credit for the rest of the team. So, she didn't say anything; she went up there and got her award and shook the man's hand."

I shrug. "You know your mom. She doesn't like to brag about herself."

"I thought it was funny they gave Dozer an award too."

I nod. "He deserved it, didn't he?"

"Yeah, he's the second-best dog I've ever met."

"I bet I can guess who you think the best dog is."

"Well, duh! Atlas got third place in the agility competition. The guy who ran the competition said I was the youngest trainer to place." Maya shows me the ribbon and medal around her neck. "He said because I won third place, I could come back next year and try again. The man said if I keep practicing, I might win first place next time."

"You might at that. You and Atlas have made a ton of progress."

"Did I show you Sol's latest trick? Sol doesn't like the stuff on the agility course as much as Atlas. So, I asked Mitch what else I could train him to do. Mitch took me on a tour of Hope's Haven and introduced me to the service dogs. Then he showed me how he teaches them to do stuff for people. They have a cool dog trainer there named Zoe. She's a girl like me. Anyway, I copied Zoe and taught Solstice how to do awesome stuff too. I can't wait to show Mitch and Jessica. Are they bringing Nikita?"

"As far as I know." As soon as the words leave my mouth, I can hear the front doorbell ring. "You better go get the door, I bet it's them. They probably have their hands full."

Maya takes off running toward the front yard. I shake my head. That girl has two speeds: stop and go and nothing in between.

Darya opens the sliding glass door and comes out on

the deck. "Where is everybody?"

"Maya went to go see if Mitch and Jessica are here," I answer as I let my gaze linger on my fiancée. "I see you had a slight wardrobe change."

"Heck yeah!" Darya answers as she glances at herself. "A halter top and cut-offs are the only appropriate dress for a backyard barbecue. I never stay in a dress and heels long."

"Too bad, because you looked beautiful and sexy as heck," I comment with a wink.

"Are you saying I don't look sexy now?" Darya asks as she pops her hip out provocatively.

"No, I would never say that. You look amazing," I assure her as I walk over to give her a kiss.

"Cover your eyes. They're at it again. Those two are always kissing. It's gross," Maya warns as she comes around the corner from the side yard.

Jessica's eyes widen as she looks at Darya. "If I were a betting woman, I would say you two have been doing more than kissing—"

Darya cradles her abdomen. "Yeah, it started out as fun and games. I found out the hard way what happens when you have the stomach flu for five days and can't keep any food or meds down. It turns out birth-control pills don't work well when they are at the bottom of the toilet bowl."

"Oh wow! So, you guys were taken by surprise?" Jessica asks with her mouth agape.

Maya butts into the conversation. "Yeah, Mom couldn't figure out why she kept yakking every time Dad made her pancakes."

Darya shrugs. "I thought it was nerves from working on such a big assignment. We've been trying for months to establish all the ties between the suspects. Every time we thought we had it sewn up, we ran across more. Klar is now operational in seventeen states. The threats against our department were only the tip of the iceberg."

"Were you finally able to round up everybody?" Mitch asks me.

Darya rolls her eyes. "Who knows? We'll probably never get everyone involved. By the time the task force and the feds got to the bottom of it all, there were four different gangs involved. Even so, I believe we got most of the major players."

I nod as I confirm, "I think so too. Dashonte says there's less seedy activity in his neighborhood and I've had no new cases of animal torture in a while."

"How do you feel about how everything went down?" Mitch asks Darya.

Darya blows her hair out of her face and sits down on the lounge chair. "I don't know if I'll ever stop looking over my shoulder since the incident at the mall, but I am relieved we could unravel their tactics and stop them at the source. I'm breathing a bit easier these days."

"I heard a rumor Isaac and Tristan want to lure you away to work for Identity Bank. Are you going to?"

Darya shakes her head. "As much as I admire what Tristan and Isaac have accomplished with Identity Bank, I am proud of the 'public' in the public servant part of my title. For now, I'm planning to stay put."

Mitch turns to me. "And you? I know this must be tough."

"I try not to hover over Darya too much. After all,

she's done this before, and I haven't."

Darya grins indulgently. "He tries, but he's not always successful. For the most part, he's doing pretty well."

"I am learning to roll with the punches. Even though the pregnancy was a surprise, it was a welcome one. I know this little one can't replace the one I lost, but it makes me happy to think about Maya having a sibling."

"I am so thrilled for you guys. It sounds like you've finally struck a balance," Jessica observes.

I nod. "We have. Everything about our relationship has been unique and challenging. I don't expect being a parent of a little one to be much different. Being Maya's step-dad-to-be has given me great practice."

"I'm a great kid. You might not get so lucky this time around," Maya teases.

"I'm fortunate to have you in my life. You are a real rock star," I reply. I grab a few cans of soda out of the cooler and hand them out. "I am so proud of my little family. I've come to terms with the fact that because of Darya's efforts, our children will grow up in a safer world. That's all I can ask for." I place my arm around Darya's waist and pull her in for a kiss.

Out of the corner of my eye, I see Maya roll her eyes. "See? What did I tell you? They're always kissing."

I grin at Maya. "If you've got a problem with that, don't look, because I plan to be kissing your mom for as long as I live."

Mitch holds up his soda and clanks it against Jessica's. "Hear, Hear! May there be more kissing in the world."

Jessica looks over at Darya. "Who do you think will be the next person to fall in love? We've pretty much paired off everyone we know."

Darya's eyes light up. "I don't know! Whoever it is, it'll be fun to watch."

THE END (for now)

For more on your friends at Hope's Haven and The Critter Clinic check out Freedom — available now.

NOTE FROM THE AUTHOR

Dear Reader,

Thank you for reading Hearts Set Free. I hope you enjoyed reading about all the special canines and their relationships with their owners.

…there's more.

Their stories continue in Freedom.

Phoenix can't believe his eyes when he sees a dog struck by a truck on the freeway.

Little does he know the person he calls to help will rescue more than just the dog.

Zoe is a dog trainer by profession, but she can't turn down a call for help.

She is reluctant to trust the handsome blonde stranger, but soon she will have no choice.

Will the circumstances which brought them together be the foundation for a lifetime together?

If you adore sweet romances with characters facing insurmountable odds make your heart sing, this is the book for you.

Get Freedom in paperback, e-book format or through read through Kindle Unlimited for free now.

Get it now.

~Mary

Because love matters, differences don't.

ACKNOWLEDGEMENTS

When I first started writing, I figured that I would be alone throughout the process. Given the nature of my disability, it is hard for me to be out and about. I assumed this meant that I really wouldn't have any friends in the author community. That simply isn't the case. I have found great groups of authors who support each other and help fill in my knowledge gaps. It is impossible for me to acknowledge each one by name, because there have been hundreds of people who have given me synonyms or provided an obscure fact or even a shoulder to cry on when things are not going well. To all of you I say thank you from the bottom of my heart.

Stuart has been a character in the background for a long time. I knew the first time I wrote him that he was a man of great depth but also a man who suffered terribly during his childhood and through college. I am pleased to be able to use this novel as a vehicle to tell his story. A special thanks to all of my friends and fans who have shared their story of love after catastrophic loss. You made this story better.

Thanks again to Kathern Watts who is my finder of all things obscure. You make my job much easier. I am blessed to have you in my life.

A huge shout out to everyone who takes the time to read early versions of my work or leave reviews. Your feedback means the world to me.

Thank you, Dr. Brandon Crawford, for all of your assistance with the weird, off-the-wall medical questions. To help preserve your sanity, I always try to preface my questions with "This is only for a book."

Kudos to Justin Crawford for being there with answers about all things video games. Thanks for your help.

I would be remiss if I didn't say a word about my husband, Leonard Crawford. Even though this is my twenty-fourth book, I still can't tell you how much I appreciate your love and support. I love you

To all my fans who support diversity in fiction, thank you for buying my books. One word, one chapter, one book at a time — I hope to change the world with your help

About the Author

I have been lucky enough to live my own version of a romance novel. I married the guy who kissed me at summer camp. He told me on the night we met that he was going to marry me and be the father of my children.

Eventually, I stopped giggling when he said it, and we've been married for more than thirty years. We have two children. The oldest is a Doctor of Osteopathy. He is across the United States completing his residency, but when he's done, he is going to come back to Oregon and practice Family Medicine. Our youngest son is now tackling high school and where he is an honor student. He is interested in becoming an EMT.

I write full time now. I have published more than thirty books and have several more underway. I volunteer my time to a variety of causes. I have worked as a Civil Rights Attorney and diversity advocate. I spent several years working for various social service agencies before becoming an attorney.

In my spare time, I love to cook, decorate cakes and of

course, I obsessively, compulsively read.

I would be honored if you would take a few moments out of your busy day to check out my website, MaryCrawfordAuthor.com. While you're there, you can sign up for my newsletter and get a free book. I will be announcing my upcoming books and giving sneak peeks as well as sponsoring giveaways and giving you information about other interesting events.

If you have questions or comments, please E-mail me at Mary@MaryCrawfordAuthor.com or find me on the following social networks:

Facebook: www.facebook.com/authormarycrawford

Website: MaryCrawfordAuthor.com

Twitter: www.twitter.com/MaryCrawfordAut

www.ingramcontent.com/pod-product-compliance
Lightning Source LLC
Chambersburg PA
CBHW032112180726

48284CB00002B/543